A Sleep of Spies

For the first time, Palma Harcourt forsakes the glamorous diplomatic background of Embassies abroad and sets her latest thriller – no whit less gripping than its predecessors – in the grimmer, greyer world of London and the Ministry of Defence.

Her narrator, Philip Camplin, a senior civil servant, helps successfully to defuse the tense diplomatic situation which follows a disaster in Northern Ireland in which civilians are accidentally killed by British troops. Thereafter he and his young wife are subjected to harassment by an organization allegedly dedicated to avenging the victims. The harassment ends in tragedy.

Still reeling, Camplin is contacted by a scientist missing from a government research establishment. The man has been a security leak, but is now trying to escape being framed by his Russian masters. By revealing the cynical reality behind the victimization of the Camplins, he blackmails the MoD man into helping him. And he names the mastermind responsible for the Northern Ireland killings aimed at discrediting Britain in the eyes of the world. The name strikes chill into Camplin's heart. How can such an accusation against so impeccable a figure be proved?

Once again, Palma Harcourt has chosen to write about a world she knows all too well. The cold horrors of the unseen war waged unsleepingly among us have seldom been better portrayed.

by the same author

AGENTS OF INFLUENCE
AT HIGH RISK
DANCE FOR DIPLOMATS
A FAIR EXCHANGE
CLIMATE FOR CONSPIRACY

Palma Harcourt

A SLEEP OF SPIES

COLLINS
St James's Place, London
1979

William Collins Sons & Co Ltd
London · Glasgow · Sydney · Auckland
Toronto · Johannesburg

First published 1979

ISBN 0 00 222496 8
Set in Imprint
Made and Printed in Great Britain by
William Collins Sons & Co Ltd Glasgow

For Dorothy and Harry

This book is fiction. All the characters and incidents in it are entirely imaginary.

A hood of graduates,
A turn of traitors,
A conviction of ideologues –
A sleep of spies.

Anonymous

PART I

Claire

ONE

Concorde had seemed the obvious answer, though it was bound to raise a question in the House. Some MP was certain to ask why a civil servant in the Ministry of Defence had been allowed to waste the taxpayers' money on a luxury flight to the States. And as certainly the Minister in his reply would disguise the truth under a cloak of clichés.

In fact, there had been no practical alternative. It had taken the whole of the last forty-eight hours – a hectic, nerve-stretching, desperate forty-eight hours – to assemble everything that might be needed at the all-important meetings on Ireland scheduled for tomorrow in Washington. I was carrying documents, tapes, signed statements, filmed interviews, even what could be called a death-bed confession. These had to reach our Ambassador before he met the Secretary of State and the White House staff. I had to brief him in depth. Time, as the Minister could truthfully tell Parliament, was of the essence.

But time was running out like sand, and Concorde sat, a beautiful broody bird, on the runway at Heathrow, her flight delayed by a technical fault.

I could have done without the trip altogether. I was bone weary, I had just spent a harrowing three days in Northern Ireland and I didn't want to leave Claire again. She swore she was all right, but tension and lack of sleep had painted black smudges under her eyes.

Unfortunately, it had to be me. Somehow I had become an expert on the ghastly tragedy in Belfast ten days ago. Without immodesty, I knew my presence in Washington could make a real difference. Anyway, I told myself, there was nothing seriously wrong with Claire. I worried too much about my wife.

I turned my thoughts to the more immediate problem of the flight's delay. At this very moment Concorde should have been coming in to land at Dulles Airport, but she was still at Heathrow and I was still in this Concorde lounge. We might both be in the same place tomorrow morning when the Ambassador went into the meetings, cold. Something could be done with telegrams and the telephone, but he would lack the first-hand material I had with me. The possibility was appalling, but I couldn't think of anything constructive I could do about it.

Hopelessly I watched the British Airways hostess chatting into her telephone in half-a-dozen languages. I waited for a lull, then stood up and limped over to her. My leg was hurting; it always hurt more when I was tired or tense.

'Any news?'

'I'll ask for you, Mr Camplin.'

She gave me a small, bright smile and, while I leaned patiently against her desk, had a long conversation with someone called Fred. Eventually she put down the receiver. Another phone rang and she switched from English to Polish, but she put her hand over the mouthpiece.

'You'll be boarding within twenty minutes, Mr Camplin.'

'Thanks.' Relief flooded through me; I could have kissed her prissy little mouth.

I went to the telephone booth at the far end of the lounge. It was a narrow glass box with a folding door for privacy and I had some difficulty getting my bulky briefcase inside with me.

Listening to the purr of the phone, I pictured Claire sitting in the big wing chair with her feet tucked under her. She was wearing the grey wool dress that matched her eyes and she was reading, her dark hair hanging over the page. I waited to hear her voice; she had been asleep when I left for the office this morning and there had been no answer when I had tried later. There was no answer now. Reluctantly I saw the empty flat, the dark rooms, the desolate tortoiseshell cat. I put down the phone, got myself and my briefcase out of the booth and went back to my seat.

Fifteen minutes later the girl at the desk announced that British Airways Flight 189 was ready for boarding. She said goodbye to each of us by name and wished us a pleasant journey. She must have been glad to see the backs of us; she had had her fill of Concorde's passengers that day.

The flight was uneventful and, given the difference in time zones between Britain and the States, we arrived an hour before we left. If only we had taken off on schedule . . .

At Dulles International I was met by an Embassy car with a driver, a security man, and the Ambassador's Personal Private Secretary. The PPS was efficient, the red carpet thick. I was whisked through the airport formalities into the waiting limousine.

'The traffic's heavy this evening, sir. It may take us an hour or more to get into Washington.'

'That's a pity.' I settled myself comfortably in my corner. 'Still, I'm so late already I dare say the Ambassador won't mind waiting a little longer.'

'Sir, the Ambassador will have left for a cocktail party before we arrive, and after that he's due to dine with Senator – '

'What? I thought there was meant to be a crisis?'

I let my temper flare. I was angry and I didn't care who knew it. If His Bloody Excellency was going to put up any sort of show tomorrow – and, God knows, he must – he needed more than a fifteen-minute look-see at the stuff I had brought him. Granted, we couldn't win outright, but given our cards and some playing skill and a bit of luck we could force a draw. Whatever happened we couldn't afford to lose by default. If we did, it wouldn't be only our worst enemies who believed that the British had intentionally and with malice used a killer gas in Northern Ireland, and thus finally proved themselves unfit to be there. Many of our friends would believe it, too. And if the President of the United States decided to take action . . .

'The Ambassador asked me to apologize for him, sir.' The PPS leaned forward and made sure the glass partition that separated us from the two men in front was securely closed. 'And to explain why he couldn't wait for you. As you know, the situation's bad at the moment. The disaster in Belfast caused a bitter reaction right across the States, and after the film of it was shown on TV feelings really ran high, especially in Washington. There's a strong Irish lobby here. So, on H.E.'s instructions, we're all doing our best to behave normally and keep everything as low-key as possible. Which means, I regret to say, sir, not cancelling engagements however unwelcome or inconvenient they may be.'

'I understand,' I said, my spurt of anger subsiding. 'I apologize. Sorry if I sounded critical.'

'That's okay.'

For once he didn't add 'sir', and I was grateful. His constant use of it made me feel old. It emphasized the gap between thirty and forty. Yet, at a glance, Claire was two or three years younger than he was. Suddenly I was aware that he was appraising me.

'I know your brother, sir.' There was that damned 'sir' again. 'You don't look very much like him, do you?'

I nearly asked which brother he meant, but I knew it would be Andrew who was in the Foreign Service. He was unlikely to have met William, the European Parliamentarian, or Patrick, the psychiatrist. Anyway, they were all the same in appearance, big men over six feet, fair-haired, blue-eyed versions of my father. I was short by comparison, small-boned, dark – and I had been born with a wizened right leg; since I was a child I had worn a heavy built-up shoe.

'I take after my mother,' I said. Not wanting to be too abrupt. I asked him where he'd met Andrew.

'In Oslo, when he was Counsellor there. I was only a Third Secretary but he was very kind to me. He used to take me ski-ing . . .'

For the rest of the drive he talked, with equal enthusiasm, about Norway and the Andrew Camplins. I was amused but I found myself relaxing, and I was startled when for no apparent reason he reached across me and checked that the car door was locked.

Seeing my surprise he said: 'We've just turned on to Massachusetts Avenue, sir. We're not far from the Embassy.'

To me this explained nothing, but I noticed the security man and the driver trying their door. Five minutes later I knew why. A demonstration was in progress in front of the British Embassy.

It was dusk, and the words on the banners were largely indecipherable, but I could see a motley crowd brandishing huge green shamrocks. And I could hear the chanting. Rather it was a sullen, menacing hum, sporadically broken by shouted slogans. 'Murderers, go home!' appeared to be the favourite.

We were turning into the Embassy gates before they spotted us. At once there was a roar of anger, shamrocks and banners waved violently in the air. There was no danger. The police had the situation firmly under control. Nevertheless, I felt a mixture of fear and revulsion; no one likes to be hated, even at second hand.

Suddenly one of the trestles that the police had erected as a barricade crashed to the ground. A woman came running towards us. Two policemen dashed after her but she was fast and she had taken them by surprise. She reached the car with seconds to spare.

Finding the door locked she first beat on the glass with her fist, then pressed her nose against it. Her face and mine were only inches apart. She was a pretty woman, or would have been in normal circumstances, young, with dark hair and light eyes. Now she was made ugly by hatred, her features distorted, her mouth gaping. She screamed obscenities.

The car moved forward. The policemen were trying to drag her away, but she clung to the door-handle, reviling me. Finally she threw back her head and spat. A glob of spittle spread itself on the glass, and I shied as if I had been hit. Then we were through the gates and they were shutting behind us.

'I'm sorry that happened, sir. It was horrible.'

'Not very pleasant – but not your fault.'

My voice was level. I sat back in my seat and forced myself to breathe slowly. I didn't want him to know how shaken I was. I had to make an effort to keep my eyes averted from the spittle on the window and my hand from wiping my face. I could feel myself sweating. The encounter had been extraordinarily personal.

It was after midnight when I was summoned to the Ambassador. In the interval I had showered, shaved and put on fresh clothes. I had also slept for three hours. I was a new man, the memory of the spitting, cursing woman pushed to the back of my mind.

The Ambassador came forward to greet me and we shook hands. He was a tall, distinguished-looking man, and a career diplomat. He had changed, too. He was wearing slacks, an old jacket and leather slippers. Beneath his left eye there was a three-inch strip of plaster.

'Sorry for the long delay, Camplin, but as my PPS will have told you I had to wave the flag this evening.' He fingered the plaster on his cheek. 'You'll find coffee, drinks, sandwiches on the side-table. Help yourself to whatever you want and come and sit down. Make yourself comfortable. I imagine we're in for a long session.'

'Thank you, sir.'

I poured myself a whisky and soda and, turning round, caught His Excellency studying the reflection of his face in a silver rosebowl. He grinned at me wryly.

'A fellow guest tonight threw a glass of champagne in my face. She said I was a murderer and she wouldn't eat at the same table with me. She was a little tight but it was very embarrassing for everyone, not least my host, who's an Anglophile and a good friend to the UK.' He shook his head sadly. 'This Irish business has really inflamed the Americans – all our allies for that matter. And, of course, it has delighted our enemies, given them a lot of grist for their mills.'

'Yes,' I said, and at once wished the monosyllable hadn't sounded quite so flat.

But the Ambassador appeared not to notice. At any rate he didn't comment. He watched in silence while I unlocked my briefcase and arranged its contents on the coffee-table in front of me. When he still said nothing, I asked him how he wanted to proceed.

'I'd like you to tell me what actually happened on Massacre Day, as they're calling it – the truth, as far as you know it. Even the facts seem to be matters of dispute. After that we can consider our defence. Tomorrow, at these meetings, no one's going to throw glass in our face or spit at us.' He gave me a sympathetic nod to show his PPS had kept him fully informed. 'But we're going to be arraigned. That's what it amounts to, though it'll be done with politeness and discretion. And it'll be up to me, with your help, to put our case. We've got to convince them that the British are not guilty of either inhuman behaviour or criminal negligence, that what happened was – an accident. Do you think that's possible?'

I chose my words carefully. 'I believe the Scots have a verdict of "not proven", sir. If we achieved that, would it be good enough?'

'Probably yes. I'm pretty sure the President won't take positive action unless his immediate advisers urge it, and they're not rash men. Of course, there's a lot of pressure on him – from the Irish Americans, from Congress, from well-meaning people shocked at what happened, from public opinion generally. They all want him to use his influence, to intervene, to "help" the Irish. But he knows that active intervention would at best do irreparable damage to US-UK relations, which would please our mutual enemies, and at worst might turn Ireland – the whole of Ireland – into a battlefield like Vietnam. God help us, it mustn't come to that.' He picked up his coffee-cup, found it empty and put it down again.

'I would say our chances of "not proven" are high, sir.' I wasn't sure I believed this but I hoped I was right.

'Good. Let's get down to it.' He rose and went to pour himself a whisky.

'First, the facts,' I began. 'Needless to say, they've been distorted. The march was yet another March for Peace, mostly women and children or young people, and to begin with it was disciplined and orderly. There should have been no trouble. However, shortly after the march set off a warning was received that bombs had been planted near Dunmarnock Street. This turned out to be untrue. No bombs were found. But it meant the army had no choice but to divert the marchers.'

'What about the IRA's claim that we invented the bomb scare after the disaster, so as to cover ourselves?'

'At least that charge can be disposed of. I have a statement from the girl at the exchange who took the message, and timed it. Her sister was paralysed by the gas so she has no reason to lie.'

'Good.'

'I also have sworn depositions from some of those who were only mildly affected, a local reporter and a woman who was watching the march from her window. They agree broadly on what happened next.' I paused to take a sip of whisky; my throat was still dry after the flight. 'The army lieutenant in charge addressed the marchers through a loud-hailer. There was shouting in response, people at the rear pushed forward, a stone was thrown and then another and another. At this point the whole thing mushroomed. The lieutenant, afraid some of the marchers would break through into the threatened bomb area, ordered his men to disperse them with gas grenades. And here's where we come to the film.'

'Yes, that damned film!' The Ambassador swore. 'It's done us more harm than any newspaper or radio report. It was shown on the news, you know, networked right across the US in prime time.'

I knew. I knew, or was in process of finding out, far more about the film than he did, but I didn't want to discuss it with him. I shuffled some papers and said nothing, waiting for him to continue.

'What can we say, Camplin? No provocation could justify the awfulness of it. Fifty-four dead, mostly women and children, and a couple of hundred in hospital, many permanently crippled, not to mention those who escaped with a very light dose and recovered fairly quickly.'

'The figure's gone up to fifty-five, sir. Another of our soldiers has died.'

'How many of the casualties were in the army?'

'Ten dead, and about another twenty still in hospital.' I thought this would surprise him. The deaths of the soldiers had been almost ignored in the UK, and I suspected they hadn't got much coverage in the States.

'I've a tape here, made by the last chap to die – a corporal. He describes his horror when the gas cloud seemed to clear and he saw the marchers lying on the road. He ran forward to help them and – blank, until he came to in hospital. He swears he had no idea that the grenades he'd been issued with were anything but ordinary tear gas. So do all his chums, including two who are partially paralysed, and the lieutenant in charge.'

'That should help to support the accident theory. But our enemies will argue – and with truth – that if we were deliberately trying out an experimental gas in Northern Ireland, only very senior officers would have known anyway.' The Ambassador stood up and began to walk about the room. 'What's been done to trace the source of these grenades? I assume we know what they were.'

'We think we do, sir, yes.' We were on delicate ground again, but I had to consider tomorrow's meetings; the man must be properly briefed.

'We believe they were part of a batch of experimental grenades developed by a firm that also makes tear gas. How they got muddled with a shipment to Northern Ireland we don't yet know. It's difficult, because this particular lot of trial material was ordered to be destroyed over two years ago.'

'Why? Tell me about it.'

'Well, it seems to have been a failure. What the scientists were looking for was a truly safe instant knock-down weapon, something like Mace or Lance – quick acting, but with no lasting injury, even in the highest concentrations. Certainly stuff that killed in relatively low concentrations and maimed when it didn't kill wasn't within their terms of reference . . .'

It was four a.m. before we went to bed.

Things went better than I had expected. The Ambassador was impressive. He spoke with calm assurance, ignoring provocative criticism and refraining from smugness when he scored a point. Inevitably there were some sticky moments, but by the end of the meetings it was clear that he had persuaded the Secretary of State and most of the White House contingent not to turn thumbs down on us. If they weren't fully prepared to accept that the Belfast tragedy had resulted from a combination of unfortunate accidents, they were willing to withhold judgement. The case against us was 'not proven'.

The Ambassador was jubilant, and generous with his thanks for the help I had given him. For my part I was glad I hadn't let him suspect what was probably the truth of the matter. It would only have confused the issue.

I was leaving Washington that night. There were one or two people I should have liked to see – Hal Runce, an old Oxford friend now in the CIA, for example – but I wanted to get home. I went to say goodbye to the Ambassador, and he thanked me again.

We were shaking hands when he said: 'By the way, Camplin, there's something I'd like to know. My scientific adviser's due for a posting pretty soon. Would you and your wife be interested in three or four years in Washington?'

I swallowed hard. I didn't know what to say. The work would be fascinating, and it was exactly what Claire and I wanted, needed. I heard myself make some non-committal reply, but he understood.

'Don't count on it. There may be someone else lined up for the job. Just consider it – as a possibility.'

I considered it, savoured it, all the way out to Dulles International. I knew what the odds were. I didn't need the Ambassador's warning. Still, if he were to back me . . . I was tired and it did no harm to dream. I didn't intend to mention it to anyone, not even to Claire.

At Dulles I checked in and found a telephone. I tried to get through to Claire, to tell her I would be home tomorrow morning, but her number was engaged. I tried Hal instead. I expected him to be out, partying somewhere, but he answered at once.

'Philip! Say, this is great! Where are you? I'll come and get you. Is Claire with you? How are you both?'

The questions poured out of him, and I had to laugh. But I was touched, too. We didn't meet often these days and we never wrote, but it made no difference. Hal was always the same and we could pick up an old relationship instantly. If I did get this job in Washington, having Hal as a neighbour would be one of the big attractions.

I explained what I was doing at the airport and why I couldn't possibly change my flight, and he pretended to be hurt. But when I told him to stop berating me as I'd already had enough argument for one day – over Ireland – he changed the subject abruptly. This set me back. I didn't understand his reaction. I had assumed he had a good idea of what I was doing in Washington and, whatever his feelings about the situation, he wouldn't hold it against me. I told him that my brother Patrick and Denise, his French wife, were flourishing.

'That's fine, Philip, just fine,' he said, a little too heartily, I thought. 'And what about John?' John Telsey was a mutual friend from our Oxford days. 'When did you last see the old bugger? He was on the box the other night, pontificating on some panel programme, but I was out with my latest girl – you knew I was between wives, didn't you? – and I missed him.'

'He spent a weekend with us at the beginning of last month.'

It hadn't been a very successful weekend, I remembered. Claire had been annoyed when John phoned to invite himself, and she hadn't made much effort for him. When I remonstrated she said that John Telsey, university professor, scholar, wit, befriender of students, was fine, but John Telsey, the TV personality with his charm and his know-all views on foreign affairs, was a bore. I didn't agree. I liked John. Besides, I owed him an unpayable debt. It was through him I met Claire, who had been one of his pupils.

'Philip! Philip! Are you still with me?'

'Sorry, Hal.' I wrenched my thoughts back to the present. 'I must go. I haven't bought my duty-free liquor yet, or a present for Claire.'

'You sure you won't change your mind and stay over? I'd fetch you in no time and – '

'Quite sure, Hal.' I laughed. 'Goodbye. Take care of yourself and come and see us soon.'

I put down the receiver. The warmth that Hal's original greeting had generated was gone, and the conversation had left me uneasy. I wished I hadn't called him.

Telling myself not to be stupid I dialled Claire again. I heard the hum of the transatlantic connection, a click, a pause, and the engaged tone. Claire was still talking to someone – probably to that damned Bette Aylwyn who was such a chum of hers. Irritably I banged down the phone and collected my coins. I couldn't wait any longer. My flight had just been called.

TWO

It was sleeting with rain when we landed at Heathrow and ten degrees colder than in Washington. Everything was sodden with water, the sky a sullen grey. As I lugged my overnight bag and briefcase across to the taxi rank, I shivered in a thin raincoat. I was cold, depressed, and in need of sleep.

Heathrow at seven-thirty of a rainy April morning isn't exactly a cheerful place, and I had been delayed at the Immigration desk. The man ahead of me was a Canadian, but his passport was stamped with a Certificate of Patriality, and he was damned if he was going to join a queue of foreigners to get into the UK. He was right and I sympathized, but the Immigration Officer was inexperienced and the delay was infuriating.

It cost me the last taxi and five minutes waiting in the downpour before another cab came. I threw my bag and briefcase on to the back seat and climbed gratefully after them.

'Harley Street.'

'You a doctor?'

'No, though I may be a patient if you don't get there soon.'

The driver laughed but he took the hint. Luckily it was too early for the commuters and traffic was light. We tore along the M4.

Thankful to be in the warmth of the taxi, I wrung out the bottoms of my trouser legs and dried my hair on a handkerchief. It didn't help much. Rain had trickled down into the inside of my collar. I had trodden in a puddle and my feet were soaked. I was wet, chilled, miserable – but soon I would be home. I refused to feel sorry for myself.

Home was our house in Harley Street. Apart from the years I had been away at school and university I had always lived there. My father had inherited it from his father, who had been a good businessman as well as a doctor. My brothers said they could remember when we occupied the whole house, but my memory only went back to an apartment on the two top floors with consulting-rooms beneath. Today, even the apartment had been divided. Patrick and Denise had the larger flat and Claire and I lived under the eaves in what in my grandfather's time would have been the maids' bedrooms. However, by knocking down some walls we had made a big living-room, two small bedrooms, a bathroom and a kitchen – and a minute roof garden. It had, I admit, inconveniences, but I loved the place.

Even this morning, with the rain beating off the steps and the stonework gleaming damply, the tall, grey house looked welcoming. I opened the handsome front door with its column of brass plates giving the consultants' names and went along to the lift. The lift had been put in by my father and ascended only as far as what was now Patrick's floor; this was one of the inconveniences. I had to carry my bags up the last flight of stairs.

I let myself quietly into the flat. The curtains were drawn and there were no sounds of anyone moving around. I called Claire's name; she wasn't expecting me and I didn't want to startle her by walking into the bedroom while she was asleep. There was no answer, only a piteous miaow from the direction of the kitchen. I laughed. Katy was always getting herself shut in somewhere.

'Claire!' I called, louder this time. 'Claire! It's me, darling. I'm back.'

My words echoed foolishly. Otherwise there was no response. And suddenly I sensed the emptiness of the flat. I opened the kitchen door. Katy half leapt, half clawed her way into my arms. Startled, I fell back a step and Katy began to lick my face with her rasping cat's tongue.

'What's the matter?' I said. 'Why're you so upset? You're not usually such an affectionate puss.'

The questions, I realized, were really directed at myself, not at the cat. Claire wasn't here – and I was upset. But there could be a hundred explanations. Offhand I couldn't think of one that was acceptable.

I went along to our bedroom, switched on the light and stood in the doorway, surveying the mess. There were clothes everywhere, on the floor, on the chair, on the bed. Mostly they were evening clothes, a long dress, two long skirts, a selection of blouses. It looked as if Claire had been going to a party and, undecided what to wear, had put on first one thing and then another, letting the discarded garments lie where they fell. This wasn't unusual. Claire wasn't the tidiest of girls. I half smiled and felt my face grow stiff.

Claire had gone to a party. It must have been a sudden invitation because she hadn't mentioned it before I left for Washington. After the party she hadn't come home. The bed hadn't been slept in; it was still neatly covered with its quilted spread. I gazed at it blankly, my mind a whirl of uncorrelated thoughts.

Then Katy miaowed sharply and tried to struggle from my arms; I realized how hard I had been clutching her. I let her fall and she stalked off, tail erect, back to the kitchen.

I went into the living-room and automatically drew the curtains. The flat looked uncared for. There was dust on the round table where we had our meals, and dead tulips in a vase. The telephone receiver was half off its rest. I stared at it, remembering. Last night, when I had tried to phone Claire from Dulles Airport, I had got the engaged tone and I had assumed she was gossiping with Bette Aylwyn. I could have been wrong. Carefully, I replaced the receiver.

And the telephone rang. I swallowed my saliva. My mouth was dry. I had a horrible, empty feeling in the pit of my stomach and, though I would have been ashamed to admit it, I had to force myself to answer the phone. It was, however, only Mat Harworth, to whom I reported at the Ministry.

'Hallo, Philip. I thought you might be home. How did it go?'

For a moment I didn't know what he was talking about. Then I wrenched my thoughts away from Claire. 'Better than we had a right to expect. The Ambassador was worth his weight in gold.'

'You didn't – er – give him any hint?'

'No. I played it straight.'

'Good. Splendid. Incidentally, one or two things have come

up. You'll be in later?'

'Yes. Yes. I suppose so.'

'You suppose so? What do you mean? Philip, are you okay?'

'Yes – I'm fine.' I was glad he couldn't see me. 'My wits are a bit addled, Mat. That's all. My plane just got in and I don't know whether I'm coming or going.'

'Yes. Yes, of course, old boy. Take your time.' He hesitated. 'But you will be in this morning?'

'I shall be in, Mat, in an hour or two.'

'Good.' He laughed. 'Better feed that cat of yours first. I can hear her yowling from here.'

He did Katy an injustice. Katy never yowled. But she was certainly crying piteously. I went into the kitchen to investigate and found she had neither milk nor water, and her food bowl was clean. Claire seemed to have forgotten her completely.

I attended to the cat and, catching sight of my reflection in a mirror, decided I had better do something about myself too. I shaved and washed and put on a clean shirt. I told myself that if Claire hadn't returned when I was ready to go to the office, I would have to go and talk to Patrick and Denise; at least they could do some straight thinking for me. Claire would be furious, of course, but . . .

I ran downstairs. I rang the bell twice before Denise opened the door. She was wearing a thin robe and nothing beneath it; I could see the outline of her tall, narrow body against the light. Her hair was ruffled, her lips half smiling and her eyes had that lost, dreamy look that only comes from love-making. I didn't realize I was staring until I saw colour stain her cheeks.

'Philip, what a surprise! We weren't expecting you back so soon.' She kissed me lightly and called: 'Patrick, it's Philip. Come and entertain him while I make coffee.'

Patrick appeared almost at once, in a pair of slacks and an old sweater. 'Hallo, brother. That was a short visit to the USA. Didn't you like it there?'

'I've brought you greetings from Hal Runce,' I said. 'And a bottle of duty-free gin. I haven't unpacked the gin yet.'

'Thanks. Can we take it with us to the cottage? I've got the day off and we're making a long weekend of it. We meant to drive down last night, but I had an emergency.' Patrick's ruddy face clouded and his surprisingly gentle voice became gentler. 'A twenty-year-old kid – '

He stopped, frowned at me and said: 'Sorry, Philip. I'm not fully awake yet. You've got a problem yourself?'

'I'm not – sure.'

Denise brought in the coffee. She had pulled on a pair of jeans and a sweater, washed her face and put a comb through her hair. She looked happy.

'Coffee, Philip?' she said.

'Nothing, thanks, Denise. I had some on the plane. I came to ask if you knew where Claire might be.'

'Claire? But – '

I told them, leaving out all mention of Katy and trying to make light of it, as if Claire were in the habit of spending the night out. I knew I wasn't deceiving them but it was easier that way.

'Surely the obvious explanation is that she went to visit friends for the evening and either the car wouldn't start or they suggested she should stay with them rather than go home to an empty flat.'

Patrick smiled at me hopefully and I nodded agreement. It was, as he said, the obvious explanation. Yet I found it difficult to accept; somehow it wasn't like Claire.

'Not to worry, Philip.'

'Don't be silly, Patrick. Of course he's going to worry.' Denise's voice was sharp. 'Philip, if I were you I should wait till noon. If she's not home by then, call anyone she might be staying with. Say you've returned from Washington sooner than expected – as you have. It's quite reasonable. And, Philip dear, don't even think about phoning the hospitals or the police until you're certain – ' She stopped, raised her neat, dark head, and listened. 'I heard the lift. It always gives a thud when it starts. It might be . . .'

I was already on my feet. After my brief trip to the States my sense of time was completely awry, but the clock on the mantel said ten past nine. The consultants usually started their day at ten, secretaries came in at nine-thirty. Patients, if they were up from the country, sometimes arrived early, but they were shown into the communal waiting-room – once our family dining-room – on the ground floor. It might be Claire. I hurried out to the landing.

Containing myself as best I could, I watched the movement of the cables. The lift was coming up. By peering down the shaft I could see its roof ascending. It was one of those metal affairs that exposed its occupants as if they were in a cage and, as soon as I knew it had passed the floor below, I stepped back.

Denise had followed me. I felt her hand on my arm. Momentarily her fingers tightened; it could have been a warning. Then she shut the door of the flat quietly behind me.

I saw Claire's face before she realized I was there. She was lost in thought, happy thought, because she was smiling to herself. Her expression reminded me of someone or something but I couldn't think what. The lift was already drawing level and, as she suddenly became aware of me, her eyes widened and her smile died. Her face went blank, or perhaps it was just a shadow.

'Philip! Philip, darling!'

She pushed back the gate of the lift and almost threw herself into my arms. She seemed delighted to see me.

'Where the hell have you been?'

It wasn't what I meant to say, but it came out that way. My feelings were chaotic. Relief that she was home, safe and well, fought with anger and suspicion. I recognized the anger as a reaction to the fright she had given me. The suspicion I refused to analyse.

'Philip, I'm sorry, darling. I had no idea you were home. When did you get in?'

'You haven't answered my question, Claire.'

'Where have I been?' She glanced over my shoulder and raised her voice as if she suspected Denise of listening at the door. 'I've been at Bette's. She was giving one of her parties and, since you were away, I stayed the night with her. It's as simple as that.'

I looked at her. She was wearing a shocking-pink blouse and a long black skirt – slightly crushed – with the mink jacket I had given her for her last birthday. Her eyes, grey, wide-set, candid, met mine. I didn't know whether I believed her or not and at the moment I didn't care. I knew I loved her.

We went upstairs slowly, with our arms around each other. I told her how I had found the flat empty and the cat neglected and how worried I had been. She was very upset about Katy.

'Oh, Philip, I am sorry. I couldn't guess you'd be home so soon, but I've no excuse for forgetting Katy. I suppose it was because I was in such a flap. The hairdresser kept me and I couldn't decide what to wear and . . .'

I laughed, thinking of the clothes strewn about the bedroom. I pulled her to me and kissed her, as I should have kissed her when she first got out of the lift. I wanted to make love to her then, urgently, but I was tired, Mat was expecting me at the office and, though I wouldn't have admitted it, I had an undefined fear that she might find excuses for refusing me.

'Claire, my love, I must go.'

'Go? Where? You've just got home.'

'To the Ministry. I've work to do.' I kissed her on the end of her small, straight nose. 'Expect me about six.'

Clutching the bottle of gin I had promised Patrick, I hurried down the stairs. Denise opened the door to me as she had done earlier. This was a pity, because it jogged my memory. Suddenly I knew why that lost look I had glimpsed on Claire's face as she came up in the lift had been reminiscent. It was a reflection of Denise's expression when she was warm from Patrick's bed. I felt sick.

I gave Denise the gin. I explained how Claire had stayed the night with Bette Aylwyn and apologized for having panicked. And somehow, by taking explanation and apology for granted, Denise unwittingly reassured me.

On the way to the Ministry I took myself to task. God knows why Claire had ever married me. She should have married someone her own age, someone who could do all the things my game leg prevented me from doing. But our marriage had lasted six years, six pretty happy years, and during that time she had never given me the slightest cause to distrust her. I was damned if I was going to begin now.

The following Friday it was getting on for five and I was preparing – like many of my colleagues – to leave for a long Civil Service weekend. I had at least two good reasons for wanting to be gone. One was that I had done nothing but work since my return from Washington, and I needed some time off. The other was Claire.

Claire had been unwell all the week. Last Monday, when I got home from the office – late as usual – I had found her whey-faced and unable to disguise her distress. She had pleaded a sick headache, said she would be better after a night's rest, begged me not to fuss. It was true she was much better the next day; but she was still pale and withdrawn, her nerves jumping, her temper abrasive. I had persuaded her, with some difficulty, to make an appointment with our GP for this afternoon, and naturally I was anxious to know what he had to say.

My desk was cleared. I had locked my safe. I glanced around the room to make sure everything was in order; it was a reflex habit. Then Mat Harworth came striding in, his pink face shining with satisfaction.

'Philip, they've found O'Reilly at last.'

'They have? Splendid!' I tried to sound enthusiastic. O'Reilly was the freelance photographer who was believed to have taken the film of the disastrous Peace March; a woman, watching from the safety of her house, claimed to have recognized him. 'Where?'

'The Dublin police pulled his body out of the Liffey early this morning. They say he was dead before he hit the water. Interesting, isn't it?'

'Could be – if he was killed because someone didn't want him to talk to us.'

'I think it's fair to assume that, though of course it was made to look like a mugging.'

Mat sat himself down at my desk and calmly lit a cheroot. I

stifled a sigh. Resigning myself to delay, I leaned on the window ledge and looked out.

Far below toy cars raced along Northumberland Avenue, and toy people scurried to catch their trains at Charing Cross. In spite of the stuff the Department of Works put down, the pigeons were busy nesting in the crannies of the dirty grey buildings that lined the street. And a large group of Ghanaians or Nigerians, all in their spring finery, were having their photographs taken outside the Royal Commonwealth Society. There was always something going on, which was why I steadfastly refused to move to a larger office at the rear of the building.

'Philip, will you please concentrate.'

'Sorry, Mat.'

'If it was a mugging, the muggers didn't get much. O'Reilly had a married sister in Dublin, and he'd left over a thousand pounds with her for safe-keeping. He told her he'd "got it for doing a job for someone". That doesn't sound to me like selling a film he'd happened to take. It sounds much more like being commissioned to take one. What do you think?'

'Yes. It fits.' I nodded my agreement. 'Someone knew that a very ordinary demo was going to turn into a shambles, and the only way they could have known was by organizing the whole thing in advance. But we're no nearer proving it, are we?'

'We will. We must.' Mat looked for an ashtray he knew wasn't there, then flicked his cheroot at the carpet. 'We've bought time from the Americans, thanks to the Ambassador and the ammunition we could give him. The President won't intervene in Ireland – not for the moment. But that's not good enough. The situation's too unstable. All it needs is another spark – something quite trivial – and wham! Everyone will be crying for our blood again, and I don't think the President will hold out in the face of public opinion for a second time.'

'Mat, are you still convinced this wasn't masterminded by the IRA?'

'Yes. Positive. They've nothing to gain by bringing in the Americans and making Ireland a free-for-all. Besides, it's much too subtle an operation for them, or for any of their splinter groups. If they'd got hold of those gas grenades they'd never have kept them for two years, and then used them on a Peace March so that we'd get the blame.'

'Has Special Branch come up with anything more about the grenades?'

'No. The research department that made the things seems to have been in a mess at the time. Dr Finton was taking over as director and some of the other staff were changing. I must say, Philip, I'm sorry for Bob Finton. He's terribly upset and he's being as co-operative as he can. Not that we're getting anywhere. Everyone's being re-vetted, of course, but it takes a long time to do a good job, and – '

He stopped short and stroked the top of his nose with his thumb. I knew the sign; Mat had been my boss for a number of years. He was about to offer me some titbit of information he considered important.

'By the way, there's trouble at The Park. They're doing some re-vetting there too – very, very quietly.'

I frowned. The Park, which had once been a country mansion and at present belonged to HMG, was a Ministry of Defence establishment that housed a lot of secrets. Mat had produced another problem. I hoped he didn't want to discuss it.

Surreptitiously I glanced at my watch. Mat was looking for somewhere to stub out his cheroot but he caught me. His mouth stretched in a smile that reached his bulbous eyes. He stood up. He was a kind man.

'Well, there's nothing more we can do for the moment, Philip, and it's Friday night. I'm keeping you from that charming wife of yours. Let's go.'

We walked up Northumberland Avenue together and across Trafalgar Square. Nelson, atop his column, was faintly rose-coloured in the setting sun. It was a lovely spring evening. Mat talked about his garden, and I promised myself a stroll in Regent's Park if the weather held. I thought about the weekend ahead, dinner in one of our favourite restaurants tomorrow night, perhaps a movie at the Curzon on Sunday afternoon, otherwise a lazy time. I hoped Claire was looking forward to it as much as I was.

At the corner by Canada House I spotted an unoccupied taxi. I shouted a goodbye to Mat and ran for it, waving my umbrella. The traffic swept past, cars, taxis, coaches, double-decker buses, motor-bikes, trucks. But my luck was in; the driver had seen me. Thankfully I scrambled in.

'Harley Street!'

I was home in twenty minutes. There was a gaggle of doctors in front of the lift so I went up the stairs. It was a long haul. When I reached the flat I was breathing hard. It's difficult to keep in shape if you have a sedentary job and you can't play any sport. I waited to get my breath before I opened the door.

Claire was sitting in the wing chair, with the cat on her lap. She was wearing the grey wool dress that I liked so much and she was beautiful. The thought did stray across my mind that she wasn't reading or watching the box or listening to the radio or anything, except sitting, but I didn't pay much attention.

'Hallo, darling. Don't get up. You'll disturb Katy.'

'Hallo, Philip.'

I bent and kissed her. Her mouth tasted of gin. Claire wasn't much of a drinker and she never drank alone. A knot of fear tightened in my gut.

'What did David have to say?'

'David?'

'David Holmes. Claire, you did go and see him this afternoon?

'Yes. Yes, I did. And he gave me a thorough check-up. He says I may be a little anaemic but otherwise I'm fine. I wish you'd stop worrying about me, Philip.'

Her voice was sharp, but I didn't care. The knot in my gut loosened. I poured myself a whisky and soda and sat myself down. One drink, and then I would go and change out of my office clothes. I sniffed. I couldn't smell anything cooking. I hoped Claire didn't want to go out tonight.

'That's wonderful news, darling, and I promise not to nag you any more.' I grinned at her, but she ignored me. 'What's for dinner?'

'Can I have a gin and tonic?'

'Yes, of course. I'm sorry.'

I had to go into the kitchen to get some ice. When I came back Claire had pushed Katy off her lap and was standing by the window. I handed her the glass. She took it without looking at me and drank about a third of it.

'Philip, there's something I've got to tell you. But first I want to say that I love you very much indeed.'

'I love you too, darling, more than anything in the world.'

'I know!'

'Claire – '

She didn't really have to tell me. I knew. I had known ever since I returned from Washington and found the empty flat, her clothes strewn around the room, the bed not slept in, Katy shut in the kitchen. But I hadn't faced up to it before.

'Why?' I said. 'Why?'

'Philip, it just – happened. We met by chance. He was in London for some meeting. I'd been to Marks and Sparks and . . . I hadn't seen him for six years, not since we were at Oxford. I was desperately in love with him then, but – it didn't work out. We arranged to have dinner together . . . someone had lent him a flat . . . we had a lot to talk about . . . Philip, it was sex, nothing else . . .'

I didn't listen. She hadn't understood my question. I didn't want to know why she had slept with her old boy-friend. What I wanted to know was why in Christ's name she was telling me about it. Crystallized into words, I found it unbearable.

THREE

'Philip, I think you should go to Dublin.'

'All right. When?'

'What about Thursday? You could take Claire and stay over till Monday.'

'No.'

'My dear chap, I'm offering the two of you a long weekend in Dublin's fair city, all expenses paid, and you turn me down.'

'I'm not turning you down, Mat. It's part of my job to make expeditions on your behalf. But HMG doesn't employ Claire.'

Mat, startled by my vehemence, regarded me solemnly. 'It's Dublin I'm asking you to go to, not Belfast, Philip. There'll be no danger,' he said mildly, 'and if you take your wife it'll be like a private visit.'

'What am I to do there?'

'Call on O'Reilly's sister. If you ask her the right questions you might get something out of her. She'll be over the shock of his murder by now and . . .'

I listened to what Mat had to say because I knew he wouldn't repeat his instructions, but my mind was on Claire. Claire wouldn't want to come to Ireland with me and I had no intention of pressing her. At the moment our relationship was fragile.

I hadn't wrung Claire's neck last Friday or raped her in anger or even walked out on her. I was much too civilized. I hadn't wept either. And of course she didn't understand. In the end it was she who had stormed and cried, and hating myself I had tried to comfort her – with lies. It had been a bitter scene. I was determined we should both forget it, if we could. But for that we needed time.

Meanwhile we were very polite and considerate to each other – and everything was bloody hell, at any rate for me. I didn't attempt to fathom Claire's feelings. I suspected that in some strange way she was happier than she had been before; I heard her singing in the kitchen once, something she had not done for ages. I did my best not to think about it.

'I'll get Claire's number for you and you can ask her, Philip.'

'Can't it wait until this evening?'

Mat paid no attention. He pressed the intercom button, told his secretary to ring Mrs Camplin and handed me the receiver. I waited, hoping that Claire would be out.

'Hallo.'

'Claire, it's me, darling. Listen, I have to go to Dublin on Thursday. Would you like to come? We could stay over the weekend. I shan't be very busy and you might enjoy it. But – but if you'd rather not, just say.'

She hesitated. 'What about Katy?'

This wasn't the reaction I had expected. 'Denise will look after her.'

'All right. Then I'd like to come.'

'You're – sure?'

'Yes. That is if you – you – '

Conscious that Mat was listening, I didn't let her finish the sentence. I said how pleased I was and that I would arrange everything. Even to myself I sounded stilted. I put down the receiver and gave Mat a thin smile. At once he became jovial.

'Splendid, Philip, splendid! I'm sure Claire'll love Dublin.' He paused to light a cheroot. 'Incidentally, O'Reilly left his ill-gotten gains with his sister, but it seems he also visited another lady when he came south – someone he'd known on and off for years. Perhaps you might pay her a call too?'

It was a rhetorical question and I didn't bother to answer. I would do whatever Mat wished. It wasn't as if I had been looking forward to the weekend at home.

Thursday was one of those beautiful spring days with fleecy white clouds scudding across a blue sky; it didn't look quite real. Denise drove us to Heathrow and, while the two women chatted, I thought about the last time I had travelled along the M4 – less than two weeks ago, in the pouring rain and the opposite direction. They weren't pleasant thoughts.

Luckily there wasn't much time to brood once we reached the airport. We had cut things fine, and our plane was already boarding. We joined the tail of the queue. As we shuffled along I spotted two plainclothes men casually noting everyone who passed them. I had never seen either of them before, but one of them gave me a brief nod.

We landed at Dublin Airport on schedule after a perfect flight and, since HMG was paying, I took a taxi the five and a half miles from Collinstown. The first person we met on entering the lobby of the Shelbourne Hotel was John Telsey.

John had just nodded goodbye to the receptionist and was turning to pick up his bag when he caught sight of us. He wasn't pleased. The smile faded from his face and his eyes flickered from side to side as if he were looking for the nearest exit. Only when it was obvious he couldn't avoid us did he decide to make the best of it.

'My dears, what a lovely surprise! And what are you two doing in Dublin?'

'Having a brief holiday,' I said hurriedly, probably too hurriedly because I saw his interest quicken. 'What about you, John?'

'Work – what else? I've been filming an hour's panel discussion for the box on "The Problem of Northern Ireland".'

'I didn't know you were an expert on Ireland, John.'

'My dear Claire, I'm an expert on everything, though I must admit I'm not in Philip's league when it comes to the Irish troubles.'

The remark took me aback. It was no great secret that my current work was concerned with Northern Ireland. Nevertheless I hadn't expected John, in spite of his many contacts, to be so well informed. I didn't comment. Instead, I suggested he had a drink with us.

'I'd like to, Philip, but I've a plane to catch. I have to attend a damnable College meeting this evening and I must get back to Oxford.'

'Surely we can spare ten minutes, love. We've heaps of time.'

Bette Aylwyn's soft, husky American voice was unmistakable. I hadn't heard her approach but I had been aware of turning heads and a stir of interest. Wherever she went, Bette, six feet tall and slender, with a cap of copper hair and outrageous clothes, was always a focus of interest. Today she was wearing what could only be described as a lemon-coloured jump-suit, and she looked terrific. It was difficult to believe she had a seventeen-year-old son.

'Johnny's embarrassed,' she said. 'He hoped Dublin would be a nice safe place for a dirty weekend, but these days nowhere's safe. You might as well go to Brighton or Paris – or stay in London. You're certain to bump into friends.'

'Do you have to spell it out, Bette?'

'Why not, Johnny my love? We're grown-up, aren't we?'

'I'm not so sure you are, my dear.'

John wasn't pleased. To be honest, nor was I. Another time I would have been amused; Bette liked to wife around and John could take care of himself. Now things were different. I was hyper sensitive and Bette's words had hurt. They reminded me that she had been Claire's alibi; she knew Claire had made a cuckold of me. I wondered if she had told John, if they had laughed about it together. I wished we hadn't met them.

Yet five minutes later, such was the force of Bette's personality, we were all sitting in the Horseshoe Bar, chatting, our private embarrassments forgotten. Bette, who had limitless energy, was describing the things that Claire simply must not miss. Claire protested that she would be exhausted.

'Quite right,' John said. 'On a first visit to Dublin there are only three essentials. For piety, you must go to St Patrick's Cathedral and bow three times at the tomb of Jonathan Swift. For culture, you must go to Trinity College and see the Book of Kells. And for pleasure, go to Guinness's Brewery and try that dark, dark brew.'

We laughed and he added: 'You can buy up the shops while Philip's working, Claire.'

'Working? I'm not here to work,' I said.

'But while you are here, don't tell me you won't be seeing a man about a dog.'

'I won't be seeing anyone about anything, John.'

I grinned at him, wondering why he was so interested. Perhaps he just liked to be informed. Well, he wasn't going to be informed about the two women I proposed to call on.

John put down his glass. 'Come on, Bette, we must go.'

'Thanks for the drink, Philip.' Bette got up reluctantly. 'You know, in spite of what I said before, it is odd that we should meet like this. Johnny thought he saw another old friend – a friend of you both – yesterday on Marlborough Street. An American. What did you say his name was, love?'

'I was wrong. It was merely a resemblance.' John was short.

'You're not talking about Hal Runce by any chance, are you?' I asked, suddenly curious myself.

'Yes, but I made a mistake, Philip. It wasn't Hal. In fact, the chap wasn't very like him.'

'Johnny, you were certain it was this Hal. You jumped out of the cab and ran after him. You and he disappeared into some church. What was it called?'

'St Mary's Pro-Cathedral.' John bit off the words. 'I was wrong, Bette. It wasn't Hal Runce. It was someone who looked vaguely like him, that's all.'

'As you have already said, my love.' Bette could be acid too. 'But that wasn't what you thought at the time, was it?'

'If that plane's not going to take off without us . . .' John said.

I caught Claire's eye and suppressed a grin. However much he had enjoyed himself in bed I didn't think John would be planning any more jaunts with Bette for a while. Yet I didn't understand why he was in such a state. Normally John was a casual, relaxed man, but not today. Something had got under his skin.

Claire commented on it when we were unpacking. 'It's unlike John to run after shadows. Philip – do you think Hal could be in Dublin?'

'Not very likely. When I talked to him in Washington he never mentioned coming to Europe, let alone Ireland,' I said. 'What would he be doing here, anyway? No. I think too much

Bette probably fevered John's imagination.'

The first thing I had to do was follow protocol and make my number with the *Garda*. London had been on to them about my visit, and they were correct if not particularly forthcoming. They had clearly written off O'Reilly's death as an ordinary mugging, and were hoping that any deeper issues would go away. In any case, they raised no objection to my visiting the sister, and didn't even press a companion on me. The girl-friend we had kept to ourselves.

O'Reilly's sister lived in a terraced house on the outskirts of the city. When I knocked at five o'clock the door was opened by a small boy with jam smeared across his face. He took one look at me and bolted, leaving the door ajar. I pushed it gently open. Two girls were giggling at the end of the hall, which smelt of cabbage. When I spoke to them they ran off, but an older boy, about fifteen or sixteen, appeared.

'What do you want, mister?'

'I'd like to speak to your mother.'

'You can't. She's busy. She's getting m'Dad's tea.'

He stood squarely in front of me. He wasn't being aggressive exactly, but he was taking care to occupy the whole doorway as if he were afraid I might try to push into the house.

'My name's Camplin,' I said. 'Would you please ask her if she'll see me? It's important.'

The boy hesitated. He recognized the authority in my voice but he couldn't place me. I could almost hear his brain ticking – not police, not a reporter, what? His eyes flickered over me, appraising my clothes. He frowned.

'You're British,' he said. 'The chap who came yesterday was a Yank.'

'Who is it, Rory?'

The arrival of a small, dark-haired woman and the need to introduce myself enabled me to absorb the shock of what Rory had said. Mrs O'Donovan was more welcoming than her son. I was ushered past the pram in which the youngest O'Donovan slept, and into the front parlour.

'Sit down, Mr Camplin. Sit down. Rory, tell Maureen to bring us a pot of tea.' She waved away my protest. 'I wasn't expecting you yet, Mr Camplin.'

'You were expecting me?'

'Indeed yes, Mr Camplin. The gentleman who was here yesterday said we'd be hearing from you.' My expression must have changed because she added, 'You have come about the compensation for my brother, haven't you, sir?'

'No, Mrs O'Donovan. I'm afraid not. I'm from the Ministry of Defence in London. I'm not connected with Mr Runce. It was – er – Mr Runce who came to see you, wasn't it?'

'Yes,' she said, 'and a very nice gentleman he was, very kind. He explained how it made no difference, m'self being married to a Dubliner and living in the South. The group of Americans he represents wants to compensate anyone who's suffered because of that dreadful massacre in Belfast.'

'I don't quite understand the connection, Mrs O'Donovan, between you and – '

'Well, I lost my brother, didn't I? He was given a great deal of money to go and film the March and he gave me some of it, I know. But it was because of that film he was murdered maybe, because he was there and saw it all. He said it was ghastly what happened, Mr Camplin. Mr Runce himself says the same. Mr Runce has been to Belfast to visit the families of some of the poor victims and . . .'

Her stream of words was interrupted by Maureen with the tea and, apart from a cup of black brew that must have coated my throat with tannin, I got little more out of Mrs O'Donovan. She was willing enough to talk, but she knew nothing of value. She made it clear, however, that all my questions had already been asked by my old friend Hal. The CIA was way ahead of me.

They'd forestalled me with O'Reilly's lady-friend too. When I called on Bridie Connell the following morning I discovered, not altogether to my surprise, that Hal had visited her two days ago. The only satisfaction I could get from this was imagining Mat Harworth's reaction when he heard about it.

Nevertheless, my visit to Bridie Connell was worthwhile.

Bridie – a successful prostitute with the face of a saint – was intelligent. O'Reilly had told her everything he knew or guessed, and it confirmed Mat's theories in full.

'Someone deliberately caused the massacre, Mr Camplin. Pat realized that, but he was scared not to give them the film as he'd promised. When they sent him the money with orders to lose himself he came down to Dublin and stayed with me in the flat here.' She gave me a wide, sad smile. 'I took a holiday from my work. Then Pat started making enquiries. He was still scared but he was angry at the way he'd been used, and he was curious. He wanted to know who these people were.' She sighed. 'Next thing the police were fishing his body out of the Liffey.'

'Did he discover anything?'

'Not much, except that the Provos had no part in it. He was convinced of that, and I'm sure he was right. He did say – you're not going to like this.'

'Try me.'

'He did say a pal of his, a chap high up in the IRA, told him it was organized from England. No, don't be sceptical! The chap wasn't blaming the British Government, not this time. He thought it was some outsiders trying to stir up trouble – the communists perhaps – but he swore neither the IRA nor the Provos nor any of their supporters were connected with it. He said they'd never kill or maim their fellow Irish in that way, and I believe him.'

I thanked her. We shook hands and said goodbye. I opened the front door, and she reached across me and shut it again. She looked at me with large, innocent eyes that belied her experience.

'Mr Camplin, I'm from the North myself – I didn't come to Dublin till I was seventeen – and I've known Pat O'Reilly all my life. If you can scrag the shits who killed him and caused that terrible massacre, I'll – I'll have a mass said for you, that I will.'

She laughed to hide the genuineness of her feelings, and I smiled in sympathy. I didn't want to press. I sensed she was on the point of saying something that could be vital, but was half afraid to commit herself.

'You understand, Mr Camplin, I have my regular clients. I don't do one-night stands. But occasionally one of my regulars will ask me as a favour if I'll accommodate a friend or even a – a business acquaintance of his.'

'They know they can rely on your discretion?'

'Yes.' She nodded. 'This may not be important, and I didn't mention it to Mr Runce. But a night or two after Massacre Day I had a special like that – he was an Irish American – and of course we talked about the tragedy. He pretended to be very concerned but I don't think he was really. He said: "You mustn't worry your pretty head over these things, my dear. They happen and they'll go on happening as long as – as there's an Oxford and Cambridge." Then he roared with laughter.'

'As long as there's an Oxford and Cambridge?'

'It sounds silly, I know, Mr Camplin, but I'm sure it meant something to him.' She made a face. 'He was a horrible man. I asked my regular who he was, and my regular said he's returned to the States and, if I had any sense, I'd forget he existed. Mr Camplin, you won't – '

'No. Don't worry.'

It was a facile remark. Twenty-four hours later Bridie was dead – strangled, apparently by one of her customers, though he was never to be found. I didn't hear about her death until Monday.

Claire and I enjoyed the weekend. My conscience pricked me a little, but I had telephoned Mat and given him a carefully-worded account of my progress, and he had urged me to stay on in Dublin. So we went sight-seeing. We went to the theatre. We had some excellent fish meals. We made love. We seemed close again. And on Sunday we went to church.

We went to Evensong at Christ Church Cathedral, which is at the top of Lord Edward Street and a pleasant walk from the hotel on St Stephen's Green. We decided to do this at the last moment. Neither of us is religious, but Claire hadn't seen the supremely beautiful interior of Christ Church and I wanted to hear the choir.

Because we wanted to look round the Cathedral we lingered after the service until the congregation had left. When we came out, a few minutes later, the priest was still standing near the great door, chatting to some of his parishioners. At the kerb a woman was loading a large family into a station wagon. And, not far from them, a youth in a green crash helmet sat on a motorbike, waiting.

I took Claire's arm. We started down the steps. The youth in the green helmet had been waiting for us. As soon as he saw us he waved his gloved hand above his head and roared away. Immediately a parked car drew out into the road and accelerated past the Cathedral.

A split second before it was level with us I saw the gunman at the nearside window. Instinctively I thrust Claire to one side, out of danger. My weak leg gave under me, and I fell. The bullet hit me in the chest high above the heart.

It didn't hurt. I couldn't feel it. I lay on my back and wondered where all the people had come from and what the fuss was about and why someone was screaming. It wasn't Claire. Claire knelt beside me. Her face was paper white, her eyes enormous and she was biting her bottom lip. A great scarlet smear stained her suit. It was blood, I realized, my blood. Everything was growing dark. The priest knelt on the other side of me. Someone put a coat over the lower half of my body and someone else made a pillow for my head. I shut my eyes. The sweet salt smell of the Liffey seemed very strong.

Then, after a while, I was lifted on to a stretcher and put in an ambulance. Claire sat close to me, holding my hand. There was something I had to tell her, but I couldn't think what it was. A man in a white jacket was cutting off my shirt and inexplicably this hurt. He had already jabbed me in an arm. I was losing consciousness again. But I remembered what it was I had to tell Claire. With a great effort I managed to whisper to her.

'Phone Mat – Mat Harworth. He'll cope with – everything.'

Claire's face contorted and she turned her head away, tears streaming down her cheeks. I wanted to reassure her but I couldn't. I was falling through clouds, slowly, slowly . . .

I came to in a hospital bed, in a private room. A nurse was sitting near. I tried to move my hand and found it was bandaged to a board. My eyes followed the tube that snaked from the bandage to the plastic bottle above my head. I was being fed intravenously.

'You can see we're taking good care of you, Mr Camplin,' the nurse said, with a brogue so thick as to sound like stage Irish. 'The bullet came out cleanly and did little damage, but we're guarding you against shock – and other things.' She nodded towards the door. 'There's an armed man in the corridor to protect you. No one will be harming you in here.'

'Good.' I managed a smile. 'What about my wife?'

'She's fine, asleep – as you should be. The doctor gave her a sedative. She'll visit you in the morning.'

I would like to have seen Claire for myself, to have talked to her for a minute, but I was too tired to argue. I let my eyes close. I slept.

The morning brought a succession of visitors – nurses, doctors, police, Claire, a representative from the British Embassy, and Mat Harworth. To be honest, none of them was welcome, not even Claire. Except for her they wanted to ask too many questions. She sat, wan and empty-eyed, and I was tempted to snap my fingers in front of her face to wake her from her seeming trance. I supposed it was a form of shock.

'Claire, darling, it's all right. There's no permanent harm. I'm only temporarily damaged.'

'If you hadn't pushed me out of the way I'd have been killed.'

I stared at her, momentarily puzzled by her remark. 'I very much doubt it, darling. I know it's not easy to shoot accurately from a car, especially if the target's moving too, but it would have been bad luck if you'd been hit. He wasn't aiming for you.'

'Philip – ' She shook her head as if in exasperation. 'Do you really believe it was meant for you? Because of your bloody job? Because you've been involved in this enquiry into – into Massacre Day?'

'That appears to be the general opinion, yes, though it's conceivable they could have been after the priest. He was quite close.'

'I – I hope you're – Oh, Philip darling!'

Suddenly she bent and kissed my hand. I was touched. It was a surprising gesture coming from Claire, who was inclined to despise overt sentiment. For a second I was tempted to tell her about the possibility of my posting to Washington, but Mat Harworth interrupted us.

Mat had no doubt whatsoever that the bullet had been intended for me and that it had been intended to kill me. The idea didn't seem to depress him and I resented his cheerful attitude to what might have been the end of me. When I said so, he grew serious.

'But, Philip, surely you understand. If they're gunning for you now, it must be because you're getting hot.'

'The IRA – the Provos?'

'Certainly not. Of course they're getting the blame, but that merely exacerbates the situation. No, I mean the real enemy, the one – God rot his soul – who organized the disaster in Belfast.'

'If I've become a threat to him – or them – I wish I knew why,' I said bitterly.

Mat ignored the comment. 'It wasn't a very efficient attack on you,' he said. 'It was probably planned in a hurry.'

'No one could have known we were going to Evensong at Christ Church Cathedral.'

'You might have been followed from the hotel. Apart from your family and obvious people at the Ministry, who knew you were in Dublin?'

I thought carefully before I answered. 'John Telsey, the political commentator and an old friend of mine.'

'Also a don, at Oxford.'

'For God's sake, Mat, are you going to distrust anyone who

is or ever was at Oxford or Cambridge on the strength of Bridie's story?'

'She gave us a lead, a positive lead.'

'Perhaps. Anyway, John had been staying at the Shelbourne with Bette Aylwyn. She's the American widow of Sir George. You remember the eccentric MP who died a couple of years ago? They were about to catch the London plane when we met them and we had a drink in the bar together.'

'Who else?'

'Mrs O'Donovan and her brood. Conceivably Hal Runce.' I grinned at him. 'Another Oxford man, Mat, and an American of Irish descent, though not the same as Bridie's special.'

'Runce is CIA.'

'My dear Mat, you know there are bad apples in every barrel.' I enjoyed mocking him. John, Bette, Hal – I might as well suspect Mat himself; after all, he had been at Cambridge. 'For that matter Bridie knew – '

'No, not Bridie.'

And he told me how Bridie had died. It wiped the grin from my face.

FOUR

Claire went back to London with Mat Harworth. She had protested, but half-heartedly. She was yearning to get out of Ireland.

Because she had a sense of guilt at leaving me, she phoned each day and we had long, difficult conversations. The situation became more and more unsatisfactory and finally my patience burst. In the face of my doctors' advice, the objections of the Irish authorities who were making fruitless enquiries into the shooting and the concern of the Ambassador – yet another friend of my brother Andrew – I decided to remove myself.

The security which accompanied me to the airport at Collinstown would have done justice to a Cabinet Minister. It seemed to cease, however, on the Aer Lingus flight somewhere over the Irish Sea. I was an ordinary passenger again.

I realized this when, without apology, a man slid into the empty seat beside me. He was a short, solid individual with a pock-marked face, reddish hair and a walrus moustache. His breath smelt of cigarette smoke and I noticed that the fingers of his right hand were heavily stained with nicotine. He wasn't what one would call an attractive personality.

'My name's Derwent,' he said. 'I'm a journalist. Freelance. I'd like to interview you, if you don't mind, Mr Camplin?' He had a strong Irish accent.

'I do mind, Mr Derwent.'

'But why, Mr Camplin? Why do you shy away from the media? No photographs, no interviews, everything under wraps. It's not as if you'd been a coward. You were very brave, throwing yourself dramatically in front of your wife like that.' Somehow he made my behaviour sound ridiculous. 'You didn't do so good by Bridie Connell, did you?'

My instinct was to say 'who?', but I managed to swallow the

word. It would have amounted to an admission that I knew what he was talking about. I wondered who the hell Derwent was. Not even the Irish police had been told that I had visited Bridie the day before her death. I signalled to the steward.

'Would you ask this gentleman to return to his own seat and stop bothering me, please?'

'Sir.' The steward looked from me to Derwent and rapidly decided in my favour. He addressed the self-styled journalist. 'Do you have a first-class ticket, sir?'

'You know damn well I haven't.' Derwent showed his yellow teeth in a grin. 'Okay. I'll go quietly.' He stood up and, as he got out of the seat, he leaned over me so that the steward couldn't hear what he said.

'Just a demo, Mr Camplin, to show how vulnerable you are. Next time your wife might not be so lucky.'

His face was close to mine and I was aware of his unpleasant breath, his wet lips and his small red eyes. Angrily I jerked my head aside. And he laughed. He was genuinely amused. He wasn't like the woman who had spat at me in Washington, but I was equally revolted by him and I sensed that he was the more dangerous.

The steward returned. 'I'm sorry about that, sir. It won't happen again.' He looked at me anxiously. 'Is there anything I can get you? A whisky, perhaps?'

'Yes, please.' I was conscious of my thumping heart and the sweat on my skin; I was still weak. 'A whisky would be fine.'

For the rest of the flight I sipped my drink and pondered on Derwent's words. As a message they were ambivalent. They could mean that next time the job would be done properly and Claire would be made a widow; or they could mean that next time the danger would be to Claire herself. Neither prospect was encouraging, especially as I hadn't the faintest idea how to appease the enemy – even supposing that I were willing and able to do so.

At Heathrow I was met by Mat in a chauffeured Ministry car, and by Claire. I was delighted to see them both. However, each acted as a brake on the other. Mat was yearning to talk shop but couldn't in front of Claire, and Claire was restricted by Mat's presence. As a result our meeting was constrained, and it wasn't till I was home that I thought of Mr Derwent again. I hadn't seen him at the airport.

I would have to tell Mat about Derwent, though I was reluctant to do so. I didn't want police protection. And finding Derwent, even if it were possible, would achieve nothing. Derwent would maintain that he was a freelance journalist and that all he had done was give me a friendly warning which I had misunderstood. He was too clever to provide us with a lead. I sighed. It was absurd that I – and Claire, because of me – should be in danger, but it seemed that we were. If only I knew why . . .

It was three days before I found out about the telephone calls. Our number is unlisted but of course we've given it to family and friends, and a lot of them phoned to ask how I was and to commiserate. The telephone was ringing constantly. Claire always seemed to answer it and, if there was an inordinate amount of 'wrong numbers', I didn't notice.

Then, over the weekend, Hal Runce phoned. He was in London on duty, and when could we meet. I was tempted to ask him if he intended to offer me compensation for being shot, but instead I invited him to dinner at the flat. We agreed on the following Wednesday.

I said goodbye and was about to suggest to Claire that we consider what other guests we should ask with Hal, when the phone rang again. My hand was within inches of the receiver. Claire had no excuse for intervening.

'Hallo.'

There was a pause, heavy breathing and a muffled laugh. 'That's Mr Camplin, isn't it?' The voice was dimly familiar.

'Yes. Who are you?'

'Derwent here, Mr Camplin. You remember me?'

'What do you want?'

'Who is it, Philip?' Claire's voice was high.

'It's all right, darling.'

'Ah, it's not me you'd be calling darling, is it now, Mr Camplin?' He mocked me. 'Claire must be with you. Good!

Tell her she's liable to have a little accident if she's not careful, will you?'

He didn't wait for an answer. The line went dead. And I sat, holding the receiver and remembering Derwent's wet mouth with its large discoloured teeth and weeping moustache, his bad skin, his foul breath, his angry eyes. The knuckles of my hand were white. I hated him, not least for his familiar use of Claire's first name.

'Philip, who was it? What did he want?'

'Do you know anyone called Derwent?'

'Derwent? No. Who is he?'

I described him, and how I'd met him on the plane, but she continued to shake her head. She wasn't lying. Yet she was scared. She sat on the edge of the chair, tense and miserable. Katy rubbed against her leg but she paid no attention.

'Darling, if you're never heard of this man why are you so frightened because he phoned?'

Claire moistened her lips with her tongue. Then she opened her mouth as if she were about to speak. No sound came. She made a feeble attempt to smile.

'What – what did he say, Philip? Tell me, please.'

The truth hit me. Claire didn't know Derwent, but she knew – or was afraid she knew – why he had telephoned. It wasn't the first threatening call he had made to us. I cursed myself for my obtuseness at not realizing this at once.

'He said – ' I stopped. I couldn't tell her what Derwent had said. I had to lie. 'He said I should be careful or I might have another accident.'

'Oh, God!'

'Claire, how often has Derwent phoned?'

'Three – four times. It isn't always Derwent, though. Sometimes it's a woman. She phoned the day after I got back from Dublin.'

'The threat was the same?'

'Yes.'

But Claire had hesitated and I guessed she was prevaricating. She wouldn't want me to worry about her. In all likelihood both of us were being threatened. I wished I knew how they had got hold of an unlisted number.

'Darling, I'm sorry. This is some form of harassment because of my bloody job. I'll put a stop to it, I promise you.'

'Don't be silly! You can't! It'll go on and on – ' She shook her head hopelessly.

I said I would have the phone disconnected temporarily and the number changed. Then, wanting above all to reassure her, I told her of the possibility of being posted to Washington.

And she began to laugh. She became semi-hysterical. I poured her some brandy, made her sip it, wondered if I should fetch Patrick. Gradually she grew calmer, but it had been a frightening experience. I had never seen Claire in such a state before.

Wednesday was the day of our dinner-party for Hal Runce. At the office it was a day of petty irritations, interruptions, nothing achieved. I was meant to be 'taking things easy' still, but this was impossible. I was showered with work.

And Mat didn't help. He kept on referring people and problems to me, wandering in and out of my office, making the place stink of his cheroots. It was far into the afternoon before I discovered what was bothering him. The leak at The Park had been narrowed to half-a-dozen suspects. Of these, one of the most likely was the son of a friend of Mat's, whom Mat himself had sponsored for the job. I agreed this was unfortunate. I sympathized. But I wished Mat would leave me to get on with my work.

Because of all these frustrations I was home later than I intended. Claire had already changed. She was wearing the same blouse and long skirt she had worn the morning I had returned from Washington. That hurt.

I kissed her hurriedly and made for the bathroom. I would have liked a leisurely soak, but only had time for a quick shower and shave. Five minutes before our guests were due I was ready. I found Claire in the kitchen, busy adding wine to a casserole that smelt delicious. While she put out dishes of olives and nuts,

I filled the ice-bucket. Everything was under control. Suddenly I realized that I was looking forward to the evening.

'By the way, Philip, your friend from the Institute for Strategy Research – Monique Laroche – phoned to say she had flu and couldn't come.'

'Damn! I hoped she'd balance the party.'

'Yes. I asked Bette instead. I had to explain we'd been let down at the eleventh hour, but she didn't mind.'

I looked at Claire in exasperation. Bette Aylwyn was the last person to replace the scholarly Miss Laroche. I could imagine her flirting madly with Hal, annoying Denise with anti-French remarks and shocking Margaret Harworth. In the event, however, though she did all these things, I was glad of Bette. Without her we might have been mourners at a wake.

The Harworths were the first to arrive. Mat was as glum as he had been at the office. Margaret, blue-haired and sharp-nosed but still retaining traces of the prettiness of her youth, had obviously been told the bad news. Usually she chattered about her grandchildren and her garden and her dogs and the church and the Women's Institute; tonight she sat, absentmindedly playing with the clasp of her evening bag. It wasn't a good beginning.

Denise came next, alone. Patrick had been called out unexpectedly. He sent his apologies. He would do his best but we weren't to wait dinner for him; it was possible he would be very late indeed.

I had scarcely absorbed this depressing fact when the doorbell rang again. I went down in the lift and found Hal on the doorstep with an enormous bunch of long-stemmed roses, a present for Claire. We greeted each other with a certain amount of constraint, though Hal was boisterous as ever. Neither of us mentioned Ireland.

In the flat Hal kissed Claire and Denise and I introduced him to the Harworths. There were exclamations from the women at the beauty of the roses. But the flurry of excitement died quickly. Claire went to arrange the flowers. Margaret returned to her discussion of children with a bored Denise. Mat, pretending not to know that Hal was CIA, questioned him about his work and what he was doing in London. Apart from my duties as a barman I was redundant.

Bette's arrival changed everything. When I brought her into the sitting-room, conversation ceased. Hal leapt to his feet and offered her his chair. Mat stood more slowly, but bowed lower over her hand. Margaret regarded her disapprovingly as I had expected, and Denise, who knew Bette but didn't like her much, made some charmingly catty remark about the dress-suit-costume Bette was wearing.

I suppressed a grin. Denise's supposed confusion was understandable. Bette was more suitably clothed for a *fête de nuit* than a small dinner-party in Harley Street. She was swathed in chiffon from neck to thigh, baggy trousers tight at the ankles covered her legs, and slippers with long curling toes adorned her feet. The whole of this creation shaded from pale mauve to purple. But, as always, Bette looked incredibly beautiful. Hal couldn't take his eyes off her.

Bette pirouetted slowly and unconcernedly before her audience. 'This,' she said, 'is my harem *ensemble*. They're all the rage in the States. You must buy one when they get to Paris, Denise.'

Hal laughed aloud; he was charmed by Bette and would have laughed at any witticism she attempted. Unjustly, Denise gave me a quick suspicious glance. I hoped my face was a blank.

Claire came back with the roses and Bette, having kissed her, held her at arms' length. 'You're a bit black under the eyes, sweetie. Have you been getting more of those threatening phone calls?'

The question caused shock waves round the room. Everyone reacted differently. Mat glared furiously at me; I looked my reproach at Claire, who was flushed with embarrassment; Denise shook her head in disgust at Bette's remark; Margaret gazed at Mat as if in expectation of an outburst; and Hal tried to look as if the question was being asked every day by people all over England. Only Bette seemed unaware that she had said anything out of the ordinary.

Realizing the need for immediate intervention, I answered for Claire. 'No, the nuisance has stopped – at any rate as far as we're concerned. Of course, the nut may be bothering someone else.'

'You're sure it was a nut, Philip?'

'My dear Bette, quite sure.' I smiled at her. 'Now, what can I get you to drink?'

Bette returned my smile disbelievingly. 'I'd adore a Martini, but you're not very good at mixing them, are you, love? I wonder if perhaps Mr Runce – ?'

She turned to Hal, who at once oozed gratification. His pleasure was to be short-lived. Bette had scarcely tasted and approved the Martini he had made her when she said casually: 'Did you enjoy your visit to Dublin, Mr Runce?'

Momentarily Hal was thrown. 'My visit to Dublin?' he repeated.

'John Telsey saw you there,' Claire explained. 'He abandoned the taxi he was in and ran after you, but you vanished into a church.'

Hal was quick to recover. 'John told you that?' he said as if mildly surprised.

'No, no.' Claire corrected him. 'Bette – ' She hesitated.

'I see.' Hal's voice was cool. 'You're a friend of John's, Lady Aylwyn?'

'I surely am. And I happened to be with John at the time. He knows Dublin and I don't. He was showing me some of the sights.' Bette was all innocence. 'Were you sight-seeing too, Mr Runce?'

Hal didn't answer. He glanced at Mat, who was studying his nails, then at me, then back at Bette. His eyes were thoughtful.

'Hal represents an Irish-American Trust that provides compensation for those who've suffered, directly or indirectly, as a result of Massacre Day,' I said unkindly.

'What a fantastic idea! Tell me about it,' Bette invited.

'It isn't that interesting.' Hal turned to Margaret. 'Have you ever been to Dublin, Mrs Harworth?'

After that our dinner-party didn't have a hope. Even if

Patrick hadn't caused confusion by arriving with the cheese, I doubt whether anyone would have remembered it as particularly enjoyable. Bette continued to make an effort, but Hal was disenchanted, Mat brooded, Margaret talked nervously and Denise kept looking at her watch. Claire, never a relaxed hostess, began to feel the strain. When the bell rang loud and violently, she started, and upset the cheese board.

Denise let her husband into the flat. Patrick, his cheeks flushed, his generous mouth set and his fair hair ruffled, barely acknowledged her kiss. He glared at me.

'I could vomit!' he said.

'Give him an enormous gin and introduce him to the others,' I said to Denise, and disappeared into the kitchen.

By the time the cheeses had been cleared up, Patrick had poured half his drink down his throat and was feeling better. He gave me a wild grin.

'How is your patient, Doctor?' Margaret asked inevitably.

'Dead, Mrs Harworth. Well and truly dead.'

'Oh dear!'

'He hanged himself. The details will be in tomorrow's papers, if you're interested.'

'Was he famous, then?'

'Infamous, you might say. He was the lieutenant who gave orders for the gas attack in Belfast on Massacre Day.'

'He was your patient?' Mat said sharply in the sudden silence.

I knew what he was thinking. He wasn't going to have the name of Camplin colouring the headlines again, not in relation to Ireland, not even if it was a different Camplin – not if he could help it. There was no chance of a 'D' Notice; he wouldn't be able to quash the story, but if need be he could keep Patrick out of it. Mat was prepared to take action.

Patrick shook his head. 'Not really. I'm just one of the army consultants. They called me in as a safeguard, in case questions were asked. In fact I was superfluous. One of my colleagues beat me to it.'

Mat relaxed. 'Ah, yes. I see. Poor chap blamed himself for

what happened, I suppose. Very sad.'

'Very sad!' Patrick didn't bother to hide his disgust. 'It was a waste – a bloody waste.'

'I only meant . . .' Mat was offended.

As I said, it wasn't the most successful party that Claire and I had ever given.

I was thankful when the Harworths left. They were the first and they broke up the party. Denise and Patrick followed them almost immediately. And, as soon as the family had gone, Bette offered Hal a lift. He refused, politely but without obvious regret, saying he wanted to have a word or two with me in private.

I took this to be an excuse to let Claire see Bette downstairs. As a formality I offered Hal a nightcap. To my surprise he accepted with enthusiasm, flung himself into an armchair and settled himself as if he intended to stay till the small hours.

'Well, Philip me old son. I owe you an apology. I've been devious with you and I shouldn't have. Hell, I could plead the exigencies of my job, but we're on the same side, aren't we? I should have told you of my interest in Ireland.'

'You mean, for instance, why you were dodging into Dublin churches to avoid John Telsey?' I asked.

'Sure.' Hal grinned sheepishly. 'Curses on John's head. I made him swear he'd not seen me, that he'd mistaken someone else for me. I didn't want it to get around to your people that we were involving ourselves. That's fair enough, isn't it?'

'Sure,' I mimicked him. 'Incidentally, don't blame John. He did his best to cover for you, but Bette gave him away.'

'Ah – the fatal Mata Hari.'

'Mata Hari? You don't mean Bette Aylwyn, do you? You don't think – ?' I began to laugh.

I was still laughing when Claire came back. She refused a drink, pleaded tiredness and went to bed. Hal and I resumed our conversation. I assured him Bette was a most unlikely candidate for British Intelligence, and he agreed he hadn't taken the possibility very seriously. For a minute or two we joked together. Then he began to talk seriously of Ireland.

It was after one when Hal prised himself from his chair and said he must go. Rain was beating gently against the windows. I couldn't turn him out into an inhospitable street to wait for a taxi that might never come. Weary though I was I would have to drive him back to Highgate, where he was staying with friends from his Embassy.

Overriding his polite protest I went along to the bedroom to tell Claire I wouldn't be long. I expected to find her reading, but she was already in a deep sleep. I bent and kissed her. Her skin was cold. I pulled the bedclothes higher round her shoulders, removed the bottle of sleeping pills from the bedside-table and put out the light.

Hal was waiting for me in the hall. He had on one of those see-through plastic raincoats that I abhor. He grinned at me, his eyes bright in his red, shiny face. Inexplicably I felt a rush of affection for him.

'Where do you keep your automobile, Philip?'

'In a mews, not five minutes away.'

'Fine. You drive to work, do you?'

'No. Parking's too difficult. I usually walk as far as Wigmore Street and catch a bus from there. If I'm in a hurry or the weather's foul, I get a taxi. I scarcely use the car during the week.'

We went down in the lift. As I opened the front door the wind and the rain forced me back. In the sudden squall I had to fight to open my umbrella. Hal seized it from me and, holding it like a shield in front of us, succeeded in protecting me more than himself. We battled our way up Harley Street.

The squall passed before we reached the corner of Weymouth Street but the rain was heavier. Two private cars swished by and a taxi, having deposited its passengers, drew away from the kerb some twenty yards ahead of us. Hal ran after it, shouting and waving the umbrella, but the driver ignored him; he had had enough for one night and was going home. I was more disappointed than Hal.

We turned into the mews where I kept my car. It was dark

and quiet, no light shining from any window. Our footsteps sounded loud on the cobbles and we kept our voices low.

'Thank God for London,' Hal said. 'If this were Washington or New York I'd be scared stiff of being mugged in an alley like this.'

'You're pretty safe around here,' I said and thought 'famous last words'; but there was no one about.

I found the key for the garage, fumbled it into the lock, turned it and pulled up the handle. The door was the sort that folds itself upwards and backwards so that it lies under the garage roof. It was an old door and inclined to stick. It stuck now. I bent to get a better leverage.

'Here, let me, Philip.'

Unless I let him try, Hal would never believe that opening the bloody door was more a knack than a question of strength. I stood aside.

'Be my guest.'

'Thanks.'

Hal gave me the umbrella, pretended to spit on his palms and doubled himself over the handle. He heaved. The door zoomed up and over, crashing against the back wall of the garage.

At the same time there was another sound, a dull, soft sound as if air had rushed out of a large bladder. It was followed almost instantaneously by a bang and a spurt of violet-coloured flame. Instinctively Hal and I jumped backwards. Bigger and heavier than I, he was also quicker – too quick, because he knocked me down and then fell on me. His elbow caught me in the very place where the Irish doctors had extracted the bullet from my chest and, sick with pain, I blacked out.

Seconds later I was aware of Hal trying to lift me. I pushed him aside and struggled to my feet. The car was burning. If the petrol tank exploded the flat above the garage would be wrecked and the fire would spread. Thoughts of people happily unconscious in their beds raced through my mind.

'There's an extinguisher on the wall to your right,' I said to Hal. 'Hurry!'

It was superfluous to urge him. He was already reaching for

the bright red canister. I banged on the door that led to the flat above and shouted 'Fire!' As soon as I heard footsteps on the stairs I roused the neighbours on either side. The man opposite threw open his window and leaned out. I called to him to phone the fire brigade.

Within minutes lights came on everywhere. People appeared in various stages of undress. Those with garages next to mine ran to move their cars. Their wives watched anxiously from the flats above or sought shelter with friends. A child, suddenly wakened, began to scream. Two men, seeing Hal's efforts, brought their own fire extinguishers. A passing patrol car turned into the mews. It was closely followed by the fire brigade. By then the fire was out, the danger past.

Three-quarters of an hour later, having answered innumerable questions, I limped back to Harley Street by myself; a police car was taking Hal to Highgate. I was wet, dirty and tired. Above all, I was frightened.

I tried to think logically but my thoughts scurried like mice. As I had told Hal, I rarely used the car during the week. Claire did, most days. The booby-trap had been intended for her. It was the 'little accident' Derwent had threatened. The enemy was trying to get at me through Claire. But why? What did they want of me?

At least one thing was certain. Mat had been wrong; no one was trying to kill me because I had become a menace, like poor Bridie Connell. The shooting in Dublin had been a threat, like the booby-trap – an attempt to terrorize. I had more or less stumbled into the bullet, and tonight's explosion had been too small to do any real damage. But why terrorize me? What did the enemy want of me? Surely the men who could organize Massacre Day must know how relatively unimportant I was to them and their plans.

Cursing softly, I let myself into the house. It made no sense, no sense whatever.

FIVE

Mat was livid. He strode up and down my office flicking ash from his nasty little cheroot as if he imagined himself scattering hot coals on the unrighteous. He paid no attention when I opened the windows, nor when I shut them again; I could bear the petrol fumes rising from Northumberland Avenue, but the roar of the traffic was impossible. I sat behind my desk and watched Mat prowl.

It wasn't the bomb that had made him angry. We had been through all that this morning. It was the lunch-time papers. An enterprising reporter had put two and two together and made a story.

'. . . on the front page, Philip, your face, and right next to it a photo of that poor young lieutenant who hanged himself. And a great black headline screaming: "An Irish Revenge!" '

He stopped his perambulation and turned to point a stumpy finger in my direction. His eyes were popping from their sockets.

'God knows what the later editions will come up with, and the mornings – and the other media.' He groaned. 'More publicity. And that's the last thing we want. You can't work under a floodlight, not on this job, Philip.'

He paused as if he hoped for some comment, but I didn't oblige. I wasn't feeling my best after a white night, and it was easier to let him blow himself out. It happened sooner than I expected, perhaps because his cheroot had come to its disgusting end. Reluctantly I produced one of those scallop shells that HMG provides for its servants and he ground out the butt.

'Philip, I'm taking you off Ireland. I've arranged a leak to the Press to that effect. It'll be interesting to see how the enemy reacts. Personally I believe the threats will cease. I hope they will.'

'Considering we haven't a clue what they want of me – ' I shrugged. 'Anyway they won't believe it. Why should they?'

'Because it's the truth. Parson's going to take over from you. I want you to brief him fully, give him everything you have – down to the last niggling suspicion.'

I emptied the remains of the cheroot into some tissue and consigned the smelly thing to the bottom of my waste-paper basket; I thought how lucky it was for Margaret Harworth that Mat only smoked in office hours. Then I stood up slowly behind my desk and opened my mouth to protest. Mat forestalled me.

'It's no use arguing, Philip. Everything's fixed. You're going to the Cabinet Office, on a temporary basis.'

'Then what?' I managed to grin. 'You can't fire me. I'll appeal to my union.'

'Then you go to Washington – adviser to His Excellency.'

'That's definite?' I held my breath.

'Yes, though it won't be announced for a while. You can tell Claire, of course.' A shadow passed across his face; he must have remembered Bette Aylwyn's familiarity with our affairs. 'She mustn't gossip to her friends.'

'I don't know what to say. I was hoping, but – '

'I know how you feel. It's a plum. But you deserve it. You've been short-listed since January, and when H.E.'s report came in that settled it.' He smiled at me benignly.

I gave him a wide, inane smile in return. I felt slightly light-headed. 'In that case, Mat, wouldn't it be simpler all around if I stayed on Ireland till – '

'No.' The emphatic monosyllable brought me up short. 'When you've done what you can for Parson, take a few days' leave. Call it sick leave, Philip. You need it by the look of you. They're not expecting you at the Cabinet Office before – ' he shrugged – 'Monday or Tuesday week.'

And it wouldn't matter a damn if I didn't turn up then, I thought, as Mat nodded his goodbye and strolled out of the office. They wouldn't have anything for me to do when I got there. Mat had sicked me on to them to get me out of his hair.

The prospect of a long, dull summer stretched ahead of me.

Yet later in the day, briefing Parson who was wagging his tail at the chance of replacing me, I admitted to myself that what really riled me was the inevitable black-out on the Irish scene to which I should be subject. I wouldn't know what was going on any more. I wouldn't know if Derwent had been picked up or if Bridie Connell's unpleasant 'special' had been traced or if there was any further info on the gas grenades or if anyone had an inspiration about the 'Oxford and Cambridge' lead or a hundred other things. All my sources would dry up. I would be dependent like everyone else on the news media – for what they were worth. Suddenly I realized how important the problem of Massacre Day had become to me, and how personal.

I tried to concentrate on the compensations. Not least of these was that with luck there might be no more 'incidents'. Claire had been devastated by the news of the fire in the garage and the destruction of our car. When I told her about it at breakfast, she had been literally sick; I had heard her vomiting in the lavatory. It was worth a lot that that shouldn't happen again.

And on Friday when I left Parson to the files and set off for home at three o'clock in the afternoon, I felt an unexpected sense of freedom. I was looking forward to some leave in the country. Usually in the spring I only managed to snatch odd weekends. Ten days would be splendid, especially if the weather was good. Today it was glorious. We should be at the cottage in time for drinks before dinner if there wasn't too much traffic and if Claire was ready.

I found Claire and Denise loading up the Renault, which Denise was lending us. Denise was being practical and efficient as usual – and very kind in giving up her car. Claire, I was happy to see, was fairly relaxed and cheerful. I kissed them both.

'Do you want tea before you go?' Denise asked.

'No, thank you. I'd like to get away as soon as possible. Avoid the worst of the rush. Are we all set, Claire?'

'Yes, apart from Katy. She's sniffing round her travelling

basket rather doubtfully.'

'Fine. Ten minutes for me to change and you to corral Katy. Okay?'

'Yes. By the way, Philip, a parcel came for you – just after lunch. It's on the dining-room table.'

The front door of the house was open and at the end of the hall Patrick's secretary was showing a patient into the lift. She waited for me and the three of us went up together. We didn't speak. But when we reached the floor where Patrick had his consulting-rooms, the girl said: 'There was a parcel for you on the hall table, Mr Camplin. I took it up to Claire.'

'Thanks.'

Idly I noticed that she called me 'Mr Camplin', while she called Claire, who was her own age, by her first name. Then, as I continued upwards, I thought of the parcel. My mind raced. I took the last flight of stairs faster than I had ever done.

The parcel was on the dining-table, where Claire had said it would be. I stood, looking down on it and ignoring Katy who wound herself between my legs in the hope of some attention. It was rectangular, wrapped in olive green paper, the corners very neat, more a box than a parcel. My name and address had been scrawled on it with a felt pen. The white lettering blurred as I stared at it.

Perhaps I was mad. Perhaps the parcel was perfectly innocent. But I wasn't prepared to take risks, not at that moment. I put my ear on a level with the table and listened. Nothing. No suspicious ticks. There was a smell though, vaguely familiar. Feeling an awful fool, I sniffed. The parcel smelt of chocolate.

I went to the kitchen and got a sharp knife from the drawer. I reminded myself that the parcel had been delivered to the house, carried upstairs, given to Claire. It wouldn't explode because I touched it. Nevertheless, I slit the outer wrapping with care and slid it gently off the box. The inner wrapping was printed all over with gold lettering – Fortnum & Mason – and a small gold envelope was attached in the exact centre. It looked expensive and reassuring.

More hurriedly now – I thought I heard Claire on the stairs –

I cut off the envelope. The card inside read: 'Love to you both. Bette'. I tore off the last wrapping and opened the box. Bette Aylwyn had sent us two pounds of liqueur chocolates. I detest liqueur chocolates, but never had a gift been more welcome.

'Lovely,' Claire said, seeing the open box. 'But who's sending you chocolates?'

'They're from Bette,' I said. 'For you too. They were wrongly addressed.'

I left Claire, who had a sweet tooth, making her choice among the little bottles, and escaped to the bedroom to change. I was shaking and the palms of my hands were damp but, thank God, Claire hadn't noticed. I would have been furious with myself if I had upset her unnecessarily. As it was, only Katy and I knew what a stupid performance I had just been through. I smiled wryly. Mat was right. I needed some sick leave.

It took us an hour to get out of London. Although we left before four, the Friday traffic was already building up and I wasn't used to the Renault. But once we were clear of London and I had got the hang of the car, we made good time. I began to enjoy the drive.

Katy was on the back seat in her travelling basket. The basket was made so that she could curl up and go to sleep or, if she wished, sit and poke her head through the opening to see what was going on. She was accustomed to it and usually slept, but today for some reason she was fretful. She kept miaowing to make Claire turn round and rub her behind the ears, which she loved. Eventually, however, she grew tired and settled down. Claire, I noticed, continued to turn round.

'What's the matter?'

'I – I think we're being followed.'

'My dear girl, of course we're being followed. We're in a stream of traffic on the M40. What do you expect?'

'I meant by one particular car, a fawn-coloured Rover. They've been behind us ever since we left London. They've had several chances to pass but they don't take them. They stay on our tail and – '

'For heaven's sake, Claire! Why on earth should anyone be following us?'

My voice was sharp with irritation, tinged with fear. Claire was right. I had been watching the fawn-coloured Rover in the driving mirror for some while. If I accelerated it accelerated. If I slowed, it slowed. It seemed to be attached to us by a piece of elastic that stretched or took up the slack, but never broke. I had been wondering what the hell to do about it.

As long as we kept to the motorway, the problem was academic. This was no corniche road where they could force us over the edge of a cliff. I caught myself up, shocked by the melodramatic turn my thoughts had taken and I remembered the box of chocolates I had opened so carefully. I didn't intend to make a fool of myself twice in one day. Nor, if I could help it, did I intend to lead the Rover to the cottage.

'I think we'll get some petrol in Woodstock,' I said, 'and we might have a drink at The Bear. The pubs should be open by the time we get there.'

'All right, Philip.' Claire's voice was expressionless.

I bit my bottom lip to stop myself from cursing aloud. The day had been so promising, the beginning of my leave. Now it was in ruins. I glanced sideways at Claire. There was tension in every line of her body and her knuckles were white as she gripped her hands together. I yearned to do something or say something that would make her relax, but it was impossible. Instead I trod viciously on the accelerator and the Renault leapt forward. Behind us the Rover smoothly increased its speed. We were in Woodstock within the half-hour.

We drove in tandem past the creamy stone walls bordering Blenheim Palace. There was no longer any attempt to disguise the fact that we were being followed. The Rover sat on our tail. At the traffic lights it stopped directly behind us. I was able to take a good look at its occupants. The driver was young, darkish, athletic-looking. His passenger was older – about my age – with a large fleshy nose and a straggle of mousey hair. They were both nondescript types and not in any way frightening. Yet they frightened me.

My mind churned over the possibilities as I drove on slowly. All of them had snags. However, the sight of some thirsty patrons disappearing into The Bear decided me. We would go and have a drink; and I would phone the number the Special Branch chap had given me when he questioned me about the shooting in Dublin. If necessary, we would stay the night here in Woodstock. It mightn't be heroic but it was the sensible, safe thing to do.

The difficulty was the car. Since it belonged to Denise I couldn't just abandon it. I would have to find somewhere to park it, somewhere close and public where the two men would be discouraged from playing tricks. But first I had to drop Claire. We were almost at the pub and I was crawling along. My intention must have been obvious.

'Claire darling, I'm going to stop in front of The Bear. Get out and go straight into the bar, quickly! If either of the men follow you, appeal to the barman, scream, do anything. If I'm not with you in five minutes, phone Mat. Do you understand?'

'Yes, but – what about you, Philip?'

'Don't argue! Just do what I say!'

I stopped the car as near the entrance to The Bear as I could. Claire opened the door, got out, turned and got back in again. She was kneeling on the seat beside me and reaching for Katy's basket. I tried to help her with the basket and, at the same time, I urged her to go without it. I was aware that the door of the Rover was open and the passenger – he was a bigger, heavier man than I had thought – was already on the pavement. When Claire straightened herself, clutching Katy's basket in front of her, he was there waiting.

I flung open my door, narrowly missing a passing car that hooted furiously. There was a fair amount of traffic and quite a few pedestrians, people going home after work, even the odd tourist. More people were going into the pub. It was a peaceful, ordinary scene that should have been reassuring.

I seized Claire by the arm. I could feel my nails digging into her skin through the thin material of her suit. Katy, rudely wakened from some fishy heaven, thrust her head through her basket and miaowed plaintively.

'Nice cat.' The big man put out his hand, stroked Katy behind the ears. The miaow changed to a purr. 'I used to have a puss the spitting image of you once.'

'Who are you?' My throat was hoarse. 'What the hell do you want?'

His face went blank. 'I'm sorry, sir. I thought you knew. Special Branch.'

He produced his warrant card, and showed it to me. There was no room for doubt. It was the box of liqueur chocolates over again.

'Okay, darling,' I said to Claire, releasing her arm and patting her on the bottom. 'It seems there's nothing to worry about after all. Go and order our drinks.' My voice shook.

He was quick. As soon as Claire had gone, he said: 'Gawd, I'm sorry, sir. There must have been a balls-up somewhere. We were ordered to see you down to your cottage safely and make sure you hadn't any unexpected visitors waiting for you there. After that you'd be on your own. But if no one told you – Christ, when you found us on your tail, you must have been piss – '

He didn't finish the sentence but I knew what he had been going to say. You must have been pissing yourself. It was as near the truth as made no matter.

'And your poor wife. She was as white as a sheet, but game. She wasn't going without the cat, was she?'

I sketched a smile. 'Let's forget it. We'll be in the pub for about twenty minutes. Then we'll push on to the cottage. All right?'

'As you say, sir. If you give me the keys, I'll park the Renault for you. And I really am sorry. Please tell your wife.'

I nodded. I believed him but it didn't help much. What did help was the double whisky that Claire had waiting for me – and the next. We debated whether it was possible to be charged with drunken driving when accompanied by the Special Branch. We sniggered into our glasses. We were weak with relief.

The SB men didn't have a drink, not in The Bear at any rate. They may have sneaked a quick one somewhere else. When we came out of the pub, the big-nosed character who liked cats was waiting on the pavement for us. He led us down a side street where his colleague was propping up the Renault. They ushered us into the car as if we were infirm and incapable. I was half expecting them to suggest I shouldn't drive.

We reached the cottage later than we had originally planned, but it was good to be there. Lights were on downstairs, and I could see the flame of a wood fire through the living-room window. The welcoming sight made me believe that in spite of its awful beginning my leave could still be salvaged.

'Nice place you've got here, sir.'

'Yes.' I didn't explain that it belonged to my brother William, who had married a rich wife.

The cottage was, in fact, a solid Cotswold house, which I'd known on occasion to sleep twelve, plus innumerable children. It was on the edge of a village, still unspoilt except for television masts, and included two acres of land and a small stream. William and Anne were generous. The house was never let, and was at the disposal of all the Camplins. It was Patrick who had started referring to 'our country cottage', and the ironical name had stuck.

'Someone living here, sir?'

'Yes. The housekeeper – and her husband.' I didn't add that they were old-age pensioners, both pushing seventy.

'But we thought – ' the younger SB man began.

'In that case, sir, you won't need us any more. We'll be getting along. We didn't realize the cottage was occupied.'

The interruption was smooth, and there was no inflexion whatever on the word 'cottage'. I gave him full marks. They had expected a labourer's two-up, two-down, made over for the city slicker, in some lovely inaccessible place. This time the laugh was on them.

'Come in and have a drink,' I said. It's a long way back to London.'

They refused, with thanks. But they waited till the front door was open and Mrs Moreton had come out to help us unload the car. They were being conscientious. They would be able to report that they had carried out their instructions. Smiling grimly, I thought what I would have to say to Mat when I saw him next.

We had a pleasant, lazy evening. For dinner, as a treat, Claire had bought us some smoked salmon. Mrs Moreton made us an omelette and a fresh salad, and we had cheese and wine. It was the sort of meal I liked. Afterwards we had coffee by the fire, listened to some music and watched the ten o'clock news. I turned the TV off when we were shown an interview with a woman whose daughter had been killed on Massacre Day; she was saying she hoped the parents of the lieutenant who had hanged himself were suffering as much as she was. It was a bitter note.

'I'll put Katy out. Then let's go to bed, shall we, darling?'

'Yes, let's.' Claire reached a hand towards Bette's box of liqueur chocolates, unwrapped a large bottle, and put it back. 'I really shouldn't, should I? But they do tempt me and you won't eat them, Philip.'

'Darling, you've had too many already. You'll be getting drunk on them.'

Claire laughed. Her reaction to the fright the SB men had given us had been intense, and ever since Woodstock she had been in the brightest, happiest mood. It made me happy too.

I started on the going-to-bed chores. There were always more of them at the cottage. I picked up a reluctant Katy, took her to the front door and tipped her on to the gravel. She ran, protesting, to the shelter of some bushes. It was a beautiful night with a full moon, but cold – at least five degrees colder than in London – and Katy was unlikely to linger about her business. She was a sybaritic cat. I waited for her.

I was listening to the country sounds – the sough of an old tree, the wind whispering in the grass, a splash in the stream, the hoot of a distant owl – when Katy returned. Ignoring me, she stalked past my legs and up the stairs. I took one last look around at the peaceful, moonlit garden and went inside.

I locked the front door, double locked it, put on the chain. I checked the back door and the downstairs windows. If I was more meticulous than usual, there was no one to see me. We had never had any trouble at the cottage, but William was security-minded and tonight, tonight I was nervous. It was absurd, but I couldn't help it. I made sure Claire had set the guard in front of the fire and that all the lights were out. I went slowly up to bed – to Claire.

We took a long time making love – it was the best it had been since before I went to Washington – and we didn't get to sleep until well past midnight. When I woke, I had the impression that day had already come. I was surprised that the bedside clock showed only a quarter to three. For luxurious moments I lay there, warm and contented. Then I saw the strip of light under the door of the adjoining bathroom and heard the noises.

I was out of bed, across the room, flinging open the bathroom door. Claire lay on the floor. She was clutching the lavatory seat with both hands, so that she could hold her head high enough to vomit into the pan. Before I could reach her, her body contorted. She cried out. A stream of liquid, greenish-brown and thick with flecks of food, poured from her mouth. I felt the tightening, the contractions in my own stomach. I knelt beside her. I put my arm around her, held her, supported her, willed the spasm to pass.

Inevitably it did. She leaned against me, gasping softly, her eyes closed. Her skin, greyish-white and glistening with sweat, was cold to the touch. The smell was revolting. Still cradling her in my arm, I reached out with my free hand to flush the pan and pull a towel from the rail. I wiped her face.

'Oh darling, my poor darling, are you feeling any better?'

She nodded and her lips twitched in an attempt at a smile. 'It must be – smoked salmon,' she said. 'A tainted bit. Do you remember, Philip, in Florence – doctor said – only needed one – one mussel?'

I remembered. Claire had been horribly sick on that occasion too. The hotel had got us a doctor. In fact she was improving when he arrived, but he had given her an injection and she had slept for twelve hours. Should I try to get a doctor now? There wasn't one in the village. The nearest would be – where? The Moretons would know, but I would have to go and ask them. I wasn't sure what to do. I didn't like leaving Claire. She clung to me when I tried to stand up. She was shivering. I pulled her dressing-gown, which she had discarded, towards me, and found it filthy with vomit.

'Claire, how often have you been sick?'

'Don't know. Three – four times. Oh – God!'

Her body arched with the pain. She groaned aloud. Eventually she vomited and collapsed on to the floor. Tears ran down her cheeks. She gasped for breath. In the next half-hour this happened again and again until she could produce only black bile and retch dryly. She was getting exhausted.

Between the spasms I managed to wrap her in a blanket and arrange a pillow for her head so that she could lie down more comfortably. I scrambled into some slacks and pulled a sweater over my pyjamas. I beat up the Moretons. The doctor was out on a maternity call, his partner was away, the locum didn't answer. When I returned with Mrs Moreton, Claire was semi-conscious.

'If I was you, sir, I'd get her into Oxford – to the Radcliffe Hospital – as fast as you can.' The soft Oxfordshire burr made it sound easy, but it would be three-quarters of an hour's drive in the Renault and . . . For one of the few times in my life I envied my brothers. Any one of the three of them could have picked Claire up and carried her downstairs to the car, with ease. For me, even with the Moretons' help, this required an enormous effort. We achieved it at last. Claire was belted into the seat beside me and we set off.

I made it to the Radcliffe in forty minutes.

SIX

The hospital was expecting us. Mrs Moreton had telephoned. As soon as we arrived Claire was whisked away on a stretcher. I answered questions – full name, age, address, telephone, next of kin, local doctor and so on. None of this seemed immediately relevant. A nurse took me to a waiting-room. To my surprise, this was full, but a place was made for me and I was able to sit at the end of a wood bench. It was uncomfortable and my leg hurt. I tried not to fidget. Time passed.

At intervals a nurse or an aide put her head round the door. Immediately the murmur of conversations ceased. She mentioned a name and, with fearful expectation, its owner followed her. The door shut. The murmuring recommenced. Bodies shifted in an effort to get more comfortable. There was nothing to read. A child began to cry. I asked myself what on earth a child was doing at this time of night in a hospital waiting-room, but I wasn't really interested. I didn't care about anyone except Claire.

Gradually the room emptied. When there were only five of us left and the child, talk became general and confidences public. The elderly woman's husband had had a heart attack. The young couple's baby had had 'a sort of fit'. The wife of the man with the child had fallen downstairs and was having a miscarriage. When they had exhausted the details they turned to me.

I didn't want to discuss Claire. I said my wife was suffering from food poisoning, some bad fish, and didn't elaborate. They began to tell me of their own experiences, first, second or fourth hand. If a nurse hadn't interrupted a graphic description of a stomach pump, I think I would have vomited myself.

The nurse checked our names against a list. She was a large blonde girl with a wide smile. She looked tired.

'We've had a busy night with that multiple car crash on the

Banbury Road,' she said cheerfully, 'but things are nice and quiet again now. I'll get you all some tea.'

We muttered our thanks and she went, colliding in the doorway with a young doctor in a white coat. I saw him pinch her bottom, and she yelped.

'Mr Camplin?' His face wore a mask of bland sympathy. 'I'm Dr Collins.'

I stood up. I felt like a small boy before the headmaster on his first day at school. Everybody else had been fetched by a nurse. A doctor must mean – must mean – I couldn't formulate the words even in my own mind. I stumbled after him into the corridor.

The corridor was unending and he walked very fast. I thought at first he was taking me to Claire and I made a great effort to keep up with him, but he turned into a small, cluttered office. He pulled out a chair for me.

'Sit down, Mr Camplin.'

I sat. I was cold and I began to shiver. The doctor glanced up from the papers he was shuffling on his desk. He kicked on an electric fire, gave me a quick smile.

'There's some tea coming.'

'My wife – '

'No need to worry about her. She's going to be fine. Ah, here we are.' He had found the paper he wanted and was giving it his attention.

I absorbed what he had said. Claire was all right. She wasn't going to – The world was suddenly recoloured. I could have wept for joy.

The blonde nurse came in with a tray of tea and biscuits. She poured the tea. It was strong and she added milk and sugar without asking. Normally it would have revolted me, but now I gulped it down, scalding my throat. It tasted wonderful.

'Mr Camplin, I'd like your wife to stay in hospital for the next twenty-four, thirty-six hours so that she can have bed rest and we can supervise her intake. She's okay but she's had a bad time. Her stomach will be over-sensitive for a week, and she'll have to be careful what she eats and drinks. After that you can both forget what, I'm afraid, has been a nasty experience. The moral would seem to be don't indulge in smoked salmon.' He grinned at me.

'You think it was that?'

He shrugged. 'Probably. Without analysing the stomach contents one can't be certain. Did she have a lot to drink last night, rich food?'

'We had a simple dinner, but she did have more to drink than usual, yes.' I thought of the stop at The Bear, the wine, all those liqueur chocolates.

'What about medicines? Is she taking anything?'

'Tranquillizers. Valium. She uses them as sleeping pills. And something for anaemia. That's all.'

'You're sure? She – ' Whatever he was about to say, he decided against it. 'Well, there's been no lasting damage anyway.' He stood up. 'I see you gave a Harley Street address, Mr Camplin. You're not Patrick's brother by any chance, are you?'

'Yes. Do you know him?'

Rudely I showed my surprise. The easy familiarity with which the doctor had spoken of Patrick suggested that he knew him well, but it seemed unlikely that their careers would have crossed.

'Yes. I met him when I was an undergraduate at St John's.' A dull flush suffused the milky skin that went with his red hair. 'He – he treated me. I had a run of bad luck. My girl-friend took an overdose of pills and then I fell out of a car – the week before my finals. I'd never have got through if it hadn't been for Patrick.'

'I'll give him your regards.'

'Thanks. I used to have a drink with him once in a while – before he gave up his consultancy work for the University – but I haven't seen him for ages. How is he?'

'Extremely busy, and flourishing on it.'

'Great!'

At this point, if it hadn't been for my connection with Patrick, I should probably have been escorted to the door. As it was, I was allowed to see Claire for a brief minute. And all the way back to the cottage her pale face, framed in its dark, sweat-stained hair, haunted me. It was so bloody unfair! Why, on top of everything we had been through lately, did Claire have to buy that particular piece of tainted salmon? I cursed aloud, and took my anger out on the Renault.

Shortly after seven, thanks to the empty roads and my furious driving, I reached the cottage. It was difficult to believe it was still so early. I let myself into the house. There was no sound of movement anywhere. The Moretons weren't up yet. I went along to the kitchen and helped myself to a large glass of orange juice from the refrigerator. The sight of a row of brown eggs and a wedge of bacon slices made me feel hungry. I put on some coffee. If Mrs Moreton hadn't appeared by the time I was ready I would make my own breakfast.

Clutching the orange juice, I wandered into the hall. The door of the living-room was ajar. I pushed it open, went in and threw myself into the nearest comfortable chair. I yawned and stretched prodigiously. As I opened my eyes I saw that our box of liqueur chocolates had been knocked off the side-table where Claire had left it, and its contents scattered on the floor. Some of the liqueurs were squashed into the carpet.

I got up and looked at the mess. Mrs Moreton wasn't going to be pleased. I had better do something quickly, for the culprit was obvious. Katy, tempted by the smell of chocolate, must have pushed the box off the table and bitten her way through the silver paper wrappings. She adored chocolate, anything sweet. She must have had an orgy.

'Katy!' I called. 'Where are you? You're a bad cat!'

There was no sign of her and I went to the kitchen to fetch some paper and a damp cloth. Then I thought of those plastic bags that fit inside the rubbish bin. If I could discover where Mrs Moreton stored them, one would be ideal for holding the remains of Katy's carnage. Cursing the cat, I started to search, but without success, and I had almost decided to settle for newspaper when I remembered the cupboard by the garden door.

In the back hall I forgot about the bags. Katy was there. She was lying on her side, her legs stretched out stiffly in front of her. I knew before I touched her that she was dead.

Slowly I straightened myself and leaned against the wall. My heart was bumping against my ribs. For what seemed forever I stood there, staring down at Katy. Claire was in hospital and Katy –

A distant sound, the creak of a stair, a cough, something roused me. In a moment the Moretons would be in the kitchen. Without conscious thought I seized a dish towel, wrapped it round Katy and, overcoming my repugnance, picked her up. Then hurrying, fumbling with the lock, I let myself out into the garden.

Once outside I made straight for the Renault. When the Moretons appeared at the front door, full of anxiety for me and for Claire – they must have seen me from a window – Katy's body was safely locked in the trunk of the car.

I heard myself say: 'Yes, Mrs Camplin's going to be all right, thank you. And thank you very much, both of you, for all your help. I'm all right too – a little tired, perhaps. I'd – I'd love some breakfast when you're ready. I've put the coffee on.'

I was babbling but it didn't matter. I was backing them gently into the hall and past the sitting-room door, which I had left open. At my request for breakfast Mrs Moreton hurried off without a sideways glance. Old Moreton, who was a great talker, would have lingered to tell me about his own experiences at the Radcliffe, but fortunately she called him and he shambled after her. I was alone.

I stared doubtfully at the sticky mess of chocolate and silver paper on the carpet. It looked different from when I had first seen it. Then it had been evidence of Katy's greed. Now it was evidence for – what? At dinner Claire and I had each given Katy a tiny piece of smoked salmon, but it seemed improbable that this could have killed her. The chocolates might not have come from Bette Aylwyn at all. I knew she was in Scotland, so I couldn't check immediately. But I had to know what – if anything – had poisoned Claire and Katy.

The Times which we had brought down from London

yesterday was lying on an occasional table. I divided it into three. In one section I put the horrible squashed bits of liqueur chocolates which bore no resemblance to their original shapes. In the second section I collected those which were reasonably whole, even if they had been scratched or bitten or had lost most of their contents. The third I reserved for the box itself, the moulded trays in which the various sized bottles had nested and the untouched chocolates. There were a surprising number of these, that had cascaded themselves under the sofa and under an antique commode out of Katy's reach.

When I was positive I had found every stray I took the three packets out to the car and arranged them on the front seat. Later I would have to bring out some sticky tape and do them up more securely. And I would need a bag for Katy's body. Checking over the items in my mind I hurried back to the house. I had to make some attempt to clean the carpet.

In the cloakroom off the hall there was hot water, soap and – my luck was in – even an old towel that no one would miss. By the time I heard Mrs Moreton calling up the stairs to me that breakfast was ready, the carpet had a very damp patch but the stains were no longer visible. They would probably reappear as the wool dried, but they ought not to be too noticeable. Most important, it would probably be impossible to detect what had caused them. I thrust the soap in my trouser-pocket and concealed the filthy towel behind my back.

'Here I am, Mrs Moreton.'

'Ah! I thought you were in your room.' She gave me a long look that made me conscious of the fact that I was sweating. 'You – you've not washed yet, Mr Camplin, and I've taken in your breakfast.'

'I won't be a minute.' Smiling fatuously I started to sidle past her so that she wouldn't see the towel I was hiding behind me. 'By the way, Mrs Moreton, I won't be in for lunch. I'm going in to Oxford later this morning and I hope to spend most of the day at the hospital. I'll be back for supper – unless I telephone.'

'All right, Mr Camplin. You'll give Mrs Camplin our best wishes, mine and Moreton's, if you please.' As an afterthought, she added: 'And don't either of you worry about your cat. We'll take good care of Katy.'

'Thank you, Mrs Moreton, thank you very much.' The words nearly choked me.

It was just after nine when I called goodbye to the Moretons and drove away from the cottage. I let the Renault loiter through the village. At the first opportunity on the narrow road – an opening to a field – I stopped. As quickly as I could I taped up the three packets. Then reluctantly I got out of the car.

I had with me an airline bag I had been thankful to find at the back of a wardrobe. It probably belonged to one of William's boys, but ten to one it had been forgotten. If not, it was too bad. Katy's body fitted it very nicely.

The grinding of the clutch as I set off would have caused Denise to raise her eyebrows. Purposely I turned on the radio. Music, snippets of news, disc jockey jokes, more music – some of it ear-shattering – filled the car. I didn't care. It all helped to drown my fears.

In Oxford I managed to park in Broad Street. To find a public telephone that worked and was unoccupied wasn't so easy. I had to walk as far as the Post Office. I knew the number I wanted but there was no reply. I dialled again and, after a long pause, I asked to speak to Mr Havant.

'No. Not now. Impossible. Absolutely impossible.'

'Could you tell me when it will be possible? I'm only in Oxford for twenty-four hours, and it's extremely important I should see him.'

'You can't – see him or speak to him. He's very ill. The doctors don't expect him to live beyond the weekend.'

'I'm sorry, truly sorry.' What else could I say?

I put down the receiver slowly. Dick Havant had lived in Oxford all his life and had shown hospitality to successions of undergraduates, but he wasn't connected with the University. He was a retired schoolmaster with private means, who spent most of his days working in a laboratory he had built in the garden of his North Oxford house. I had hoped . . .

In the circumstances the most sensible thing for me to do was to go up to London, tell Mat my suspicions and give him the evidence. But I was loath to do this. I had panicked twice yesterday, once over opening the box of chocolates and once over the Special Branch men. I didn't want to make a fool of myself again. And I could be wrong. It could have been the smoked salmon that had caused the trouble.

Besides, there wasn't time to get to London and back. Claire would be expecting me at the hospital this afternoon. If I had wanted to go to Mat I should have gone straight from the cottage. But I had been counting on Dick Havant.

Without warning, the door of the telephone box was suddenly pushed open, pinning me beside the instrument.

'If you've quite finished – ' the girl said belligerently.

'I haven't,' I said, glaring at her.

'Look, mate,' another would-be telephonist intervened, 'you've not bought the bleedin' phone. There's others want to use it.'

I shoved the door shut and leaned against it. The girl started to tap on the glass. I found some change, inserted it in the slot, dialled. It was a very long thirty seconds before John Telsey answered.

'Hallo, John. This is Philip Camplin. John, I need help. Will you do something for me? It's important.'

'Of course, if I can. Where are you, Philip?'

'In Oxford – at the Post Office. I'll be with you in ten minutes, if that's okay.'

'I'm expecting you.'

I hung up the receiver with a sigh of relief. I had done the right thing. John hadn't asked me what I wanted or why. He hadn't asked any questions at all. He would help me, if he could – and he almost certainly could. As I pushed my way through the Saturday morning crush of shoppers on Cornmarket Street, I wondered why I had ever hesitated about appealing to him.

I picked up the three packets and the airline bag from the car and made my way along the Turl. John had come down to the lodge to meet me. As we walked across the quad to the staircase where he had his rooms I dropped one of the packets.

'Let me take that for you, Philip.' Before I could stop him he had seized the bag from me and was swinging it backwards and forwards at the length of his arm. 'You've come to spend the night. That's splendid.'

'No!' I said sharply, reaching for the bag. 'No! Don't do that!'

'I'm sorry,' he said at once, startled by my vehemence. He gripped my shoulder. 'I didn't mean to behave like a bloody clown. Is it all right if I carry the bag carefully?'

I nodded and let him lead me up the familiar staircase to his rooms. His face, when he discovered what was in the bag, would be worth watching. He was carrying it now as if it contained a Ming vase.

'Where do you want me to put this, Philip?'

'Anywhere – not in the sun.'

He gave me an odd look and moved the bag a yard or so. I put the packets down on his desk. Lack of sleep was catching up with me, and I was feeling incredibly tired.

'It's a bit early to start drinking, but if you'd like a whisky – ?' I shook my head. 'Coffee, then?'

'Yes, please. Black and strong.'

He set about preparing the coffee, and I sprawled in a chair and stared at nothing. I was wondering how to word my request. Dick Havant would have done what I wanted without asking questions; it was one of the advantages of going to him. John was different. He was a curious man. He also knew far more than Dick about my work and what lay behind it. But I couldn't confide in him completely.

'How's Claire, Philip? Is she in London?'

It was the perfect opener. 'She's in Oxford, in the Radcliffe. We're staying at the cottage and she was taken ill during the night. Suspected food poisoning. We'd had smoked salmon for dinner.'

'My dear chap! I am sorry. What – '

'It was the hell of an experience, but she's okay. John – ' I leaned forward in my chair to impress him with what I had to say. 'I'm far from sure the smoked salmon was to blame, or that it was an accident. To tell the truth, I suspect Claire was deliberately poisoned with some liqueur chocolates that were sent to us as a gift.' Seeing his expression, I added quickly: 'Look, maybe I'm going mad, but during the last few weeks I've been shot at, my car's been destroyed and I've received a variety of threats. Now Claire's in hospital and Katy, our cat, is – is in that airline bag. She's dead.'

'Christ!' John breathed. He eyed the bag with distaste. 'Christ!' he repeated.

I gave him an outline of what had happened, and he asked some pertinent questions. Why hadn't I checked with Bette? Why hadn't I eaten any of the chocolates myself? Could Claire and I have got help if we had both been taken ill?

'It seems such a chancy way of trying to poison someone,' he said doubtfully. 'If you'd phoned to thank Bette for her gift, which you could easily have done, she'd have denied any knowledge of it and you'd have been suspicious at once.'

'Yes. But a lot of trouble was taken over the other attacks, and it wouldn't have required much effort to find out that Bette would be away and that I probably wouldn't be able to contact her. It was an obvious thing to check. The fact that I happen to dislike liqueur chocolates was much less obvious.'

John began to pour the coffee. 'Okay. A bigger snag is that you might easily have offered the box around – to Patrick or Denise or any visitor who happened to have dropped by.'

Knowing John I should have realized that he would want to analyse the problem. In different circumstances I might have done the same myself. Now it irritated and disturbed me.

'It's a ghastly thought, I admit, John, but unlikely to distress my Irish chums. Why should it? They've not distressed themselves over Claire. In fact, in their campaign against me they've used her as a threat.'

I had purposely used the phrase 'Irish chums'. It was the first overt reference that either of us had made to the Irish. Seemingly we had both taken it for granted that they were responsible. I was astonished that John didn't raise the obvious objection –

that not even the wildest Irish group had ever been known to use poison. Mat would leap on it at once as evidence that the Irish situation was merely being used. It was hard to believe that the same thought hadn't occurred to John. And, if so, why hadn't he voiced it . . . But it was too late to change my mind.

'John, you said you'd help.'

'And I will. But how, Philip? What do you want me to do?'

'Do you know anyone here at the University who could do an autopsy on – on Katy, and analyse what's left of the chocolates? It must be someone you can trust, someone who'll keep his mouth shut. We can't have any gossip.'

For an appreciable minute John didn't answer. I was positive he was going to refuse. If he did I would have to go to London, today. And Claire would have to be told, which was the last thing I wanted. In her weak state, she would be distressed beyond measure.

'John, if I'm wrong – if it was the smoked salmon – we can forget it. No one need know I pressed the panic button. More important, Claire won't be unnecessarily upset.'

'And if you're right?' He was withdrawn, lost in his thoughts.

'Then I'll have to tell Mat Harworth. The authorities will be informed. There'll be an enquiry – ten to one it won't get us anywhere – and it'll be very hard to keep Claire out of it.'

He shook his head in mild irritation. 'You flap too much about Claire, Philip. She's tougher than she looks.'

'Maybe, but that's irrelevant.' I controlled my temper. 'John, if you can arrange this for me, I'll be eternally grateful.'

'I can. I will. I said I'd help, didn't I?' He didn't sound very happy about it. 'Give me five minutes on the phone. There's a chap in College who'll do it. He owes me a favour. He got into a spot of bother last term with one of his pupils, and I managed to fix it for him.'

Smiling wryly, John went into the bedroom and shut the door behind him. I could hear him on the telephone, but not what he said. I drank my coffee. I was both enormously relieved and enormously uneasy . . .

'Wake up, Philip.' John was shaking me gently.

'Sorry. Your coffee can't have been strong enough.'

'You're dead beat. That's what the trouble is. Go and lie down on my bed and get some sleep. I'll wake you for a late lunch.'

I stood up, too quickly. The room revolved. I staggered and would have fallen, but John seized me by the arm. He was right. My bullet wound was still taking its toll and I was out of everything except will-power. I made an effort.

'What did he say – the chap you were talking to?'

'It's all arranged, Philip, so for God's sake try to relax. I'm to take the cat and the other stuff over to him and he'll start work on them this afternoon. I told him a friend of mine suspected someone had been playing an unpleasant practical joke on him, but he wanted to be sure before he raised a stink. Fair enough?'

'Fair enough, yes. Thanks, John.'

I sighed. It was, I thought, as good an explanation as any. I only wished it could have been the truth.

SEVEN

On Monday morning I caught an early train to London. Because of a futile argument with Claire, who wouldn't accept that Mat had commanded my presence, I was late leaving the cottage. As the Renault came over the crown of the hill the train was just drawing into the toy-sized station below. I rammed down the accelerator and roared the last four hundred yards into the forecourt.

I didn't bother to lock the car – it would be safe enough in this sleepy place – but I had to spend precious seconds rescuing the remains of the liqueur chocolates from under the driving seat where I had hidden them. Clutching the packet, I ran as fast as my game leg would let me.

The train had already begun to edge along the platform. But my fingers were on the handle of the carriage door and, with a violent effort, I managed to swing myself inside. Someone stopped me from falling on my face. Someone else slammed the door shut behind me. Yet a third person fielded the packet which had skidded across the floor. Muttering my thanks, I stumbled over their feet into the corridor. It wasn't an auspicious start to my day.

The train was full. I pushed past people and suitcases and haversacks and a folding pram and things tied together with string and yet more people. I began to regret my decision not to drive up to London. An almost empty first-class carriage tempted me. I had intended to get a cheap day return when the ticket collector appeared, but I wasn't going to stand all the way to London. I slid open the door and collapsed thankfully into the corner seat.

The other occupants of the carriage, having looked their reproach at my intrusion, retreated behind their newspapers. I didn't have a paper to retreat behind, and I soon caught myself watching the middle finger of my left hand massaging the ball of my left thumb. It was a nervous mannerism I had recently developed and one which I deplored. Hurriedly I took from my inside pocket the analyses of the chocolates and the results of Katy's autopsy that John Telsey had given me yesterday. They made depressing reading, but I had nothing else.

Because of the moulded tray in which the liqueur chocolates had lain their original number and size were apparent. Most of them had been in the form of small bottles and these were uncontaminated. But there had been six larger bottles. Claire had eaten three of them. She had unwrapped a fourth, I remembered, and put it back in the box. Katy must have eaten it. Of the two remaining bottles, both had been tampered with. The silver paper had been carefully peeled off their bases. Then some of the liqueur had been syringed out and a poison with a multisyllabic Latin name had been substituted. Enough had been found in one bottle to cause the death of a small animal. Afterwards the needle-holes had been sealed with chocolate and the silver paper replaced. It had been a finicky job; someone had taken a lot of trouble.

And someone had given the operation a lot of thought. The choice of liqueur chocolates had been deliberate. They were suitable vehicles for the poison and they had the added advantage that anyone, if offered the box, would almost certainly pick a small bottle. In fact, they made it a safe bet that no one but Claire or I would be poisoned – and that neither of us would die.

But what the hell was the purpose of it all? What was the point of trying to frighten me, to intimidate me, if no demand was made? What was I expected to do? I wondered if John could conceivably be right.

'The bastards are playing with you, Philip,' he had said, 'as a small boy plays with a fly, pulling off its wings and legs, one by one, before he squashes it flat. Sooner or later, when they reckon you've suffered enough, they'll squash you flat – and probably Claire too.'

The bastards, according to John, could well be relations or friends of people who had been gassed on Massacre Day. They had got hold of my name, and they had decided to make me, the hated Englishman from the Ministry of Defence, the target of their personal vengeance. It was an interesting theory – and to my relief it explained why John hadn't immediately commented on the unlikelihood that the IRA would use poison – but . . . I must have dozed.

I was disturbed by the ticket collector, who pretended to think that I was trying to defraud British Rail by boarding the train without a ticket. The altercation riled me, and my temper was not improved by the long queue for taxis at Paddington. I limped angrily out of the station into a drizzle as fine as a cobweb. It had been a lovely morning when I left the cottage and though I had a light raincoat I hadn't brought an umbrella. Soon I was hot and sticky and damp, and more exhausted than if I had driven up to town. I caught a bus going in approximately the right direction, walked a few blocks and finally caught a taxi which took me to the corner of St James's Square.

Mat had arranged to meet me in the Army and Navy Club. It was supposed to be a security measure. He didn't want me coming to the Ministry. But I was scarcely in the hall when I met the wife of one of my colleagues. She was having her voluminous handbag searched – a precaution since the Club had been bombed – and I tried to hurry past.

'Your parcel, sir – if I may.'

'It's only chocolates. Smell them if you doubt me.'

He gave the parcel a perfunctory sniff, and handed it back. 'Thank you, sir.' A smile edged his lips.

'That's not fair. You went through my handbag as though . . .'

Grinning to myself I escaped to the cloakroom and hung up my raincoat. I gained nothing by it. She was holding the lift for me and I was subjected to a torrent of words – complaints about the Club's security measures, questions about my bullet wound, questions about Claire's reactions to the booby-trap in the garage, personal questions which I resented, especially as they were interlarded with expressions of horror at the way so-called political prisoners in Northern Ireland were being 'tortured', The woman was a menace. Chalking up a black mark against her husband, I thanked my gods for Claire.

I found Mat occupying a small sitting-room reserved for male members of the Club. Presumably he had chosen it because at this time of the morning we were unlikely to be disturbed. When he saw me he jumped to his feet and asked at once after Claire. Reassured, he then went to order coffee, and returned with a large brandy, which he set in front of me. I smiled my thanks.

'You look as if you could do with it, Philip, and judging by what you told me on the phone I'm not surprised. Are those the chocolates?' He nodded towards the packet I had put on the coffee-table. 'Where's your poor cat?'

'Incinerated, courtesy of the University.' My voice was blank. 'I wasn't prepared to bring her corpse up to London, Mat. I brought the box of what remains of the chocolates because I assumed you want to have your own tests done. But I do have the report on them and on Katy's autopsy.'

'Who did it?'

'I don't know. A friend of John Telsey's. He'll keep his mouth shut. John vouches ior him.'

'And you vouch for John?' The question was barked unexpectedly.

I found myself explaining about Dick Havant and how, since I couldn't leave Oxford and Claire, I had appealed to John. The arrival of coffee interrupted what was beginning to sound like an excuse. I buried my face in the brandy glass and waited for Mat's comments. I didn't think I was going to like them. But, when he had paid for the coffee and the waiter had gone, Mat was silent. He read the reports I had given him, put them in his briefcase, lit a cheroot and sat back in a corner of the leather sofa, smoking. I poured myself some more coffee.

After a while he said: 'Philip, I'd like a complete record of everything that happened from the time you got back to your flat on Friday afternoon. As much detail as you can.'

He produced a small battery-operated recorder, switched it on and handed it to me. Taking a deep breath, I began. I included everything I thought he needed to know. There were some points, like the ludicrous fashion in which I had dealt with the parcel of chocolates, that only torture would have extracted from me. For the rest, he was welcome to it. Unfortunately I didn't think it would help much.

Nor did Mat. He dismissed John's idea of a personal vendetta with contempt, on the grounds that no private cabal from Belfast would have the experience or the means to mount such elaborate attacks on me. But he couldn't produce a better theory. If I were a menace to whoever had organized Massacre Day, why not kill me, as O'Reilly and Bridie Connell had been killed. Threats without demands were meaningless and there had been no attempt to approach me. Mat ground out his cheroot in the ashtray and at once lit another; it was a measure of his concern.

'Between you and me, Philip, we've made no progress, and I see no prospects of making any. The Special Branch will go through the motions but I doubt whether they'll have any more luck tracing the poison in those chocolates than they did tracing Derwent.'

He sighed and lapsed into thought. We finished our coffee in silence. God knows what Mat was thinking about. I was contemplating the lies I had told Claire, lies about the smoked salmon and the box of chocolates she had missed on her return to the cottage, and above all about Katy's apparent disappearance. It had seemed the right thing to do, to save Claire from more worry and anxiety – she was already under too much strain – but now I was having doubts. With the SB sherlocking around, a trivial word could collapse my deception like a card castle. I ought to get Claire right away – for a complete holiday.

I caught at the idea. We could go to Paris where we had spent our honeymoon, to Strasbourg to stay with William and his family, or to the British Embassy in Bonn; Andrew had been urging us to visit them. There was nothing to stop us. I wasn't chained to my Ministry desk any longer. The Cabinet Office wouldn't miss me for a few weeks. I wondered why I hadn't thought of it before.

'Philip, you remember I told you there was a security leak at The Park?'

I adjusted my mind to the change of subject. 'Yes – Wasn't the son of a friend of yours – someone you'd sponsored – supposed to be involved?'

Deliberately Mat inhaled the smoke from his cheroot and let it drift out through his nostrils. 'You're referring to my wife's nephew,' he said coldly. 'That was an error of judgement on some fool's part. He's been completely cleared.'

'Good. Margaret's nephew? I thought you said he was the son of a friend.'

'He's both. His father, with whom I was at school, is married to Margaret's sister.'

'Then you must be doubly relieved.' I couldn't resist the dig. I didn't like Mat when he was being pompous. 'I assume we haven't caught the agent yet?'

'Not yet, but we're getting close. You didn't discuss the matter with John Telsey by any chance, did you?'

'I most certainly did not! I'm not in the habit of – '

Mat cut short my indignation. 'Pity. He might have given you some information about our latest suspect, who happens to be a former member of your college. Telsey refused to help our security people. He said he'd co-operated with previous vettings but if they'd been bloody inefficient, it was our own damned fault. Then he delivered a lecture on the rights of the individual and kicked our people out.' Mat gave a grunt of disgust. 'How I hate these liberal dons with their pink politics! Take my advice, Philip. Don't ever trust them.'

Mat lumbered to his feet. 'It's past twelve. The bar will be open. Let's go and have a drink. I booked us a table in the dining-room for a quarter to one. You'll be my guest, I hope?'

I thanked him, gave a feeble smile and followed him from the room. I felt ashamed. He hadn't given me much chance to object to his innuendo or to defend John Telsey. Nevertheless, considering the concern John had shown for me yesterday, I was disconcerted that I had made no effort to protest on his behalf. What Mat had implied was absurd, libellous, completely unfounded. But, as the unspoken apologia formed in my mind, I couldn't help recalling my own doubts.

Angrily I renewed my resolution to take a month's holiday in Europe, away from all problems. Mat had been right to take me off Ireland. My judgement was getting warped.

Claire and I spent the rest of the week at the cottage. It was a peaceful, if not an idyllic, time. Nothing untoward happened but there were too many reminders of the unpleasant. Claire's diet had to be observed strictly. The Moretons continued to reproach themselves for the loss of Katy; they made a great effort to find a tortoiseshell kitten for us, but Claire refused to keep it. Mat telephoned, and John Telsey. Claire had a violent nightmare from which she woke crying. And constantly I found myself watching, waiting, anticipating another attack.

After the weekend we went back to London. Things improved. Claire recovered from the effects of the poison and began to eat normally again. She was delighted with the idea of a long holiday on the Continent. I got in touch with William and Andrew who offered us unlimited hospitality. I arranged my leave, booked us a room at a small hotel near the Etoile and picked up our airline tickets. Denise telephoned her half-sister who lived at Versailles. We were all set to fly to Paris.

On Thursday, the day before our departure, I put in a token appearance at the Cabinet Office. As I had suspected, there was nothing for me to do, though I was made welcome. I thought longingly of Washington. I was looking forward to Paris and visiting the family, but I would have wished the summer away.

At three o'clock I decided to go home. There was a flower-seller at the corner of Downing Street and Whitehall, and I bought some roses for Denise, who was cooking us a *bon voyage* dinner. Almost at once I regretted the impulse. The bus was crowded and I had to go upstairs, where I sat on a third of a seat beside a very fat woman with innumerable parcels that constantly endangered both me and the flowers. At Oxford Circus I got out and walked.

It was a beautiful day and I was in no hurry. I enjoyed the

walk. As I turned into Harley Street I saw Denise leaning out of her sitting-room window, and waved to her. She waved in return and abruptly withdrew her head. She was waiting for me as I got out of the lift.

'Philip – come in!'

Immediately her agitation communicated itself to me. 'What is it? Has something happened? Is it Claire? Denise – '

'No, no! Claire's all right. She's having her hair done. She'll be back soon.'

I was enormously relieved, but still tense. 'There is something wrong, though?'

Denise nodded. Automatically I handed her the flowers and she put them down on a table. She was too preoccupied to thank me.

'The laundry came this afternoon, and I took yours upstairs for you. Claire was packing and she was in something of a flap. She said she'd changed her mind about the clothes she was taking to Paris and there were a couple of dresses that needed an iron, but she had to go to the hairdresser's. So I volunteered.'

Denise paused, and her tongue flickered over dry lips. Normally she was composed, a rather sardonic observer of other people's emotion. Now she was badly shaken. Her words tumbled over each other, and a Normandy accent betrayed her usually impeccable English.

'For God's sake get to the point,' I said roughly.

'I – I was on the second dress when the phone rang. A voice said "Mrs Camplin?", and without thinking I said "Yes", and she – '

'It was a woman?' I interrupted out of surprise.

'Yes. She sounded Irish – or rather as if she were pretending to be Irish as a nasty kind of joke.' Denise was astute. 'But it wasn't a joke. She was frightening. She said: "Claire, if we'd put a different poison in those chocolates, you'd be well and truly dead at this moment. You realize that, don't you? We were giving you a last chance. Think about it. Think hard." There was something else I didn't get. I was angry. I said "Go to hell!", and banged down the receiver. It was a feeble gesture, I'm afraid.'

I cursed. We had a new telephone number and, like the last, it was unlisted. But these damned people had got hold of it just the same. They were making fresh threats – and their threats were usually followed by action. Thank God we were getting out tomorrow.

'It's a blessing it was you and not Claire who answered the phone,' I said, my concern solely for Claire.

'But you'll have to warn her, won't you?'

'No! What good would it do? She's fraught enough as it is.'

'She's not the only one.' Denise was tart. 'I don't think you realize how much Patrick worries about you, Philip.'

'Well, don't tell him either!' I couldn't cope with Patrick's problems. Then, seeing Denise's expression, I added: 'Look, my dear, I'm sorry. I know I'm being an awful curse to you and Patrick, but Mat's taken me off Ireland and with any luck by the time I've had a month's leave and I'm back working in the Cabinet Office, this bloody business will be over – at least as far as I'm concerned.'

'You mean the IRA, or whoever it is that's hounding you, will have got tired of it?'

I glanced at her sharply – in my attempt to comfort her I had said too much – but her puzzled face was innocent. Suddenly I felt an urge to confide in her, to tell her what we believed to be the truth. Of course it wasn't possible. Yet I hesitated for so long that she was looking at me curiously, and I was trapped into explanations. Resenting the need for the deception, I told her about John Telsey's idea of personal vengeance. She was horrified. She couldn't conceive of anyone hating like that. She asked questions. And, while I answered them with great care, I yearned for tomorrow to come.

The week in Paris passed very quickly. Claire and I did the sort of things tourists do, the sort of things we had done on our honeymoon. But we were lazy rather than adventurous. We spent a lot of time strolling along the boulevards, hand in hand, and idling in sidewalk cafés. The May weather was perfect, the chestnut trees in full candle – and our old relationship seemed fully re-established. Gradually we unwound.

On Friday afternoon I was sitting under the umbrella of a café on the corner of the Place Vendôme, slowly sipping a *crème* and waiting for Claire. Denise's half-sister, who was married to a Parisian lawyer, had taken Claire shopping and we had arranged to meet here.

It was our last day. Tomorrow we were renting a car to take us to Strasbourg and the William Camplins. From there we proposed to drive up the Rhine Valley to Bonn and Andrew's family. I thought of the weeks ahead with pleasure, tinged with some sorrow at leaving Paris. It meant a quarter of our holiday was already over. I hoped the rest would be as good.

The café was beginning to fill. I glanced at my watch. Claire was late, but that was to be expected. She was probably drooling over some beautiful, unobtainably expensive garment. As I grinned to myself, I caught sight of her on the other side of the street. She was waiting for the little red man to become a little green man and the traffic to halt.

I waved to her, but she didn't see me. Her attention was concentrated on the lights. When they changed she walked very quickly across the street, her head up, her dark hair swinging, a half smile on her lips. Suddenly, for some inexplicable reason, I was reminded of our first meeting.

I had been standing, talking to John Telsey, at the bottom of his staircase when Claire came out of the porter's lodge and hurried across the quad towards us. She was wearing a green suit not unlike the one she was wearing now, and carrying her commoner's gown as she carried the couturier's box. John had introduced us – Claire was his pupil – and we chatted while he fetched the book she had come to borrow. Before I left her in the High Street she had promised to have dinner with me that night. Three months later we were married. I couldn't believe my luck. I still couldn't believe it.

'Hallo, darling.' I kissed her. 'Had a good afternoon?'

'Fabulous, absolutely fabulous.'

She sat down and put the box carefully on the chair beside her. Her face was bright like a happy child's, her eyes shining. I had to laugh. Even the waiter, who brought us a couple of Dubonnets, smiled at her.

'Claudine sends her apologies for not joining us, Philip, but it's late and she wanted to get home. She looks forward to seeing you again in July when she comes to stay with Denise.'

'Fine. Anyway, I'm grateful to her for not letting you buy up the whole of Paris.' I nodded towards the box. 'I was expecting to see you laden with parcels.'

'Only one dress.' She sighed with delight. 'It's super, Philip, absolutely super. But you're going to be horrified at the price. It cost the earth.'

'Well, we can always go home on the Métro, and as long as we've got enough money to get us to Strasbourg tomorrow . . .' I teased her while we drank our Dubonnets.

And, as it happened, we had to settle for the Métro. It was impossible to get a taxi. The nearby rank was empty and had a long queue, and all the cabs on the street seemed occupied.

Without a car we had used the Métro a lot during the week, and as we walked to Concorde we joked about how economical we were in not wasting our last two tickets. But I regretted the taxi. Concorde is always a busy station and in the late afternoon it was seething with people. We had to push our way along the platform to the place where the first-class carriages would stop. It was less crowded here, but we were constantly jostled, and I was glad when we heard the gentle rumble of the approaching train. I hoped it wouldn't be so full that we should have to stand.

As the long silver tube emerged from the tunnel like a dragon on rubber wheels, we edged towards the front of the platform. Claire was concentrated on protecting her new purchase and I had a firm grip on her wrist. I didn't intend us to get separated.

The blow came without warning, a crippling chop on my upper arm that was to leave a livid bruise. It must have hit a nerve end, because momentarily I was nauseated. I released my hold on Claire's wrist. I felt myself sway forward, saw the shining killer rails rush up towards me, sensed the nearness of the train. Then a powerful arm was flung across my chest, holding me back, preventing me from falling, saving me.

Nobody saved Claire. I watched her precious box describe a parabola in the air and her body arch with it. Together, seemingly in slow motion, they fell on the track and the train passed greedily over them. There was nothing I could do.

Above the shouts and the cries and the confusion I still heard her terrified, agonizing scream. Kind hands were reaching for me, anxious faces peering at me. None of it was real. None of it was happening. Or, if it were, it was happening to someone else, not to me, not to Claire – not to Claire.

EIGHT

It was the day of Claire's funeral and the cottage, full of family for the occasion, was already stirring. I stood at the window in my pyjamas and gazed across the garden to the stream that sparkled in the early morning sun. I would have wished for a day of beating rain, grim sky, sodden ground, weeping trees, cowering flowers – a cheerless, sunless, hopeless day. Instead it was beautiful.

I stood there for what seemed a long time. I didn't see what my eyes looked at, nor think the thoughts that scurried through my mind. I was in a vacuum of unhappiness.

A rap on the door roused me and I leaped for the bed. Anne, William's wife, brought in my breakfast tray – orange juice, boiled egg, toast, marmalade, coffee. No posy this morning; flowers might remind me of wreaths and she had removed the vase that Mrs Moreton had put on the tray. I could see the small round indentation where it had stood on the cloth.

'Good morning, Philip. How did you sleep?'

'Very well, thank you.'

It was our ritual question and answer. The family insisted on treating me as an invalid. During the days since Claire's death my brothers had organized my affairs, their wives had cosseted me, their children shown me affection. As many of them as could would be here today. And I was grateful to them, though I knew they came for my sake, not for Claire's. Apart from Patrick none of them had ever really liked Claire. They had thought my marriage a mistake.

'Philip!'

'Sorry, Anne. What did you say?'

'I said you should be downstairs by twenty to eleven. That gives you heaps of time to have breakfast and bathe and dress in as leisurely a fashion as you please. We'll be leaving for the church about ten to.'

'All right.'

I did as I was told. I ate breakfast, showered, shaved, dressed. My dark grey suit, white shirt and black tie couldn't have been less suitable for a lovely spring day in the country. At precisely twenty to eleven I arrived in the sitting-room, where everyone was waiting for me. I greeted Patrick, and Denise, who had just driven down from London, and an assortment of relations. They were all kind, solicitous, loving, and I tried to respond. But I felt as if I were playing a part; none of this was relevant to Claire and me.

We left the cottage in a sort of procession, myself bringing up the rear with William and Anne. Even at our mourning pace it only took us five minutes to reach the church. They didn't talk on the way, for which I was thankful. I was steeling myself for the moment when I would have to look at the coffin.

The funeral was meant to be private but the church – a small, part-Norman building of Cotswold stone – was surprisingly full. Many of those present I had never seen before but, as I limped down the aisle to the front pew, I noticed – apart from members of the family – the Moretons, Mat and Margaret Harworth, John Telsey – and Bette Aylwyn. Bette, in vivid green, was the one bright splash of colour in the congregation and my heart warmed to her. She distracted my mind from the flower-covered coffin until I was settled in my seat and could bury my face in my hands, pretending to pray.

Mercifully the service was short and I was able to disregard most of it. I let the prayers and hymns wash over me. At least the sound was pleasing, and the vicar had a good voice. I listened to it during the eulogy, and tried to ignore his actual, meaningless words. He had met Claire a few times in the village but he didn't know her. He didn't even know how she had died. He kept on repeating the phrase 'a tragic accident', as if he believed it. I supposed he did – it was the official explanation – but it made a mockery of what he had to say.

I was glad to be in the open air again, even though outside the church another farce was being played. A man holding a cine-camera was having an argument with the verger. As soon as I appeared he ignored the verger and began to take movies. This incensed William, who objected strongly. The altercation became heated, but the cameraman held his ground and continued to take pictures as people came out of the church porch and fanned around us. The audience grew. Several of them, including the parson, tried to intervene. Patrick made a grab for the camera but was fended off.

The scene was beginning to have the makings of a first-class brawl when I noticed one of the mourners raise a hand above his head. The cameraman acknowledged the signal and simultaneously stopped his efforts at filming, pushed his way roughly through the group surrounding him and ran off. The man who had signalled was the big-nosed Special Branch chap I had originally met that evening in Woodstock, the one who had made friends with Katy. His presence jolted me.

Order restored, we walked up the hill behind the church and ranged ourselves around the grave. I watched the coffin lowered into the gaping ground. I heard the formal prayers and the symbolic handful of earth spattering on to the wooden box. I had said goodbye to Claire days ago in Paris, days without time, but it was still hard to bear.

As I turned away the vicar shook me by the hand and murmured perfunctory condolences. Others came up to say how sorry they were, to ask how I was, to walk a few steps beside me. I found myself shaking hands with a young woman I didn't recognize at all.

'You don't remember me, do you, Mr Camplin?' She didn't wait for any polite noises I might feel obliged to make. 'You used to know me – at Oxford years ago. I'm the Provost's daughter, Rose.' She smiled.

She had a sweet smile. It wiped the worry lines from her face. She was, in fact, a pretty girl, fair, blue-eyed, plump and about Claire's age. Perhaps I had met her with Claire. In any case I remembered her now as a solemn, fat child – the Provost's darling who used to invade the polite tea-parties her mother gave for the College's undergraduates. I wondered if John

Telsey had brought her today and why.

'It was good of you to come,' I said. 'You were a friend of Claire's, when she was at Oxford?'

'Oh no. I – I scarcely knew her. I wasn't up myself, you see. I was far too stupid to get into the University.' She laughed, but it was a tired remark that she had made too often.

I tried to think of a suitable response. I couldn't imagine what she was doing here if she scarcely knew Claire. The sun glittering on her wedding ring, which she was twisting nervously round and round her finger, prompted me.

'Well, now you're married I don't suppose not having a degree makes much difference to you.'

'Oh, but it does! A clever husband needs to talk to his wife, to be able to tell her about his work.' She stopped abruptly and brushed her face with the back of her hand as if to wipe away the shadow that had fallen on it. 'Mr Camplin, I'm sorry. Perhaps I shouldn't have come but I felt I had to. You see, I – I hated – '

I wasn't to know what she hated. Patrick had borne down on us and had taken her by the arm. He was talking volubly about the Provost and Oxford. He seemed to know who she was. I said goodbye but she didn't answer. Patrick was leading her away, and as I turned to go in the other direction, I bumped heavily into John Telsey, who was right behind me.

'The stupid little bitch!' he said. 'What was she saying to you, Philip?' He was angry.

I sighed. 'Nothing much. She was explaining who she was. I didn't recognize her.'

'Why on earth should you? She ought never to have come. Philip, I am sorry. It's all my fault. The Provost asked me about the funeral and I told him. It didn't occur to me he'd pass the information on to his bloody daughter.'

'It doesn't matter, John. Half the people here are William's neighbours or security men or something like that.' I let my bitterness show. 'They don't really care a damn about Claire.'

'As long as Rose didn't – didn't bother you,' he finished weakly.

I looked at him in exasperation. 'For Christ's sake!' I said between my teeth. 'Why are you making such a fuss about her? Forget her. She's not important.'

'As you say, Philip.' His face was blank.

Abruptly he turned on his heels and left me. I nearly called after him. I wanted to apologize. But Andrew had come to collect me; seemingly it was time we went back to the cottage for the conventional baked meats. William had already gone on ahead with the women.

Andrew walked me slowly along the gravel path towards the churchyard gate. 'None of Claire's family came,' he said.

'No. There's only a sister, who lives in the Lake District.'

Andrew grunted. He didn't point out that the village was no less accessible from the Lake District than from Bonn or Strasbourg, and I was grateful. I had written to Mary, Claire's elder sister, at the only address I could find for her. It was the address to which the invitation to our wedding had been sent; she hadn't come to that either, as I recalled. But she had written and sent a present. This time she hadn't even acknowledged my letter. Perhaps she hadn't received it. I supposed I would have to write again, make an effort to get in touch with her. It was a damned nuisance.

'Mr Camplin.'

The big-nosed Special Branch man had suddenly appeared from behind a marble angel, a superb Victorian monstrosity that dominated the churchyard and could be seen from most of the village. Not long ago, to amuse ourselves, Claire and I had made a special expedition to visit it. We had asked ourselves what sort of people Margaret Mary and James Edgar George had really been, and why he had thought fit to lavish so much money on his wife's memorial. Laughing together, we had invented a whole history for the long-dead couple. It had never occurred to us that Claire Elizabeth, wife of Philip John Camplin, would so soon be lying in the same churchyard.

'Mr Camplin, I just wanted to say how truly sorry I am, sir. She was such a game lady. A game lady.' He made it sound as if he were paying the highest tribute that he could. 'She wouldn't leave her cat behind, would she?'

He bobbed his head at me and was striding away before I could thank him or offer him my hand. I was touched. He had genuinely meant what he said.

'That was a rum chap, Philip. Who is he?'

'A friend of mine.'

'What did he mean about the cat?'

I didn't want to explain. 'God knows. People seem to behave oddly at funerals.' And that, I thought, was true enough.

Andrew didn't persist, and we walked in companionable silence down the hill, past the church and on to the road, where there were several parked cars. Bette Aylwyn was leaning against a white Jaguar. She had taken off the surprising hat she had been wearing, and her red-gold hair gleamed in the sunlight. She could have been modelling for a fashion photograph. But when she hurried to us and brought her face close to kiss me I saw how ravaged she was. She was wearing no make-up and her skin was blotchy, her eyes red-rimmed and swollen from weeping. I hadn't always liked Bette – she was an extravagant, selfish, amoral creature – but she had been very fond of Claire.

'Oh, Philip love, I hope you weren't too surprised at my being dressed like this,' she said without preliminary. 'I wanted to wear green because it was Claire's favourite colour. I didn't realize it was going to be such a – a starchy English funeral.'

My heart warmed to her and I laughed. Beside me Andrew cleared his throat. I introduced them, explaining that Bette was American, and Andrew gave her his best ambassadorial bow. He also gave her a wide grin and assumed that she was coming back to the cottage for a drink, though it was obvious she had not been asked. Bette responded. She thrust her arm through mine and, walking along the village street between the two of them, I felt – not happy, but at least a member of the human race again.

The feeling didn't last long, in spite of two short whiskies that I downed in quick succession. The William Camplins were nothing if not hospitable, and the baked meats – in the form of an excellent buffet lunch – were only rivalled by the flow of liquor. Champagne was not served, but there was what William apologetically described as 'a modest rosé'. It was, in fact, a good party. Unfortunately I wasn't in the mood.

I was glad when Mat, looking more bulbous-eyed than ever, drew me to one side and said he 'must have a word' with me. It was so typical of him, whatever the occasion. I was mildly surprised, however, when he added, 'In private, please, Philip.' I led him into the garden.

'I'm afraid I've something unpleasant to tell you,' Mat said drily.

'Go ahead.'

'There's going to be a lot more publicity about Claire's death.'

'Why? I'd have thought every ounce of interest would have been sucked out of the "accident" by now.'

'I know, Philip, but – ' I must have looked bleak because he gave me an encouraging smile. 'There's been a fresh development. Letters, or rather duplicates of the same letter, have been received by the heads of the BBC and ITV and the editors of the leading dailies. It doesn't warrant a "D" Notice; there's no question of national security. But they've been persuaded to keep the story under wraps for twenty-four hours. I – I wanted to tell you about it myself.'

I nearly said: 'For Christ's sake get on with it then', but Mat could never be hurried. To hide my impatience I bent to pick up a stone and lobbed it into the stream. When the widening circles of ripples had died away I turned back to him. He was holding out a sheet of paper.

'Here's a photocopy. It might be best if you read it for yourself, Philip.'

'All right.' I took it with reluctance.

The letter was typed, single-spaced, neatly, without error. It was dated and signed, if 'Those who loved Kevin' could be called a signature. The only address was 'Northern Ireland'. I read it very carefully.

'Dear Sir,

On Massacre Day our beloved Kevin was murdered by the English soldiers in Belfast. He died in great pain as a result of poison gas forbidden by international law, but authorized by the Ministry of Defence in London. He died for Ireland, an innocent victim. He was ten years old.

We who loved him decided that in return an English life should be taken, the life of Claire Camplin, wife of Philip Camplin. After several threats, by gunfire and bombing and poison, she was finally thrown under a tube train in Paris. She too was an innocent victim.

She was chosen because of her husband. Philip Camplin is a senior civil servant in the Ministry of Defence and the prototype for the murderers of Kevin. Nevertheless, we decided not to assassinate him – it is easy to die – but to let him live and grieve for his wife as we grieve for Kevin. He need fear nothing more from us. He will suffer enough. Justice has been done.

Please, sir, give this letter as much publicity as possible, so that the English may never again murder and cripple innocent women and children as they did on Massacre Day.

Yours truly,

Those who loved Kevin.

P.S. This was a non-political action.'

Convulsively I crumpled the paper in my hand. I was shaken and I heard myself repeating a meaningless stream of blasphemy. It must have been a full minute before I regained control. Mat had found a stick and was crouched on the bank, idly drawing patterns in the water. As he straightened himself – he made a big thing of it, though I knew thirty-six holes of golf didn't faze him – he said quietly:

'Now you've spewed that out of you, Philip, you might try using your brain. This could be what you need to get it going again – '

It was a brutal remark, but it had the desired effect. Although

I yearned to get my hands round his fat throat and squeeze, I knew Mat was right. If I was incapable of rational thought I was no use, to myself or anyone else. I couldn't spend the rest of my life in a morass of self-pity.

'Whoever was responsible for that letter,' I said slowly, 'was also responsible for Claire's death and – and the other things that happened. He knew about the poisoned chocolates, and that was never made public.'

'Philip, you're not suggesting the letter's genuine, are you?'

'No – though it's difficult to say why not. It seems to fit the known facts. But no, I don't. Somehow it lacks compassion – even for the child. Besides, no collection of private people would have the resources to do what's been done, and cover their tracks so efficiently.'

'I agree, completely. But what's the point of a phoney letter? That's what I'd like to know. Why bother to publicize a nonsense story about personal vengeance?' Mat heaved a gusty sigh. 'I suppose every little helps to exacerbate the general situation in Ireland, but there must be more to it than that.'

'Presumably it's meant to divert us.'

'Yes, but what from? There are so many questions, and when we do get answers they don't fit.' We had turned and were walking back towards the house. Mat kicked savagely at an unoffending daisy. 'Why Claire, Philip? Why did they kill Claire, and not you?'

I had asked myself that a thousand times, but it was a useless exercise. I said harshly: 'What do you want me to do, Mat?'

'I'd like you to come back to the Ministry.' Mat's mouth shaded a smile. 'Somehow the Cabinet Office doesn't seem your style, Philip.'

'To work on Ireland again?'

'Yes – if that's what you prefer.'

I nodded my assent. I didn't really care what I did; without Claire there was little purpose in anything. But, assuming I was no longer in any danger – if I ever had been – it was necessary to earn a living.

'Good. I'll expect you next Monday then.' He hesitated.

'Philip, there is one thing. It's been suggested that Claire's murder could really represent a final threat to you, and that now you'll be approached directly.'

I stared at him in amazement. I thought it a preposterous suggestion. But it explained why Mat wanted me back at the Ministry, under his eye. He wasn't acting only out of kindness. I laughed aloud, without humour.

'Let's hope they do,' I said. 'It should prove interesting.'

Before Monday there was a long weekend to be got through. I didn't want to stay on at the cottage or go back to Harley Street or accept any of the invitations I had received. I wanted to be alone. As Mat had said, I needed to think.

In the event I drove back to London with Patrick and Denise and spent the night in their flat. I warned them about the letter, and said I must avoid the newshounds. The next day I borrowed Denise's car and set off for the Lake District. I had told them I planned to drive around, to stop at whatever pubs I chanced on, to do some gentle walking. Having failed to argue me out of the plan, they had been as helpful as they could.

What I didn't mention was that I intended to call on Claire's sister. The idea had come to me suddenly when I was wondering how to fill in my time, and wouldn't be dislodged. The more I thought about it, the more eager I became. It was absurd that after being married to Claire for more than six years I had never met her only near relation.

On the Saturday morning, armed with instructions from the small hotel near Windermere where I had found a room, I went in search of Auburn House. This wasn't a part of the country that I knew and, in spite of my maps, I got lost several times. Eventually, however, thanks to a friendly postman, I found the two stone pillars that marked the driveway to the house.

I parked at the side of the road. Suddenly I was beset with doubts. Perhaps I should have written, or at least telephoned. To appear out of the blue after all this time might well be considered an intrusion. But Mary was Claire's sister, and Claire was dead.

The trouble was that I knew so little about Mary. Claire had never made any pretence of being close to her. As I understood it, there was a gap of five or six years between the sisters, and Mary, who had been something of a fool and had resented Claire's ability, had married young. After she had left home the girls had kept in touch, but nothing more, and the last I had heard of Mary was a note in a Christmas card saying they all had flu and hoping we were well. It didn't help me now.

Still, having come so far, it would be ludicrous to turn back without making some attempt to see her. If I was unwelcome I could always cut the visit short. Deliberately I made a U-turn and pointed the Renault between the pillars.

The grounds of Auburn House were rough grass, studded with trees and bushes, but the driveway was well kept and the house itself was beautiful. Long and low, with a three-car garage and a boat house, it lay along the edge of Lake Windermere and exuded quiet opulence. Financially Claire's sister had done well for herself.

I rang the bell and waited. The door was opened by a white-jacketed houseman. I asked for Mrs White.

'Mrs White is – er – no longer with us, sir.'

'You mean she's sold the house and moved away? Do you have her new address?'

'I mean Mrs White is dead, sir.'

'Dead!'

'I'm sorry. I didn't intend to startle you, sir.' He regarded me with concealed curiosity.

'Then maybe I could speak to the present owner. Would you ask him if he could spare me – '

'Sir James is not in residence, sir. Nor any of the family. There's only myself and cook, and the new housekeeper who replaced Mrs White and naturally never knew her.'

He had corrected me without seeming to and, while I absorbed my second surprise, my mind raced. I remembered the heavy silver salver that had been Mary's wedding present to us, and the expensive Christmas cards she always sent. But none of it mattered now. Like Claire, she was dead. But when had she died, and how? She was a young woman. I thought more carefully about what I should say.

'I never met Mrs White and I seem to have been misinformed, but it's not important. Actually she's inherited a small legacy, a piece of jewellery, and as I was holidaying in this district I said I'd deliver it. I did write – '

I paused and he rose to the bait. 'Ah yes, one moment, sir. If you'll step inside.'

He found the letter without difficulty. It was on the hall table with a pile of mail. When he returned to me I was holding a five-pound note in my hand. The exchange was swift.

'Thank you very much.'

'Thank you, sir.' He became unctuously affable. 'What a pity Mrs White was killed before she received her little legacy.'

'You said "killed". Some sort of accident?' I managed to keep my voice level.

'In a car, sir. Sir James allowed her the use of the Mini to do the shopping, and the brakes failed going down the hill. Towards the middle of March it was. We were all very upset, especially Sir James. She'd been here a long time – nine years – ever since her marriage broke up. Sir James made all the arrangements for the funeral himself.'

'Poor woman.' I spoke absentmindedly. My relief was enormous. There was nothing suspicious about a car accident that had taken place several weeks before Massacre Day. 'Did she have any relations?'

'I don't think so, sir – apart from her ex-husband, who's emigrated to Australia. She never spoke of any. And she left what she had to a local orphanage.'

I thanked him and said my goodbyes. He had given me a lot to think about. That we had not been informed of Mary's death was understandable; no one at Auburn House had heard of any sister of Mary White. Nevertheless, the break between Mary and Claire hadn't been complete. There had been the Christmas cards, the wedding present. Or was it possible that Claire had deceived me about Mary, as Mary had deceived her employers? There were so many questions. I couldn't believe they really mattered, and yet . . .

It wasn't until the next day, when I was driving back to London, that an unpleasant thought hit me. Claire had been nervous and on edge as early as last January, but it wasn't until mid-March – about the time Mary had been killed – that she had become obviously unwell. Of course it was a coincidence. She hadn't known about Mary's death and, even if she had, she wouldn't have been so affected. But I had been trained to suspect coincidences. I couldn't let it rest. I would have to make enquiries.

PART II

Alan

ONE

I sat with my feet on my desk reading the latest intelligence reports from Northern Ireland. In spite of talk of reprisals and counter-reprisals things had been surprisingly quiet in the Province since Massacre Day. It seemed as if everyone had been shocked by the enormity of what had happened, too shocked to resort to the violent action that the instigators of the tragedy might well have expected and hoped for.

The Russians, fully aware that we would use our veto, had tabled a motion in the Security Council condemning our behaviour in Northern Ireland and demanding the immediate withdrawal of all British troops. This was an obvious ploy. More important was the fact that the Americans had also voted against the motion, thereby creating more dissension in their own country. But the President had been firm, and it was mainly thanks to him that at least our allies were no longer crying for our blood. Eire's official restraint had also helped. The Irish Republic didn't want a free for all in the North, probably spilling over the border, any more than we did. And they certainly didn't want any foreign interference, in whatever guise.

Nevertheless, the situation was still bad. Tension was high and there was a great deal of bitter feeling on all sides. The suicide of the unfortunate lieutenant who had ordered the use of the killing gas grenades, his mother's subsequent nervous breakdown and the claim by 'Those who loved Kevin' to have caused Claire's death had combined to create a considerable anti-Irish backlash throughout the UK, and to a lesser degree in the States and Canada. I was horrified by the hatred and vituperation shown everywhere by supposedly responsible people. Cynically I wondered how much of it was communist-inspired.

My intercom buzzed and I pressed down the switch. 'Yes?'

'Mr Harworth would like to see you in his office in ten or fifteen minutes if that's convenient,' my secretary said. 'And I've a Mr Runce on the line. Will you speak to him?'

'Yes, put him through, and tell Mr Harworth I'll be along.'

I waited for the sound of Hal's voice. Apart from a letter of sympathy over Claire, I hadn't heard from him for some time. He had sent a wreath, but he hadn't come to the funeral. When I had telephoned him at the beginning of the week his secretary had said he was 'out of town', and I knew better than to ask questions. He could be anywhere, back in the States or refusing my call from his office chair in the US Embassy in Grosvenor Square.

'Philip?'

'Hallo, Hal.'

We exchanged greetings and he invited me to lunch. We agreed on one o'clock at the Stafford. I was pleased, especially since he hadn't suggested a club. I much preferred the hotel where I wasn't known. I was determined to lead a normal, ordinary life – as normal and ordinary as it could be without Claire – but inevitably at present I was an object of interest, and I wasn't yet hardened to the fact. It was, after all, only my fourth day back at the Ministry, and only a week since Claire's funeral.

I went along to Mat's office; as usual it smelt of a mixture of cheroot smoke and the air-freshener with which his secretary tried to disguise the stale odour. He was on the telephone and he waved me to a chair. His face was grim, his voice curt as he told his listener in simple words to take his finger out. He banged down the receiver.

'Jesus wept,' he said, causing me to raise an eyebrow; Mat never swore. 'They've lost Alan Bronwell. Yesterday. And I've just been told.'

I tried to look interested. I had never heard of Alan Bronwell. It wasn't a name that had ever been mentioned in connection with Northern Ireland. But Mat was uncommonly upset; his hand shook as he fumbled for the case in which he carried his cheroots, and he scowled ferociously.

'Bronwell didn't go to The Park yesterday. He told everyone, his boss, his secretary, his wife, that he had to go up to London to visit the Ministry of Defence. He did precisely that. His wife drove him to the station. He caught a train to Paddington, a taxi to Northumberland Avenue. He showed his pass and was allowed in. He walked straight through the building and out by the door to Whitehall Gardens. The guards remember him. Meanwhile – ' Mat banged his fist angrily on his blotting pad – 'meanwhile the stupid clots who were meant to be watching him thought they had him safely sewn up. It wasn't until noon, when one of them reported in, that they had any suspicions. By then, of course, our bird had flown, though we think he's not out of the UK yet.'

I knew now who Alan Bronwell was – the suspected communist agent at The Park. The fact of his bolting made it a near certainty, and I could understand Mat's annoyance. I sympathized, but he was taking it unnecessarily hard. Bronwell's chances of slipping out of the country, if he hadn't already gone, were not particularly good.

'What's the damage assessment?'

'We don't know yet. The assumption is it's not too bad. Security at The Park is very tight, and his opportunities would be limited. But that may be wishful thinking. He wasn't a fool. It was by chance he was suspected, rather than a dozen others – a tip-off. And even when we were pretty sure about him it was being difficult to prove. That's why he wasn't behind bars.'

'Will he be any use to the Russians – if he gets there?'

'Some. He doesn't seem to have taken anything with him, but we don't know what he's copied or photographed. And, apart from the propaganda value, there's always what he's got in his head.'

It was an old story, repeated too often, and I only half listened. Alan Bronwell didn't sound especially important. I stifled a yawn. In spite of the pills prescribed by Patrick, I wasn't sleeping well. I wished Mat would get off the subject of Bronwell and start talking about Ireland.

'Have a look at this, Philip.'

I took the typed sheet of paper. It was the *curriculum vitae* Bronwell had provided for The Park. Bronwell was the only child of a schoolmaster. He had won scholarships to the local grammar school and then to Oxford, to my old college. Disappointingly he hadn't got a first. On going down he was employed as a research scientist by –

I stopped reading, and raised my head. I met Mat's gaze. He had been watching me. He nodded his head gently as if to encourage me, as if I were a backward pupil who had just seen an obvious point.

'Yes,' he said. 'Alan Bronwell worked for the firm that manufactured those gas grenades. He was there when they were ordered to be destroyed. He left almost immediately afterwards to go to The Park, but he could have taken a box or two with him. He may not have done, of course, but he was in the right place at the right time – and he's a known communist agent. We can't let him slip through our fingers now, Philip.'

'I hope to God not,' I said. 'He won't be the brains behind Massacre Day, but he could be a splendid lead.'

'Read the rest of the *curriculum*.'

I read it in one minute flat. I didn't like what I read. Not only had Bronwell been at the College, but he gave John Telsey's name as a referee. John wasn't a scientist. He hadn't been Bronwell's tutor. The connection between them wasn't self-evident.

'What am I meant to remark on, Mat?'

He didn't answer directly. He said: 'Naturally Bronwell's referees were checked when he took up his first job, and re-checked before he went to The Park as part of his Positive Vetting. They've just been checked again. They're all eminently respectable – his old boss, the headmaster of the school where his father teaches, his own headmaster, his Oxford tutor who's now in the States. With the exception of John Telsey, none of them has set eyes on him for ages. And Telsey, as I remember telling you, was most unhelpful.'

'I remember, but surely now the position has changed.'

'I hope Telsey will see it that way. Personally, I have my doubts, which is why I'd like you to go and talk to him. Will you?'

'Me?'

'Yes. I don't believe Telsey's a traitor, but politically he's a deep pink and, judging from what he says on the telly and the radio, he has some strange ideas. He might be tempted to put friendship before patriotism.'

I wondered if the last remark was meant for me but decided to ignore it. I considered Mat's request preposterous and was about to say so, when I noticed a line in the *curriculum* that I had skipped previously. Alan Bronwell was married. He had married – about the time I had met Claire – a girl called Janet Rosemary Clarke who, before the year was out, had borne him twin sons. Suddenly I had a wholly imaginary picture of the two small boys and their mother. I could understand John wanting to protect them.

'All right, Mat. I'll go and talk to John, but on two conditions. I don't attempt to deceive him. I tell him I'm there on your behalf. And the security hounds are kept off until I've seen him.'

'Agreed. I've already arranged he should be left alone. When will you go?'

I remembered my luncheon date with Hal. 'This afternoon. I'll have to phone. Make sure he's around. He could be – '

'He's around.'

The flat statement chilled me. Mat was taking nothing for granted. Maybe he had thought, as had I, of the lead that poor Bridie Connell had given me. Her 'special' – the man she had disliked so much – had said there would always be Massacre Days as long as there was an Oxford and Cambridge. He had been speaking figuratively, of course. Nevertheless, it was possible that the great universities were still as good a breeding ground for spies as they had been in the heyday of Burgess and Maclean.

I walked to the Stafford, thinking vaguely about my future. Mat had made no further mention of my posting to Washington. It could be off. After the publicity I had received from the shooting in Dublin, my booby-trapped car and the letter from those who claimed to have assassinated Claire, I was associated in everyone's mind with tragedy in Northern Ireland. This could well make me unacceptable to the American people, and thus unacceptable to our Ambassador, but I hoped not. It was surprising to discover how much I still wanted the Washington job, even without Claire.

Luckily my self-analysis was cut short. Hal was waiting for me in the lobby of the hotel. He seized me by the hand and pumped it up and down, his baby face red with sympathy and embarrassment. When I protested mildly, he patted me on the shoulder and led me into the dining-room.

'Hope you don't mind coming straight in, Philip, but the bar's crowded and we can talk better here.'

I noticed that he had reserved a corner table for us. Side by side on a banquette, with our backs to a wall, we would be able to have a private discussion – if that was what he wished. I busied myself with the menu.

'The sky's the limit today, Philip, so if you fancy caviare, order it. Believe me or not, I've just been given a raise.'

I didn't believe him, but I knew he intended to be kind. I chose what I would have done on any other occasion. Hal ordered the wine, and while we waited for the food to be cooked, a couple of double whiskies. When these preliminaries were over and our drinks had arrived, we talked about the Derby, racing in the States, the prospects for Wimbledon. Rather, Hal talked. I sat, and sipped my drink, and relaxed more in the peaceful, organized luxury of the Stafford than I had done for weeks.

I was squeezing the lemon on my smoked salmon when Hal, his mouth full of potted shrimps, said conversationally: 'I've been in Northern Ireland for the last seven or eight days, in and around Belfast, which was why I couldn't – er – pay my last respects to Claire.'

I murmured ineffectually. I had to say something about the funeral. Hal had a nice sense of the conventional, not unlike my brother William's. Then I asked bluntly: 'What were you doing in Belfast?'

And equally bluntly he answered: 'Looking for the relations of the late lamented Kevin – poor little sod.'

It was what I had expected. 'Did you find them?'

'Yes, which I guess is more than your lot has done.'

He was right. Mat had told me that an intensive enquiry concerning all known victims of Massacre Day had so far produced no results. Several Kevins had been found, but they were either the wrong age or otherwise unsuitable. We were persevering.

'Look, Philip, I'm not decrying you. I realize it's not easy for the Brits over there. They don't get much co-operation from the Irish. Protestant or Catholic, nobody loves them and everyone's afraid – especially at the moment, when the situation's so volatile. Dear God, one sometimes feels it only needs a match to start a bush-fire that would raze the entire country. How it didn't go up in flames after Massacre Day is a complete mystery to me.'

Shocked by the vehemence of his own feelings, Hal drained his wine glass and a passing waiter stopped to refill it. Mine, I found, was empty too, but I hadn't made much of an inroad on the smoked salmon. I began to eat quickly. Neither of us spoke again until our Steak Diane had been served.

'Hal, tell me about this Kevin.'

'Sure. But don't gobble your food. It's expensive and good and I hate to see it not appreciated.' He grinned at me. 'Besides, you don't get proper nourishment that way and by the looks of you, Philip, you could do with some.'

I did my best to return his grin. The concern of my family and my friends for my physical well-being had begun to rile me. No one seemed to understand how irritating it was.

'Kevin,' I said gently and, before I could stop myself, added: 'I suppose you've been promising the Irish more American largesse.'

'Promising – and giving. There really is a fund for the Massacre Day victims. My fellow Americans are very generous.' Hal waved aside my apology. 'Sometimes too generous. Anyway, it's a good cover. People will confide in you a whole lot more if they think you've a wallet stuffed with dollars they might be able to get their hands on.'

'And that's how you discovered Kevin. He actually exists?'

'Yes, to both questions, Philip. At least he did exist. He died three days after Massacre Day in a village some distance outside Belfast. He was ten years old. He was known as Pat, but he was christened Patrick Joseph Kevin. His auntie in Belfast, whom he often visited, swore she always called him Kevin. She couldn't recall if he was staying with her at the time of the march but she thinks he might have been.'

Hal thumped his wine glass on the table so that the dregs spilled, making deep pink stains on the cloth. He seized the bottle and replenished our glasses, ignoring the hovering waiter. He leaned towards me, confidentially.

'She was a bitch, Philip. A double-dyed bitch. The thought of all those lovely dollars practically gave her an orgasm.'

'How did you get on to her?'

'Questions that could have been better put. I didn't, Philip. She approached me. She was only thinking of her dear Kevin's family, of course.'

'And when you went to see the family, naturally they denied that little Kevin or Patrick or whoever had been in Belfast on Massacre Day. The little mite had died of – ?'

'Meningitis. The doctor, who says he was called in too late to be of any use, backs them up. So do the village priest and the school teacher.'

'What happened when you tempted them with dreams of filthy lucre?'

'They stuck to their story. Hopefully, I got the father alone and worked on him. I said I understood. They were afraid of repercussions if the truth became public. I swore it never would. I told him he didn't have to admit to any prior knowledge of Mrs Camplin's death, only to the fact that his boy had died as a result of being gassed by the Brits – and no one need know he'd even done that. I mentioned a sum in recompense that was a small fortune to him. And – he made me feel ashamed.' Hal put down his fork and turned to face me. 'Philip, I give you my word that child wasn't in Belfast on Massacre Day. He died of meningitis. His family are completely innocent of killing Claire or harming you in any way.'

I didn't doubt it. Hal was a shrewd man and a professional. He wouldn't be easy to deceive. But the coincidence of two ten-year-old boys . . . The *maitre d'*, asking if the luncheon was to our satisfaction, gave me a moment to think.

'Hal, you don't expect me to keep this to myself, do you?'

'No. On the contrary. I want you to ensure that when your people find the poor devils – and I suspect an anonymous phone call will put them on the right scent before long – they treat them with every care. Philip, I'm scared this could be the match to set the flash fire going. Remember – people believe what they want to believe.'

While our plates were removed, our glasses refilled and the trolley with its delectable sweets wheeled up to our table, I worked on the problem. Given the information that Hal had sworn to, it was far from insoluble. I was already half way there.

The death of Patrick Joseph Kevin had been fortuitous; but if it hadn't been this child it would have been someone else. A cripple, a pregnant woman, even a very old man would have done just as well. The letter from 'Those who loved Kevin', given a slightly different slant, could have been adapted to fit any innocent tragedy. The question of coincidence didn't arise.

Nor did it matter how vehemently those who had truly loved the small boy denied complicity. Hal was right; people believed what they wanted to believe. Kevin's family and friends would be variously considered as murderers and assassins, victims of the Brits looking for a scapegoat, or artful characters who had successfully brought off a clever coup against the enemy. Feelings would run high. There could be incidents – manufactured incidents.

'Yes, please,' I said, 'I'd like coffee.' And when the waiter had gone: 'Thanks, Hal. I'll do my best but – it may not be enough.'

'It never is,' he said sadly. 'It never is.'

I caught a later train to Oxford than I had intended. It had been a long luncheon. Then, when I got back to the Ministry, I had to see Mat again and give him a verbatim account of my conversation with Hal. This had taken time but had been well worth while. I had impressed him – and he would impress others – with the need to treat Kevin's relations with kid gloves. For the present that was all we could do.

There had been no further news of Alan Bronwell.

I settled myself in a corner seat and wished I had bought an evening paper. I had nothing to read, nothing to do but stare out of the window at the dreary view – rows of identical houses, tower blocks, pathetic back gardens with their bits of grass and their hopeful flowers and their lines of washing.

I awoke with a start. In an attempt to pick up his *Evening Standard* from the floor where he had dropped it, the man sitting opposite had inadvertently kicked me. He apologized, retrieved the paper and, fearful of conversation, quickly hid himself behind it. He began to read, leaving me to stare at the front page.

In the late edition, under a bold-face head, there were about three inches of type and a picture of a young woman with two boys. 'SCIENTIST VANISHES FROM TOP SECRET ESTABLISHMENT', the black lettering shouted. The story of Alan Bronwell had broken. Evidently a photograph of the missing man hadn't been available, and to compensate for the factual poverty of the story, one of his wife and sons had been substituted. But suddenly I wanted to see it very much.

I shifted in my seat. That didn't help. I leaned forward, only to be aware that my fellow passenger was regarding me over the top of what was indubitably his newspaper. Embarrassed, I turned away and looked out of the window.

As always the train was slowing as it passed the cemetery just outside Oxford Station. In fifteen minutes or so, if there was a waiting taxi, I should be at the College and could ask John about Bronwell's wife. What was her name? Janet. That proved

I was wrong. She had been Janet Rosemary Clarke. I didn't know her. A chance resemblance and the fact that my mind was on Oxford had caused my imagination to play tricks.

The train regathered speed. The man opposite me carelessly folded his *Standard* and tossed it on to the seat beside him. He stood up, rescued his umbrella and raincoat from the rack, picked up his briefcase and, with a casual nod to me, let himself into the corridor. I waited for the train to stop. When I saw him striding along the platform past my window, I quickly thrust his paper into my pocket and hurried after him.

In the taxi I sat and regarded the front page. The paper had been badly creased, almost diagonally across the young woman's face. I tried to smooth it with my thumb-nail but merely succeeded in smearing the print. It was useless.

I read the cutline. 'Dr Bronwell's wife, Janet, with their twin sons, Clarke and Telsey, on holiday at Paramé last summer.' That was reassuring enough. Janet Rosemary Clarke was a stranger to me. It was just something about the way she held her head that had reminded me . . . The text told me nothing I didn't already know.

I paid off the taxi-driver and went in to the lodge. The porter on duty knew me. He greeted me cheerfully by name but I saw a sour expression cross his face as his mouth reshaped the word 'Camplin' to the man standing beside him. The man could have been a new porter under training, but he didn't look the right type; he was too young and quietly self-assured, more like a Special Branch officer.

John confirmed my suspicion. The first thing he said, when he opened the door of his rooms to me, was: 'Ah, the copper let you in, did he, Philip? I didn't think you'd have any trouble. I suppose he recognized you.' It was an ominous beginning.

He took my raincoat and flung it over the back of a chair. Without asking, he went to pour me a drink. I noticed him slop some more whisky into his own glass. His eyes were bright and there was a dull flush along his cheekbones. Obviously he had started drinking early.

'I should be teaching now,' he said, 'but I cut my tutorials

Can't concentrate. I keep on thinking about Alan. Are you going to catch him, Philip?'

I noted the word 'catch' instead of 'find' – and the 'you' that put me definitely on the opposite side. I remembered Massacre Day, and Claire. I heard myself say: 'I damn well hope so.' Mat would have been horrified at my tactlessness.

John threw back his head and gave a great shout of laughter. He was drunker than I had thought. 'Good old Philip! I love you – but I love Alan too.'

He picked up the *Standard* I had let drop on the sofa and frowned at the front page. His mood changed. His mouth tightened. 'Not a bit like Rose,' he muttered. He rolled the paper into a stick and waved it in my face. 'Philip, if you'd seen the Provost and Lady T. after they heard the news, you wouldn't be so – so bloody heartless,' he said. 'They're both sick with worry about Rose and the twins – even about Alan. How dare you . . .'

I listened to his tirade. I hadn't been wrong. I hadn't imagined a likeness. Janet Rosemary Clarke, Bronwell's wife, was the girl who had spoken to me at Claire's funeral; she was Rose, the daughter of the Provost. I didn't understand.

TWO

I woke slowly, disoriented. The window was on the wrong side and too small. The door was in the middle of the wall facing me; it should have been to the left. The furniture was strange. I didn't own a valet-stand, but those were my clothes hanging on one. I propped myself up on my elbows. Immediately I wished I hadn't. The room revolved sickeningly and an agonizing pain shot through my head. Screwing up my eyes, I groaned aloud and let myself fall gently back on the pillows. I felt like hell.

But I had recognized where I was. I was in what John Telsey grandly referred to as his guest-room, a slit of a room containing a narrow bed, a chair, a chest of drawers with a mirror over it, and the valet-stand. I was under a duvet and very comfortable, as long as I didn't move. I was wearing my underpants and my socks. I had the world's worst hangover.

Considering what John and I had drunk last night this wasn't surprising, especially as we had eaten almost nothing. We had drunk and we had talked, and we had forgotten about food until Hall was over and it was too late to go out to dinner. Around midnight we had managed – between the two of us – to get together a sort of meal, toast, pâté, fruit, cocoa. The thought of it nauseated me. My stomach wasn't used to such treatment.

Gingerly I reached out an arm and felt on top of the chest of drawers for my watch. I knew it wasn't late because everything was quiet, but I was surprised that it was only six-thirty. I wondered if it were possible to get myself a glass of water without waking John.

Moving with infinite caution in order not to jar my head, I got out of bed, put on some trousers, and made my way to the bathroom. I drank a glass and a half of water without a pause. Then I opened the window to get some air, topped up my glass and sat on the lavatory seat. I must have sat there for five minutes before I realized I was looking across the quad to the Provost's Lodge.

John had explained the seeming anomaly of Bronwell's wife, Janet Rosemary Clarke. It was really very simple. Rose, always known by a shortened form of her second name, was the Provost's step-daughter, though he never referred to her as such. When his fellow don, Colin Clarke, had died of leukemia at an early age, he had married the widow and adopted the baby. Rose had effectively become his daughter; he couldn't have loved her more.

Inevitably he had been opposed to Alan Bronwell as a son-in-law, but Rose had solved the problem by getting herself pregnant. And, contrary to everyone's expectations, Alan had settled down. The promiscuous radical student had apparently become a hard-working bourgeois capitalist, a good and faithful husband, and a devoted father.

Somewhere along the line, however, he had also become a communist agent. When? Why? How? John had given me an excellent composite picture of Alan Bronwell, but it had done little to answer questions like these.

John had admitted that Bronwell had visited him the previous weekend, tired, depressed, frightened. There was trouble at The Park and he said he thought he was to be made a scapegoat; he was fed to the teeth with everything. John had been worried and had offered what consolation he could, only to be told not to be a fool. Once the authorities began to be suspicious, Bronwell had said, there was no way out.

John had been very drunk, but so had I. I had no way of knowing how honest he had been with me or how complete his story . . . The smell of coffee brought me back to reality. I yearned for a mug, strong and black. Carefully I got up, splashed cold water on my face and limped out of the bathroom.

I found John in his sitting-room, doing his morning exercises while he waited for the coffee to perc. I stood in the doorway and watched him before he was aware of me. He wouldn't have won any prizes, but he was in better condition than I. He didn't seem to have a hangover. I envied him.

'Good morning, Philip. How did you sleep?'

'In a stupor.'

He laughed. 'The price of whisky being what it is, you should be more grateful. Here, drink this. It'll do wonders for you. I was going to bring it with your breakfast.'

I took the tall glass of what looked like tomato juice and regarded it dubiously. At close quarters I noticed the bags under John's eyes and the nervous tic at the corner of his mouth. Perhaps he wasn't in such good shape as I thought. I sipped the concoction he had given me, then drank it down. I yawned prodigiously.

'Why don't you go back to bed, Philip?'

'I wish I could, but there's work to be done.'

'Ah yes!' Without warning his temper flared. 'Of course, you must hurry up to London and report everything I've told you. I hope Mat Harworth thinks you've done a splendid job.'

'John, I warned you beforehand – '

'I know.' He switched off the electric percolator with an angry kick and started to pour the coffee. 'Sorry, Philip. I take it back. That remark was uncalled for.'

To ease the tension, I said: 'I'm thinking of going to see Rose. You've given me a lot of background and some names to check out, but it's mostly old stuff and – '

'Rose!' John swung round on me, spraying the carpet with coffee. 'Why do you want to see Rose? She won't help you. She wouldn't, even if she could. But she knows nothing, Philip, nothing. She's waiting for Alan to come home. She refuses to believe what she's been told about him. You'd be wasting your time.'

'She must know something,' I said mildly. 'Who his present chums are. If he ever behaved oddly. Things like that. She's been married to him for seven years.'

Suddenly I had a picture of Rose in the churchyard at Claire's funeral, her pretty anxious face and her sweet smile – and John's anger, which he had never really explained except to say he had feared that she had annoyed or upset me. What was it that he didn't want Rose to tell me?

'She might be prepared to talk to me, as you were, John. In the long run it would be best for her and the children.'

'Would it? I doubt that. Anyway, the poor girl's been questioned enough without you adding your quota. Practically the third degree. She's at her wits' end – and wits were never Rose's strong suit.' His laugh was false.

'You've seen her?'

'As a matter of fact, yes.' He had the grace to look abashed. 'She telephoned her family first thing yesterday morning. She wanted them to collect the twins. The Provost couldn't get away – he had to wait on some wealthy graduate who's thinking of giving the College a huge sum of money – so he asked me to drive Lady T. We found the Bronwells' house being searched and Rose and the twins taking refuge in the garden. Naturally her mother urged her to come back with us, but she wouldn't. She was adamant. She said all she wanted was for us to take the boys, and in the end that's what we did.'

I nodded my understanding. It was impossible to reconcile John's contradictory descriptions of Rose, but I didn't think that further questions would help at this point. He hadn't thought of mentioning his visit to the Provost's daughter before, so I asked myself what else he was holding back. I didn't like the possible answers.

In the train I glanced through the morning papers I had bought at the station. There was nothing new on Alan Bronwell. But there were two photographs of the missing man, one in profile, the other in full face. In both he appeared to be wearing a white coat and I assumed they had been taken at The Park, probably immediately after he had come under suspicion.

He seemed a very ordinary young man. He had fair, untidy hair and his face was thin with concave cheeks and a long pointed nose; on the whole a gentle face. He was described as of medium height and slightly round-shouldered. His eyes were said to be blue. The laws of libel being what they are, it was only implied that he might be a communist agent, and as news his disappearance didn't rate the front page – not today. When he was found, or if he turned up in Moscow, things would be different.

I folded the newspapers and stuffed them in my briefcase. They could be read later. Meanwhile, in my mind I reviewed the information that John had given me. Unfortunately much of it was out of date and the people he had mentioned useless as leads. For example, a don whom Bronwell had known intimately at Oxford had been killed three or four years ago in a car crash and two other of his men friends had emigrated; John had no idea if he was still in touch with them. As for girls, Bronwell had flitted rapidly from flower to flower, but none of his affairs had been serious until he had finally settled on Rose.

Wondering how many names John had conveniently forgotten, I stifled a yawn. His pick-me-up had worked a minor miracle, but my head ached and I felt extremely fragile. I decided to abandon the problem of Alan Bronwell for the moment. I made myself comfortable in my corner and slept until the train reached London.

At the Ministry I found my secretary hard at work. 'There are two messages for you, Mr Camplin. Mr Harworth wants to see you when convenient and a gentleman telephoned. I didn't get his name. I'm terribly sorry. He did tell me but there was an awful rasping noise on the line and I missed it. He'd rung off before I could ask him to repeat it.'

'What about the message?'

She laughed. 'I didn't miss that. It's on your desk. I wrote it down because he was very insistent I should get it right. And there's a phone number so I hope you'll be able to guess who he is.'

'I'm sure I will. Don't worry.'

I gave her some instructions and went through into my office. The message was on top of my in-tray. I picked it up without much interest. It read: 'Mr – would like you to phone him this evening after nine.' Subconsciously I registered that the number was familiar, but my eye had run on: 'He was sorry to miss you but delighted to be able to entertain Mrs Camplin while you were in Washington. This time he must see you. He expects to be leaving the country soon, so it is essential you telephone tonight.'

I sat and stared at the piece of paper in front of me until the writing blurred. To my knowledge, there was only one man who had 'entertained' Claire while I was in Washington, her old boyfriend, and he was someone I never wanted to meet. Nor could I imagine why he should want to meet me. Wishing him to hell, I crumpled the paper into a ball and dropped it into the wastepaper basket.

Then a thought occurred to me. I retrieved the message, smoothed it out and reread it. I had suddenly realized that the reference to Washington took it for granted that I knew what had happened between him and Claire. Who had told him that I knew? Claire? Why should she? She had sworn she had met him by chance, that the night she had spent with him had been – an aberration, that she would never see him again. I had believed her, but she might have been lying. They could have arranged to meet again. She admitted she was desperately in love with him at Oxford six or seven years ago. Perhaps they had been meeting regularly . . . I felt the jealousy curdling my stomach.

The intercom buzzed. 'Mr Harworth's ready to see you.'

'Thanks. I'll be along.'

Distracted, I didn't pause for further thought. I found Bette Aylwyn's number and dialled. Listening to the phone ring, I willed her to answer. Bette had been Claire's closest friend – and alibi. Bette, if anyone, would know about Claire's boyfriend. Before, when Claire had started to tell me about him, I had refused to listen. I hadn't wanted to know; his name, his appearance, what he said, every detail would make him more real, more difficult to forget. Now it was different. I had to be sure Claire hadn't lied to me.

'Hallo!'

'Bette, this is Philip Camplin.' I didn't waste time on preliminaries. 'I wonder if I could see you today. There's something I very much want to discuss with you.'

'Something or someone?'

'What?'

'Why don't you come along here after the office? We can have some drinks and supper later, if you like.'

'What about lunch?'

'Sorry. I can't make it. It's Founder's Day at Lance's school and for once I'm being a dutiful parent.'

'All right. I'll be there about six. Thanks, Bette.'

'That's okay, Philip love. I've been expecting you to call.'

I put down the receiver and passed a hand over my face. I felt old. My mouth was dry and there was a dull pain behind my eyes. I yearned to put my head on my desk and go to sleep again. But there was Mat; he didn't like being kept waiting.

Reluctantly I stood up. My secretary always had aspirin to hand and I borrowed a couple, which I swallowed in the Gents' on my way to Mat's room. Their immediate result was to make me gag. And the smell of smoke in his office – the number of butts in his ashtray indicated that Mat had come in early and as usual had sought solace in his cheroots – didn't improve matters. I heaved a sigh that was half a groan.

'You sound unhappy, Philip. Was Oxford not a success?'

'Not really.'

I told him what I had got out of John. It was clear he was not impressed and all the time I spoke he watched me closely, which irritated me. If he didn't trust me, why had he sent me to Oxford?

Somewhat acidly, I said: 'I agree Telsey didn't tell me everything he knew, but I doubt that anyone else would have got more out of him. He doesn't want to help catch Bronwell. Incidentally, I assume that Bronwell's not been caught?'

'No. But they've found his belongings, including shoes, wallet, money, passport. They were sitting on the grass beside a deep, undredgeable Scottish loch. Frogmen are searching for the body, but their chances of finding it are poor – even if it's there to be found.'

'Do you think it is, Mat?'

'I wouldn't like to bet. On Wednesday he caught a train to Edinburgh and hired a car. He turned up late that evening at a small hotel not far from where he's supposed to have drowned himself. He spent the day there, and next day asked for sandwiches. He said he was going walking. He didn't come back. He left a cheap suitcase in his room with pyjamas, spare shirt and socks and change of underwear – all new, probably bought in Edinburgh. He also left his briefcase containing some papers he could legitimately have been bringing up to the Ministry. Both the barman and the woman who owns the hotel say he was morose and unsociable, but that could be hindsight though it fits with what Telsey told you.'

'So it looks like a sudden decision to run, then suicide in a fit of depression when he realized he hadn't a hope of getting out of the country.'

'Yes. That's what it looks like. But it could have been very, very carefully planned. We're taking no risks.'

'Poor Rose!' I said, unthinking.

Mat nodded. 'Of course. You know her personally. She was at Claire's funeral. I'd forgotten that for a moment.'

I gave him a quick glance, but his face was innocent. He hadn't tried to mislead me. He had merely assumed I knew that the daughter of the Provost and Rose Bronwell were one and the same.

I refused Mat's invitation to lunch. I had a sandwich at my desk and got down to some of the paperwork that was piled high in my in-tray. It was a grind. The effects of last night's drinking bout had more or less worn off, but my mind was as dull as an old razor blade and, given the least opportunity, it veered towards Claire and her former boy-friend.

I left the office early, hoping that Mat wouldn't want to see me five minutes after I had gone, and took a taxi home. Denise had sorted out Claire's clothes and belongings for me, but she hadn't touched the personal papers in Claire's dressing-table. She had said I ought to do that myself, and it had remained undone. Now, grimly, I set about the task.

Claire had never been methodical or orderly, and it was simplest to empty the two drawers on to the dining-table.

Hurriedly, not sure what I was looking for, I searched through their contents. I found old invitations, theatre programmes, a birthday card from Claire's sister Mary, a thank-you note for a dinner party we had given, two or three letters, a few postcards, our marriage certificate, receipts and bills. There were a lot of bills, some of them large and 'To account rendered', which momentarily annoyed me; I hadn't realized quite how careless and extravagant Claire had been. But there was nothing amongst this confusion to suggest she had been having an affair with anyone.

The only thing that remained was an envelope which I knew contained some oddments from Claire's handbag that the French police had found on the Métro line. Denise had put it in the drawer and there it had stayed, unopened. I had to steel myself to open it now. I found her passport, wallet, keys, make-up, handkerchief, and a diary she used as an engagement book. On the day before my return from Washington there were two entries. One was a hairdressing appointment. The other was a telephone number. It was not a London number, not the same as the number the message had asked me to phone later.

Without considering what I would say if someone answered I dialled it. The phone rang several times. Then a woman's voice said: 'Hallo. This is Mrs Bronwell.'

Taken by surprise, I made an inarticulate sound and replaced the receiver. Rose? Why had Claire suddenly made a note of Rose Bronwell's telephone number? They scarcely knew each other. There could of course be a hundred explanations, but it was an odd coincidence.

Out of the corner of my eye I caught sight of the clock. It was a quarter to six. I was going to be late for Bette. Taking off my tie and unbuttoning my shirt as I went, I dashed for the bathroom. I had a quick shower, ran an electric razor over my face and put on a clean shirt. I wondered how much longer Denise would continue to cope with my laundry.

It was six o'clock when I left the flat. Directly outside the house a taxi stood at the kerb, with a would-be passenger speaking to the driver. I heard him ask for the Dorchester

Hotel. The driver shook his head. He was going home. Luckily for me, however, home was Stanmore and fifteen minutes later he dropped me at Bette's house in St John's Wood.

Bette, wearing a jade-coloured smock over black velvet trousers, opened the door to me herself. As always she looked lovely. She kissed me on both cheeks. Her breath smelt of gin.

'I've had the craziest day, Philip. If I'd not promised my late husband that Lance should be educated at his old school I'd take the poor boy away this minute. You'd never believe . . .'

While she chatted she poured me, unasked, a large whisky and soda, and set it beside me. Collecting her own drink, she sat down, smiled at me, lifted her glass.

'To you, Philip love. As I said on the phone, I was expecting you to call. I guessed you'd want to talk.'

Forgetting my resolution to be abstemious, I took a long swallow of scotch. I wasn't sure what Bette meant. Whatever it was, I couldn't be bothered with it at the moment.

'Bette, it's about Claire,' I began hesitantly. 'I know you were close friends and she confided in you. When – when I was in Washington – ' I stopped. I couldn't go on.

'Oh, Philip! Claire was a fool to tell you. I never understood why she did. It only hurt you.' Bette leaned forward, anxious to impress me with the truth of what she was about to say. 'Claire wasn't a giving person. You must have realized that. She'd always take more than she'd give. But she loved you, as much as she was capable of loving anyone. Believe me.'

I couldn't respond. I said brusquely: 'She told me she met him by chance. Was that true?'

'Yes, I'm sure it was.'

'But they met again?'

'Not as far as I know, Philip, but Claire didn't tell me everything. She was really rather a secretive kind of girl, you know. Why do you ask?'

I shook my head. I hated to discuss Claire like this but I had to find out more. And Bette was being extraordinarily sympathetic.

'Did you ever meet him yourself?'

'Yes. The summer Claire came to me as an *au pair* to look after Lance I saw a fair amount of him. He had a vacation job too, and he used to come over on his motor-bike. He was just a few miles away. I think that's why John Telsey asked us if we'd have Claire, so that she and Alan could be near each other.'

Alan? Bette had taken our empty glasses over to the bar. Her back was turned to me and she didn't see the horror that my face must have mirrored. Alan. Alan Bronwell. What a fool I had been! I should have guessed. It explained so much – the Bronwells' phone number in Claire's engagement book, why Bette expected me to contact her, John Telsey's efforts to keep me away from Rose: presumably he didn't want me to be hurt by what Rose might tell me about her husband and Claire. John, I thought bitterly, was always considerate of his friends.

'Does Telsey know that Claire and Bronwell had – had resumed their relationship?' My voice was harsh.

Bette frowned. 'If you mean the one night they spent together while you were in Washington, nobody knows about that except you and me, Philip. And I assure you nobody will. As for the rest, it was over years ago – before your marriage – so whatever Alan's done now there's no connection between him and you.'

How wrong could one be? What Bette didn't know was that Bronwell, very much alive and regrettably not drowned in some Scottish loch, was waiting for me to phone him later this evening.

I had to get away from Bette. I needed to think clearly, to make decisions. I drank my second whisky very fast and said I must go. Bette expostulated – she had prepared supper for me – but when I insisted she was understanding. We kissed goodbye and I promised to be in touch. It was a relief to be in the street, by myself.

At ten o'clock I telephoned as instructed, and a voice said, 'The Albury Hotel.' I knew then why the number had seemed familiar; I had an uncle who always stayed at the Albury when he was in London. But Alan Bronwell was on the run. He wouldn't be . . .

'Hallo. This is the Albury Hotel. Can I help you?'

I collected my thoughts hurriedly. I couldn't ask for Bronwell and I didn't have a room number. My secretary had missed the name he had given – or Bronwell had scratched a thumbnail across the mouthpiece so that she shouldn't hear it.

'I'm Philip Camplin,' I said slowly.

'Ah yes, Mr Camplin. Mr Clarke said he was expecting a call from you. I'll put you through at once.'

There was scarcely any delay, scarcely time to feel my heart thudding against my rib-cage, before Bronwell answered. 'Hallo, Philip. Alan Clarke here. I'm so glad you phoned. It would have been most unfortunate if you hadn't because we must meet. It's essential for both of us, you understand. How about lunch tomorrow?'

'Lunch? Where?'

'At the Albury. Say twelve-thirty. And, Philip, it'll be just us, a private meeting. A party would be very inconvenient for me, and you. Don't you agree? Incidentally, have you told anyone – Mat, for example – that I'm in London?'

'No, I haven't.'

'Good. I didn't think you would somehow. See you tomorrow then.'

'Yes. All right.'

It was incredible. With half the police in the UK looking for him, Alan Bronwell was staying at one of the best hotels in London. Moreover, he had just admitted his identity to a man who had every reason to hate him – on both professional and personal grounds. And lunch tomorrow! A fugitive with no sense of urgency was new in my experience. He must, I decided, be either mad or very, very sure of himself. Sure, for one thing, that I wouldn't report the conversation and call in the dogs. And if he were so sure – and sane – there was presumably a reason why I shouldn't. It was a hell of a dilemma.

THREE

'Say, Philip, this is unexpected. What are you doing here?'

Startled, I sucked in my breath. I had resolved my dilemma temporarily and I was sitting on a bench in Grosvenor Square, watching the pigeons defile the statue of Roosevelt and waiting until it was time for me to walk along to the Albury for my lunch with Bronwell. I had decided I had nothing to lose by playing along with him for the moment, and at least discovering if his veiled threats had any meaning. But I certainly wasn't prepared to explain all this to Hal Runce, of all people. I forced a grin.

'Hallo, Hal. Don't tell me they're making you work on Saturday mornings these days.' I gestured towards the American Embassy which formed one side of the square. 'You ought to join a union.'

He smiled gently at the stale joke and, to my annoyance, sat himself down beside me. I glanced surreptitiously at my watch; I didn't want to be late for my appointment with 'Mr Clarke'. Hal noticed.

'Can you spare me five minutes, Philip, or do you have a tryst?'

'I wouldn't call it a tryst exactly.' I tried to sound amused. 'I'm lunching with a business acquaintance. But I can always spare you five minutes, Hal.'

'Thanks, old buddy.' He spread his arms along the back of the bench and stretched his legs as if we were to be there for the afternoon. 'As a matter of fact I came in to pick up my mail, or rather the Ambassador's mail. He got a letter today saying, for Chrissakes help. The Brits have found Kevin's family. They're secretly terrorizing them and their whole village and, unless you Americans are prepared to save them, a lot more Irish are going to die at the hands of the vile Brits. Please, please, help!'

I shook my head in disgust. 'Publicity to keep the bitterness boiling. Let's hope there's nothing else to it. I passed on your warning, Hal. I'm sure it's been heeded, but that's not going to stop incidents and rumours of incidents.'

'You're telling me. And the media men are gathering. As I predicted the newspapers have had an anonymous tip-off – a friend of mine in the business let me know – and Kevin will be on the front page of the Sundays again tomorrow.'

'Well, there's damn all we can do about it!' I let my irritation show.

'I know that, Philip, but I'm scared to death of what might happen in Ireland. This Kevin business could be the spark that sets off the conflagration, and we just stand by with a bucket of water.' He sighed. 'Sorry. I'm feeling depressed today. If only we could shift the blame for those goddam gas grenades to the real villains, it'd be a whole new ball game. You making any progress?'

'Not really.' It was only half a lie, but I felt surprisingly guilty.

I said goodbye to Hal outside the Canadian High Commission and hurried along to the Albury. Having at first been too early for my meeting with Bronwell, I was now late and, when I enquired for 'Mr Clarke' at the reception desk, I was informed that he was not in the hotel. He had gone out some while ago. There was no message for me. Perhaps I would care to wait.

Cursing, I went and sat down. I waited. For slow, nervous minutes I waited, watching everyone who came in or out of the lobby. At five past one, when I had decided that Bronwell had tricked me or something had gone wrong with his plans, I saw a man walk across the street and enter the hotel. He was medium height, grey-haired, not fat but with a solid body that he held rather stiffly. It gave him an air of authority. He might have been a retired major. He went straight up to the desk, asked for his key, said something to the head porter. As I lost interest in him, they both turned and looked at me.

My mouth dry, involuntarily I stood up. The man – it wasn't, couldn't be Alan Bronwell – came towards me with outstretched hand. His smile was wide but it didn't match his eyes. Brown eyes. Bronwell had blue eyes.

'Philip, my dear chap, I'm so sorry to have kept you waiting.' He lowered his voice. 'I had to delay a little after I saw you limping into the hotel – to make sure you'd not brought reinforcements with you. You understand?'

I nodded. It seemed unnecessary to say anything. Reluctantly I shook hands with him.

'Shall we go straight into the dining-room and have our drinks while we order?'

He led the way and I followed. The head porter acknowledged his smile as we passed. In the dining-room the *maitre d'* greeted him like an old friend. The waiters gathered. It was obvious that 'Mr Clarke' was a well-known and valued guest at the Albury Hotel.

Behind the shield of our menus he murmured to me: 'Pop your eyes back in their sockets. Appearances to the contrary, I am Alan Bronwell. It's amazing what a difference you can make with a padded corset, coloured contact lenses and plumpers in the cheeks and a touch of hair dye. Besides, "Mr Clarke" has been coming here regularly for the last eighteen months, so everyone accepts him. You see, I was taking precautions in advance. I'm a careful man.'

'But not careful enough, it seems.'

'Unfortunately, no. I didn't anticipate the knife in the back. Ah, well – ' he shrugged – 'I may make it yet, with your help.'

'To Mother Russia? Your spiritual home? You're crazy if you think I'd – '

'No. You've got it wrong.'

He turned and looked at me regretfully. Our faces were within inches of each other and I could see the dark marks below his eyes and the tired droop of his mouth. Beneath his jaunty carapace he was a worried and perhaps a frightened man. Excitement welled in me. I no longer doubted that he was Alan Bronwell.

'Perhaps you'll explain then. You've a lot to explain, haven't you?'

'More than you dream of, my dear Philip. But I'll try to keep it brief. First you must appreciate that at the present moment the Russians are even more eager than the British to catch me. They want to arrange a nice little "accident" for me.'

'Why?' I didn't bother to hide my disbelief.

He took a hearty measure of gin and tonic before he answered. 'The masters I've served so well have decided I'm expendable – and all because I was in the right place at the right time to have stolen those gas grenades that were used on Massacre Day. The ironical thing is, I was still a sleeper then. I didn't become active till I got to The Park.'

'You mean you didn't steal those grenades?'

'I did not. If I'd been ordered to, I imagine I would have.' He paused to consider what he had said. 'On second thoughts, perhaps not. That is, if I'd known in advance about those wretched women and kids the grenades were going to kill and maim. At any rate, I didn't. I knew nothing about them until I heard of the shambles on my car radio. But someone did, someone much more important to my masters than I am, someone they plan to save at my expense. Except that I've no intention of being made a scapegoat for anyone, especially if it means dying for him.' He laughed tonelessly. 'No. Don't bother to ask. I don't know who it is. I might make a guess but I won't tell you my guess now. Let's say it can be part payment for your help.'

'I've not promised you any help.'

'No – but you will.'

Bronwell spoke very positively, which was disconcerting. At that moment I was inclined to believe his story, but any information he might have to sell couldn't buy him immunity. At best he would get five years in jail, and he might get twenty. As for any idea of my personal intervention on his behalf – presumably for Claire's sake – he had another guess coming.

'Why do you think the Russians are selling you out?' I asked.

'Because they made an outrageous demand that was bound to show up as a security breach. I was very careful and did a brilliant job, but inevitably the finger pointed at me. In fact, I was told later there had been an anonymous tip-off. I didn't understand it, but as an act of self-preservation I decided to search my house and I found a box of gas grenades. From which it was relatively easy to deduce what I was being let in for and why.'

'Where are the grenades now?'

'Upstairs, in my suite. They're much the same as the ones used on Massacre Day, except that you toss them by hand. I know, because I tried one out on a stray cat.'

Remembering poor Katy, I winced. I didn't like Alan Bronwell, and this example of casual brutality didn't help.

'Anyway,' Bronwell continued, 'at this point I knew my only hope was "Mr Clarke". I'd created him about two years ago when there was a security scare at The Park, and it occurred to me that some day I might want an escape route. Since then I've built him up and I should have been okay, but all my plans were based on going to Moscow, and I've not had time to organize anything new. This is where you come in. As I said before, I need your help. Shall we go upstairs and discuss the matter?'

I hesitated only fractionally before I nodded my assent. I had to know why Bronwell had turned to me. Supposedly he thought he had some claim on me because of Claire – but what?

'If you like,' I said, simulating indifference.

We left the dining-room amongst respectful acknowledgements from the staff and went up to the suite. As Bronwell opened the door I noticed the backs of his hands. They were covered with an unsightly purple rash that reminded me of prickly heat. There had been no mention of it in the descriptions of him, but obviously it was something that 'Mr Clarke' was unable to disguise. It could be a useful item of information.

'Have you hurt your hands?' I asked casually.

'No. They go like this when I'm under strain. It's a form of nervous rash. It's not uncommon; I've had it since I was a child.' Unselfconscious, he held his hands out for me to see. 'I've had all sorts of treatment, but none does any good. Even the head-shrinkers couldn't do better than diagnose psychosomatic eczema.' He stopped speaking and gave me a wide smile as if he had just thought of a joke at my expense. 'No matter. Let's get down to business. Take a chair, Philip. And do try to be more amiable. It'll make everything much easier.'

'Suppose you start by giving me those gas grenades.'

'You shall have them, and a lot of interesting information – in return for twenty thousand pounds, a car in which you'll drive me – '

'You must be mad, Bronwell.'

He shook his head. 'I hold all the aces. You can't beat me.'

Suddenly cold with apprehension, I knew he was going to tell me something about Claire, something that I would hate, something that would hurt me beyond measure. But whatever it was, Claire was dead. It could do her no harm. As for me, I had no intention of letting myself be blackmailed by Alan Bronwell.

'Claire,' Bronwell said softly, 'was a sleeper too, a communist agent – like me.'

For a long minute I was silent, staring uncomprehendingly at him. Claire a communist agent. Of a thousand accusations he might have made, I would never have dreamt of this. It was absurd.

'I – I don't believe you,' I said.

It was a reflex statement, and Bronwell knew it. 'I'm telling you the truth,' he said simply. 'Let it sink into your head.'

'You're talking nonsense! I was married to Claire for six years, and I'd have known if – if – '

'Didn't you ever ask yourself why she married you?' he interrupted. 'You were twelve to fifteen years older than she was, a cripple with a built-up boot. You couldn't dance or play any games. You weren't even rich. She married you because she was ordered to marry you, Philip Camplin.'

'That's a bloody lie!' I controlled my temper. 'What would have been the point of it? I wasn't important enough for anyone to take that kind of trouble.'

'You underrate yourself. Your brothers were already in high places, and you had a brilliant career in front of you.' He threw back his head and laughed. 'You must have had something else too, Philip, something that appealed to Claire. Maybe you're fantastic in bed. At any rate, last January, when our masters decided to activate her, she refused to be activated, and thus eventually signed her own death warrant.'

I wanted to hit him. Gritting my teeth, I stood up and went across to the telephone. I had had enough. He could spew out his filthy lies to the Special Branch if he liked – if they were lies. My hand was on the receiver and I hesitated. Doubts besieged me . . .

'You're saying it wasn't because of me that Claire was killed.'

'Of course not. Surely you didn't accept that dear little Kevin rubbish, did you?'

'No, but – Bronwell, are you seriously telling me that Claire's death, the poisoned chocolates, the other things, were nothing to do with me and my job connection with Northern Ireland?'

'Absolutely bloody nothing! Our masters were trying to compel Claire to become an active agent. When that failed, they killed her. They had to. They couldn't let her go on defying them, could they?'

I drew a great breath and expelled it slowly. For weeks I had been consumed with guilt because I thought myself the cause of all our grief and finally of Claire's murder. If Bronwell wasn't lying . . . The relief I felt was natural, but it was mixed with shame and anger that I was so eager to accept his explanation.

'You expect me to take your word for this?'

'I can convince you.'

'Try.'

'Okay. Claire, I repeat, was a sleeper. When she refused to wake, our masters stopped her allowance, which had been set up as a supposed inheritance from her mother. But Claire had accounts, and I dare say you were a generous husband, Philip. It didn't affect her much. Then her sister Mary – she was a housekeeper to some plutocrat in the Lake District – she was killed when the brakes of her car failed. I would guess that was an accident, but they used it as a threat to Claire, who thumbed her nose at them. She didn't really believe they'd organized Mary's death. Nevertheless, it took guts. Claire wasn't short on guts.'

Bronwell paused, smiling ruminatively, and I suppressed my dislike of him. I had to be objective. I had to admit he had explained Claire's recent debts and that he was well-informed about her sister. Suddenly I was glad that I had changed my mind and had made no attempt to enquire further into Mary White's death. And it was at this point I realized that, however much I might pretend, I knew Bronwell had convinced me.

'Go on,' I said.

'Well, next they tried a spot of blackmail, which was where I came in. You know what happened between Claire and me while you were in Washington. It was a set-up. They figured if Claire was so keen on her life with you that she wouldn't obey orders, they'd threaten to ruin it for her. But it didn't work like that. She told you and you forgave her, which, as it turned out, was unlucky for both of you.'

'Did you see her again?'

'Yes. Once. After she was nearly poisoned by those chocolates I was coming up to London on one of my "Mr Clarke" trips, and we arranged to meet. She was scared and she poured everything out to me. I'd read about you being shot in Dublin and your car exploding, but I didn't know she'd received threats before each incident. They were meant for her, not you, Philip, and I warned her. Our masters don't give up that easily. They'd been paying her for years to be a sleeper, and now they wanted something in return. If she didn't give it to them, they'd kill her. I told her that. I told her that if she got a final warning it would mean exactly what it said. But she was stubborn as hell. She wouldn't . . .'

I sat and listened to his dispassionate analysis of the girl I had loved and cherished as my wife for six years. I had thought we had a close marriage, but I hadn't known her at all. She had been a communist agent, dormant certainly, but nevertheless an agent, with a secret life and secret thoughts. And if, by chance, the day we went to Paris, Denise hadn't been in our flat and taken that telephone call with its final warning, who knows what Claire might have decided to do.

'Why,' I said, 'why, in God's name, did she ever – ?'

'She was my girl-friend. I met her at John Telsey's. Incidentally, don't get ideas about John. He's not a communist. He's a good old-fashioned liberal and he thinks he owes me, because I held his hand when his marriage broke up. He knew nothing about my extra-curricular activities. It was another don – he's been dead for years – who recruited me, and I suggested he recruit Claire. She needed money to pay off her debts, and she was far left politically. It seemed an excellent solution.'

It was something else I had to thank him for. I fought with my emotions. I needed to think and think clearly. It was imperative. But I felt drained, incapable of making any decisions.

To gain time, I said: 'Tell me more about this recruitment.'

'What's there to tell? It wasn't on a grand scale. Very few were called, and many, many fewer were chosen. One thing I can tell you. My don friend didn't do the real picking and choosing; there was someone behind him with much more authority. I know this because Claire was an exception, and it had to be approved.'

'As long as there's an Oxford and Cambridge – '

'What?'

I didn't explain the revealing phrase that Bridie Connell had passed on to me. Instead I asked for names, expecting to get some leads, but Bronwell shook his head.

'Not for the present, Philip. It's your turn to do some giving. You know, I don't think you really appreciate the situation we're in. Your mind's too occupied with Claire. And, naturally, at the back of it is the assumption that sooner or later you're going to hand me over to the authorities.'

He grinned at me. I didn't respond. What he had said was too close to the truth for my liking, and his use of the word 'we' hadn't passed me by. Of course I was aware that if he chose to denounce Claire as a communist agent there would be an unpleasant scandal. But Claire had been a reluctant sleeper and had died for her reluctance. In the present climate of opinion there would be a lot of sympathy for her, and for me. I couldn't understand Bronwell's total confidence.

'Why shouldn't I hand you over?'

'Because you don't want to spend the next ten or fifteen years in prison, any more than I do.' He held up a warning finger as I opened my mouth in amazed protest, and again I noticed the ugly rash on the back of his hands. 'The truth is, if you won't co-operate with me voluntarily, I shall blackmail you into co-operating.'

'You think you could?'

'Yes.'

Although I had been expecting some such approach, the monosyllable was chilling. I remembered Mat saying that Bronwell was no fool. There had to be some substance to his threat. Yet whatever Claire had done or not done, I certainly couldn't be blamed.

'Perhaps you'd elaborate,' I said, with a show of indifference.

'Okay.' Bronwell smiled with seeming pity. 'Unless you help me I shall give myself up to the Brits. At least they won't kill me as the Russians would like to do. But if you force me to give myself up, I shall co-operate. I shall tell all. I shall swear that you were my controller – '

'Don't be absurd! No one would believe you.'

'Wouldn't they? Wouldn't the security chaps think it odd that a high-powered civil servant in the Ministry of Defence – in an intelligence branch too – could be married to a communist agent for six years, and suspect nothing? With a little circumstantial evidence I could readily produce, your image would be nicely tarnished, Philip – and the groundwork would be laid for my main accusation.'

'And what's that?'

'That you murdered Claire.'

A cold knot of fear twisted my gut. I tried to laugh but the laughter choked me.

I heard myself say: 'That's the most ludicrous statement you've made yet. Everyone knows I was – was – ' I couldn't finish the sentence.

Bronwell completed it for me. 'Besotted with Claire, yes. Which is why you took it so hard when she confessed she'd slept with me while you were in Washington. From what Claire told me, I suspect Bette Aylwyn would be a convenient witness to your state of mind.' He looked at me enquiringly, and I stared back at him, dumb. 'In any case, you planned a series of threatening incidents – probably inspired by the time you were shot in Dublin. They seemed to be aimed at you, but in fact they were intended to lead up to Claire's supposedly accidental death. Again, there's some circumstantial evidence. The liqueur chocolates, for instance – you dislike the things, but you knew that Claire doted on them.'

Bronwell had been speaking very quickly and when he paused for breath I said: 'Lies! All lies! If you think those sort of accusations would stick you know nothing about the law.'

He shook his head at me. 'Philip, I'm not stupid. I know there are lots of holes in the case, but it would make a splendid trial – the kind that gets written up in books. And just think of the publicity for you – and your entire family.' He underlined his last words.

'It would never come to trial.'

As answer Bronwell took from an inner pocket of his jacket two Xeroxed pages which he handed to me. 'The only copy of a letter from Claire. You may keep it. I have the original.'

I read it through twice. It was in Claire's hand, and there was no reason to doubt its authenticity. It began as a thank-you letter for the lunch Bronwell had given her, and continued: 'Philip is taking me to Europe for a month and this should be a respite from our present troubles, especially as I've received no more threats. But I'm still desperately scared. I'm beginning to think Philip will kill me in the end.'

'It's a trick. It must be a trick. Claire would never have written that. Why should she?' I spoke aloud, but more to myself than to Bronwell.

'She did write it – in her large handwriting on one side of thin paper, and she didn't number the pages. Page one ended with "Philip" and page three began with "will kill", but how could you prove page two was missing? As it stands it condemns you – or it will if you insist on condemning me.'

I stared at Bronwell with a kind of horror. Within half an hour he had turned my world upside down. He had disillusioned me about my marriage and now he was threatening to put me in the dock as a traitor and a murderer. That his accusations were grotesque made no difference. The threat was formidable, and not only to me. It could ruin William's career and Andrew's, even Patrick's; who would go to a psychiatrist whose brother . . . And what about the children, William's eldest just starting at the Foreign Office, Andrew's daughter engaged, the others at school. I would rather die than let them be hurt in this fashion.

As if he had read my thoughts, Bronwell said: 'Philip, if you're thinking of doing the honourable thing and putting your head in a plastic bag, think again. It wouldn't change anything. The same goes if you're planning to dispose of me. I've left a sworn statement with the original of Claire's letter. The fuzz would find it.'

'You've thought of everything, haven't you, Bronwell?' I was bitterly sarcastic.

'I hope so.'

His smugness infuriated me. He was sure I was beaten, but I wasn't, not yet. There had to be a way out. I couldn't let the family suffer and I was damned if I was going to help him escape. There had to be a third way.

'Look, Philip, what I've done can't be undone. Sending me to prison won't achieve anything. After all, it's not as if I was responsible for the Irish massacre. And I'm in no position to betray any more secrets. If the communists catch me, they'll . . .'

I listened. I pretended to let myself be persuaded. What I needed was time, time to think of a third way, a way out. It wasn't going to be easy.

FOUR

In spite of my protests Bronwell, in his persona of 'Mr Clarke', insisted on taking me down in the lift and escorting me through the hotel lobby. Outside, for perhaps a minute, he waited with me on the pavement while the doorman, immaculate in his fawn-coloured coachman's uniform, whistled up a taxi.

'Goodbye, Philip. See you soon.'

Bronwell patted me fondly on the shoulder and, before I could forestall him, gave the taxi-driver my address. As the taxi was swept into the stream of traffic, from its back window I saw him stop to exchange pleasantries with the doorman. Then the doorman lifted a hand to his black topper in salute, and Bronwell went up the steps into the hotel. He had done his best to ensure that the staff of the Albury would remember me.

This was something to be taken into account, but I had a more immediate problem. As soon as I reached my flat, I would be duty-bound to get in touch with Mat Harworth; any significant interval could be remembered later. I had, therefore, the time it would take the taxi to get to Harley Street to concoct an acceptable story – acceptable both to Mat and to me. Failure to contact Mat immediately would commit me to Alan Bronwell and I had already decided that was impossible. I would not play traitor.

My taxi-driver was the sort of chap who would have been happy driving an ambulance on an emergency call. He accelerated through amber lights as they turned to red, screamed round corners on two wheels, squirmed through stalled traffic with inches to spare and braked so that his taxi almost stood on its nose. None of this was conducive to thought.

However, while Bronwell had been listing his demands and giving me my instructions, the germ of an idea had occurred to me. Now, clinging to the safety handle to prevent myself being thrown about the taxi, I worked on it and it grew. It had faults, of course – some I had probably overlooked – and it needed a bit more polishing if I wasn't to be caught out, but it wasn't bad.

In Harley Street I paid off the taxi and let myself in. On a Saturday afternoon the house was deadly quiet and I thought I might well be the only occupant, but as I got out of the lift I heard music coming from Patrick's flat. Someone was at home. Grateful, I hurried up the stairs. I no longer felt so lonely.

I allowed myself five minutes' grace to review what I intended to tell Mat, and then I dialled his number. Biting my lower lip nervously, I waited. Margaret answered, breathless from the bottom of the garden. Mat was playing golf. He usually had a couple of drinks in the clubhouse after his eighteen holes and she didn't expect him back until around seven. If it was really urgent he could be reached.

I tried to think quickly. Perhaps because there was so much else on my mind I had assumed that Mat would be readily available. That he wasn't had thrown me, and I realized that I wasn't nearly as composed and clear-headed as I had imagined. It was a little frightening.

Margaret came to the rescue. In spite of her preoccupation with grandchildren and Women's Institutes and church affairs, she hadn't been married to Mat for umpteen years for nothing. She sensed that something was wrong. The length of my hesitation had betrayed me. She would tell Mat I had sounded very fraught. I smiled sardonically; in the circumstances it scarcely mattered. I accepted her invitation to supper, and she promised to phone the clubhouse and warn Mat to forgo his second drink. I thanked her with genuine gratitude.

When I put down the receiver I found that the palms of my hands were damp with sweat and I was breathing hard. Margaret, kind as she was, had undermined my confidence. I began to tremble. It must have been some sort of nervous reaction, but it was humiliating. I wondered if I would ever be able to deceive Mat.

The telephone rang. To me it was like a shot of adrenalin. My trembling stopped as I lifted the receiver. It was stupid, for it couldn't possibly have been Mat so soon.

'Hallo, brother,' Patrick said. 'We thought we heard you overhead. Can we tempt you to a cup of tea or an early drink?'

'That would be marvellous.' In spite of myself my voice shook. 'But what I'd really like would be a loan of Denise's car for the evening. I've got to go out to Mat Harworth's for – for supper.'

'Another crisis?' Patrick was quick to sense my tension.

'You could say so. Yes.'

'Well, we're going to the theatre tonight so you can certainly borrow the car, but come down and have that drink first. You'll need to collect the keys, anyway.'

I showered and shaved and put on the kind of clothes that Margaret would consider suitable for the occasion. Downstairs, Patrick was sprawled in an armchair reading the evening paper. He gestured to me to help myself and I poured a large whisky. It was a fine malt – a gift from a grateful patient – and I didn't dilute it with soda.

'Are you okay, Philip? You look a bit – '

The question had taken me by surprise and I cut him short. 'Yes. I'm fine.'

'Sorry.' He gave me a wry smile. 'I didn't mean to pry. Let's change the subject.' He tossed his newspaper on to a chair. 'I see they're still searching for the body of that communist spy who's supposed to have drowned himself in some loch or other.'

'You don't think he has?'

'No. Do you?'

For a moment I was tempted. It would be so easy to tell Patrick everything, to ask his help, to let him make the decisions. But it wouldn't be fair. I was the one who had got us into this mess by marrying Claire and, if the situation did explode, complete ignorance would be the family's best protection.

'I wouldn't bet on it.'

Patrick glanced at me shrewdly. 'Don't tell me. It's top secret and I'm being tactless again. The chap's been caught and you and Harworth are going to torture the truth out of him.'

'Not quite.'

Patrick threw back his head and laughed. I managed to grin. I was used to Patrick teasing me about my job.

'What are you two laughing at?' Denise didn't wait for an answer. 'Hallo, Philip. Would you like a sandwich or anything before you go out to the Harworths?'

'No, thanks.' I explained that I had had a large lunch at the Albury and could easily wait till supper.

'What about coming to dinner tomorrow?'

I hesitated, but it was unlikely that on a Sunday I could do more than plan. 'That would be splendid. Thank you.'

Since Claire's death, without being intrusive, Denise and Patrick had made sure I was well cared for. There was a steady flow of invitations to eat and drink, all of them casual. My laundry was done, the flat mysteriously stayed clean with little effort on my part. And almost every day one or other of them found some excuse for contacting me. If only because of them and young Jack and Nicole, I thought grimly, I would have to draw Bronwell's claws.

Driving out of central London, I again reviewed the story I intended to tell Mat. It was an abridged version of the truth, heavily censored, but approximately four-fifths fact to one-fifth fiction. The less I had to lie, the less chance there was of tripping myself up. Reasonably satisfied with my story, I turned my attention to the problem of getting hold of Claire's letter. This was the *sine qua non* of the whole enterprise, but I was still bereft of ideas when I reached the Harworths' house.

Mat arrived five minutes after me and Margaret installed us on the terrace with a couple of long scotches and a plate of crisps while she bustled away to get the meal. Mat got down to business immediately.

'Do you want to tape our talk?'

'Yes, we should.' I was glad he had suggested it; a recording would be physical proof of my good intent.

He took the recorder from his pocket and set it on the table in front of us. He gave the date, time, place and said: 'It's all yours, Philip. Go ahead.'

I began. 'You once suggested, Mat, that the threats made to

Claire and me and the attacks that culminated in her death might be the prelude to a communist approach – some sort of blackmail set-up. I must admit I didn't believe it. But you were right. Such an approach was made to me today over lunch at the Albury Hotel by someone calling himself "Mr Clarke".'

I told Mat about the telephone message that my secretary had given me yesterday and which she would certainly remember. I explained how I had returned the call and been put through to 'Mr Clarke's' suite.

'He commiserated with me over Claire's death, said he had known her and her family well though they had lost touch, and had been delighted to run into her by chance a few weeks ago. He seemed to take it for granted that I knew of him and I could hardly say I didn't recall Claire mentioning his name. In fact I was damn sure she'd never mentioned him, or having a drink with him while I was in Washington. Anyway, he pressed me to lunch with him today and, as I'd nothing better to do, I agreed.'

I paused to drink some whisky before the ice-cubes melted. Mat hadn't taken his bulbous eyes from my face since I started, but I didn't mind if my agitation showed. In the circumstances it would seem perfectly natural.

'Mat, I'm sorry. I went to meet him in all innocence. It simply didn't occur to me that "Mr Clarke" was anyone other than he said he was. I was a bloody fool. I should have been more suspicious.'

'I really don't see why, Philip.'

I gave him a thankful smile before I again resorted to the truth. I described my meeting with 'Mr Clarke', gave an accurate description of his appearance and stressed the fact – not too much I hoped – that he was well-known at the Albury. I also said that there was nothing exceptional about our lunch-time conversation, though I was surprised how much he knew about Claire and me.

'I'd have been happy to say goodbye to him after coffee but he asked me to go up to his suite,' I continued. 'He said he had something important and private to tell me. Upstairs he gave me an alternative, quite bluntly. Either I would work secretly for the communist bloc when I took up my posting in Washington – he seemed to accept that the posting was still on the cards –' I looked questioningly at Mat.

'As of now, it is,' he said.

' – or, if I refused, he would see it became public knowledge that Claire had been a sleeper.'

'What?' Mat was shaken.

'Yes. That was the last thing I expected, too,' I said dourly, 'but he put up a convincing case – at least he seemed to think my superiors at the Ministry would find it convincing.' I gave Mat more or less the same explanation of the threats and incidents that Bronwell had given me, angling the story so that Claire would appear an innocent victim, and I added some supporting details. 'He pointed out the scandal this would create, and what a horrendous effect it would have on me and all my family, even to a young nephew who's hoping to join the FCO. So there I was, Mat, in the classic situation of the unwilling traitor.'

'And what did you do?'

'I reacted as expected. Surprise, indignation, disbelief that this was happening to me – all genuine – and eventually reluctant agreement – naturally not genuine. I was then told to go away and think over the situation. I must return next Tuesday evening to make a firm commitment; in other words, I assume, to compromise myself completely by signing some documents or recording a tape or something. If I did anything foolhardy in the meantime, I knew what the result would be.'

'Tuesday? That would leave plenty of time for us to interview "Mr Clarke" and ask him some awkward questions, wouldn't it?' Mat was thinking aloud. 'But to what avail? We've got nothing on him. He'd laugh at us. Ah well, the matter needs careful consideration, Philip. Meanwhile let's have another whisky, shall we?'

Smiling benevolently, Mat pushed himself out of his garden chair, collected the glasses and went into the house. He was away a long time, much longer than it takes to make two drinks. I could guess what he was doing. He was arranging for discreet enquiries to be made at the Albury and for a discreet watch to be kept on the hotel, in case anyone fitting my description of 'Mr Clarke' decided to leave during the night. I hoped the operative word would be 'discreet'. I didn't want anyone bugging Bronwell's suite or lifting his fingerprints from a wine glass in the dining-room, not yet, not before Tuesday.

'Sorry for the delay.' Mat set the whiskies down carefully on the table. 'Margaret needed some help in the kitchen.'

It was a trivial lie, and unnecessary. It made me wonder if Mat had included a discreet tail for me, amongst his other arrangements. I sighed. I would have to remember that from now on he too was a potential enemy.

'Supper will be ready shortly. Margaret will call us, but until then let's go through it again, shall we?'

'Yes, of course.'

I took a drink, shook my head at the crisps Mat was offering me, and relaxed, seemingly. The probing was about to begin.

It was midnight when I got back to Harley Street. I was mentally and physically exhausted, and my leg hurt. However, I was reasonably contented. My story had stood up well against Mat's questioning and, as far as I could see, my options for the next three days were still wide open.

I made myself a cup of weak tea and took it to bed with me. With the last mouthful I swallowed two of my sleeping pills – things I used to despise. The rest of the problem would have to wait until tomorrow. I was in no state to make vital decisions tonight. I turned off the light and lay down.

In spite of the pills, I couldn't sleep. Here in this room, where Claire and I had spent so many loving nights, it was impossible not to think of her. And I didn't want to think of her, except objectively as Bronwell might, or Mat. It was an indulgence I couldn't afford at the moment. But, while I tossed and turned and the bed got more and more uncomfortable, memories that I had succeeded in pushing to the back of my mind during the day crowded in on me. At last I wept.

By Tuesday I had done a lot of hard thinking and taken a

certain amount of action. I was as prepared as I could be for whatever the day might bring. I had even made a new will, dividing my worldly goods between my nephews and nieces. I wasn't expecting an imminent death, but I did foresee that life might become very difficult in the next few months. I had also used my visit to my solicitor as a test for the tail that Mat had put on me. As a consequence I had been deterred from visiting a travel agent and making enquiries about cruises to South America which was one of the things Bronwell had wanted me to do for him. I had been very careful indeed.

Today, however, I intended to risk all. It was essential that I should get hold of the letter that Claire had written to Bronwell and the meeting with him this evening would be my last chance. I couldn't continue to deceive Mat about the identity of 'Mr Clarke' indefinitely, but if I denounced Bronwell before the letter was destroyed . . . Full of nervous anticipation, I set off for the office.

The morning dragged. A lot of bumph had come in on Northern Ireland. As Hal Runce had foretold there was trouble over the supposed discovery of 'Those who loved Kevin'. The family had been closely questioned but, I was assured, they had been treated with great consideration. Nevertheless, there were accusations of British brutality. Two soldiers on guard in the village had been shot and some others had been stoned while making enquiries. In revenge fire bombs had been thrown at Kevin's house and on to the roof of the presbytery, which had been badly damaged. There was sporadic violence in other parts of the Province. The whole thing made me sick. I couldn't concentrate.

I was rude to a newspaper man who rang me up, which wasn't wise of me. I wrote a scathing memo on a report by one of my junior colleagues. I refused to lunch with a friend in the FCO so curtly that I offended him. And finally I almost reduced my secretary to tears. It was at this point that I realized that unless I could control my nerves there was nothing but disaster ahead. Phone calls, invitations that might never be consummated, flowers for my secretary. I hurried to patch my fences.

The afternoon wasn't so bad. At four o'clock I went along to Mat's office and at once his secretary brought in tea, tea for three, with a chocolate cake. I don't know if the cake was in my honour – a sort of last meal – or in honour of our visitor. He appeared from Mat's private bathroom, a young man in a pink denim suit with wavy hair down to his shoulders. He was introduced as Mr Gates, but I doubt that was his real name. Mat was jovial and avuncular, not at his ease.

'Mr Gates knows all there is to know about gadgets, Philip.'

And while we had tea Mr Gates kindly explained the two gadgets he had brought for me. One was a watch, which told the time, the month, the date; it would also record any sound within a radius of fifteen feet for one hour. He showed me how to work it. It was sufficiently complicated. If the need arose, I could do the wrong thing and not record my conversation with Bronwell. I contained my relief.

The other was a genuine gold Parker pen which gave off a spray guaranteed to incapacitate its victim for ten minutes. I choked on my piece of chocolate cake. Mr Gates might have pinched the idea from a James Bond movie, but it was infinitely better than the pepper pot I had expected to use for the same purpose.

'My dear chap!' Mat said. 'We don't think there's really any danger, but it would be foolish not to take precautions. Our friend might turn nasty, you know.'

'Yes. I appreciate that – but it seems very melodramatic.'

'Not your usual line, certainly.' Mat smiled thinly at me, and let his smile warm as he turned to the gadget man. 'Don't think we're not grateful to you, Mr Gates. We are.' He was standing up, shaking him by the hand, dismissing him. 'Now, Philip . . .'

Mat began to brief me – my attitude to 'Mr Clarke', the questions I might spring on him, the questions I might back into, what I should do if . . . One of the names I was to mention was that of Alan Bronwell; Mat hoped that 'Mr Clarke's' reaction might be interesting.

I was glad when the briefing ended. It hadn't been altogether a waste of time. It had given me a certain amount of insight into the way Mat's mind was working, which might come in useful, but it had been a strain and I was already on the rim of tension.

'Well, good luck, Philip, and be careful.' Mat was seeing me to the door as if I were a VIP. This was an occasion. With his hand on the knob he said: 'There is something.'

My insides lurched. 'What?'

'It may not be important, but you should know that "Mr Clarke" is being tailed by someone other than ourselves. He didn't go out on Sunday. Yesterday he took a taxi to Piccadilly, bought a couple of English novels at Hatchards, had tea at Fortnum's and took another taxi home. He was followed by our man – and theirs.'

'Theirs? You mean a bodyguard?'

'No – o. He was very careful that "Mr Clarke" shouldn't notice him. Besides – '

I waited for Mat to complete his sentence. I didn't prompt him. I wondered if Bronwell knew that his masters had caught up with him and if it would make him more or less amenable. Either way I foresaw difficulties; Bronwell might be running scared. What's more, the shadow didn't exactly fit into the scenario I was writing for Mat.

'We weren't the first to make enquiries at the Albury over the weekend, Philip. Late Saturday night two men purporting to be Special Branch were also very interested in our "Mr Clarke". They weren't from Special Branch, and I don't understand it.'

'Well, maybe we'll solve the riddle this evening.'

Deliberately I looked at my watch, my new watch; the old one was in Mat's safe. It was a quarter to six. I had told Bronwell I would meet him between six and six-thirty, and I needed to have a pee, wash my hands, collect my briefcase, make sure my safe was locked, behave normally. Then I would get into the taxi that Mat had promised would be waiting for me outside the Ministry and . . . God help me.

I arrived at the Albury Hotel at seventeen minutes past six and asked for 'Mr Clarke'. As I expected, he had gone out a short while ago, but had left a message asking me to wait. I went and sat in the window-seat near to the front door. I had an excellent view of anyone entering or leaving the hotel. I waited.

'Mr Camplin?'

'Yes.' I turned, startled, wondering if this was some new trick of Bronwell's.

'With Mr Clarke's compliments, sir.'

The waiter put the whisky down on the table beside me, squirted the right amount of soda into it and gave me no opportunity to tip him. I would have been more appreciative if I hadn't known it would be on the bill that Bronwell intended me to pay. Nevertheless, I was glad of it. The whisky warmed me, steadied me. I wondered why I hadn't thought of it myself.

I continued to look out of the window. It was the rush hour. Traffic was heavy, but there weren't many pedestrians. Yet I nearly missed Bronwell. One moment he wasn't in sight and the next he was almost opposite the hotel, standing beside a parked taxi, waiting to cross the road. He was wearing the same pepper-and-salt suit he had worn on Saturday. There were no signs of any tails.

My mouth dry, I picked up my glass, found it empty, put it down again. I rolled my tongue slowly around my lips. So much was going to depend on the next sixty minutes. Abandoning logical thought I prayed that luck would be on my side.

There was a gap in the traffic and Bronwell began to cross the road. I stood up, ready to meet him. Suddenly I saw him jerk his head around in a quick, nervous movement. Then I saw the black Jaguar car. It came roaring out of nowhere. Bronwell lengthened his stride. He started to run but he was too late.

Helpless, I watched. The Jag hit him squarely and with such force he was carried several yards spreadeagled over the engine as if embracing it. Then, contemptuously, the car let his body drop, sped on over him and left him in the middle of the road like a pile of dung from a horse.

There was no question of it being an accident. The driver had made no attempt to avoid him, no attempt to brake. Nor, though he must have been fully aware of what he had done, did he stop. On the contrary, he disappeared into the distance, scorching his tyres as he turned a corner. Somewhere, in a quiet side street, he would abandon that stolen car and there would be no trace of him. Alan Bronwell had been right to be afraid.

FIVE

It was as if the film had stopped, then suddenly restarted. The Albury doorman raced towards the discarded heap that had once been Alan Bronwell. He was closely followed by a taxi-driver. But the first to get there was a passing pedestrian. Around them vehicles swirled and snarled. A man abandoned his car, stood in the middle of the road and waved his arms commandingly; he might have been conducting an orchestra. There was a lot of shouting. The traffic crawled.

The head porter ran on to the hotel steps, took in what had happened, returned to the lobby, called to one of his underlings to ring for the police and an ambulance – in that order – and ran out again. Immediately the lobby emptied itself of guests and staff, all curious, anxious, excited. On the pavement a woman who had witnessed the 'accident' began to scream on a high hysteric note.

For perhaps a minute the Albury, its accustomed calm shattered, was wide open to intruders. Without conscious thought I seized my chance, my one chance. If 'Mr Clarke' had been carrying Claire's letter and his statement on his person, there was no hope, but they might be hidden somewhere in his suite, together with the gas grenades. I walked over to the reception desk – temporarily deserted – lifted the flap and went behind. I took down the key of 'Mr Clarke's' suite from its hook. No one noticed me.

The hysterical woman, her scream reduced to sobs, was being helped into the hotel by the head porter and another man. She was large and heavy and their entire efforts were needed to support her. But at any moment, if only from habit, the porter might cast a proprietary eye around his domain. I stood in the lift and willed the doors to shut. I didn't want him to see me. He would immediately suspect where I was going.

At last the doors shut lingeringly and I sighed with relief as the lift carried me up to the fifth floor. There was no one about. My hurrying feet were soft on the rich pile carpet as I reached the end of the corridor and let myself into Bronwell's suite. Temporarily I was safe, but I might not have much time.

I looked round the sitting-room. There were a hundred places to hide a few sheets of paper, but not many that would hold a box of grenades. I glanced inside a cabinet, but it contained only bottles of liquor, soft drinks and glasses. Its companion piece was empty. Perhaps the sitting-room wasn't a good bet. I went through into the bedroom and began to search desperately.

It was almost impossible to be methodical. There was a huge built-in wardrobe, and a chest with long, deep drawers. The bedside-tables were on the same generous scale. But Claire's letter could have been taped behind a picture, under a chair, in the lining of a suitcase. I had started at one end of the room, but I kept noticing possibilities I had missed and going back. It was hopeless.

Against the muted roar of London's traffic I heard the sound of sirens, growing louder. This would be the police, the ambulance. I went to the nearest window and looked down into the street below. Bronwell's body was still lying in the road and someone – presumably a doctor – was kneeling beside it, watched by a circle of the curious which parted as authority arrived. There were no obvious signs of any plainclothes men, which was disturbing. I didn't want to be interrupted by the Special Branch, intent on a search of their own.

With a fresh sense of urgency, I turned away from the window and studied the room, trying to put myself in Bronwell's place. As a mental exercise this produced no result, but I found that I was staring at the king-sized bed. At least it was somewhere else to look.

I lay flat on the floor and lifted the valence. There was nothing under the bed, not even fluff on the carpet. The Albury was a very well-run hotel, a fact that Bronwell would have known. He wouldn't have put the grenades where a chamber maid might chance on them. But he had said they were in this suite, and the papers might be with them. If I couldn't find a fairly big and heavy box, I was never going to find Claire's damning letter.

A thought occurred to me and I returned to the bed. Once more I prostrated myself. Lying on my back I was able with difficulty to propel my shoulders underneath. My searching hands told me I was right; I had seen that part of the canvas covering the bottom of the box spring was hanging loose. I was hideously uncomfortable, and my muscles were cramping as I managed to reach into the tear and closed my fingers round something that surely should not have been there. I explored it tentatively, felt the tape that held it up amongst the springs, and pulled, sweating with my effort.

The tape gave unexpectedly. The box fell, crushing my hand. I swore aloud. Dragging myself out, I brought the box with me. It was about a foot and a half long, eight inches square and gunmetal in colour, but what made my heart hammer against my ribs was the sight of the brown foolscap envelope attached to the lid.

Regardless of broken nails, I tore the envelope free and opened it. Inside were two smaller envelopes, one addressed to Alan Bronwell in Claire's handwriting, the other thicker and unaddressed. I held the three pages of Claire's letter in a hand that shook. This was the original. The copy that Bronwell had made for me was already destroyed. He had said it was the only copy and I had no reason to doubt him. Relief overwhelmed me.

And then I heard the sound of a key turning in a lock. I held my breath. Someone was coming into the suite. A door shut gently. Whoever it was was being very quiet. With equal caution I picked up the box and struggled to my feet. Reflected in a mirror I saw the figure of a man bending over a cabinet. He was of medium height, slim and dark-haired, and he was searching the sitting-room more quickly and efficiently than I had done. I rejected my first instinct to hide in the clothes cupboard, and made for the bathroom.

The door was ajar and I was able to push it open and slide

myself around it. Unfortunately I misjudged the length of the box I was carrying and it made a dull clunk against the woodwork. He must have heard it. I thrust the door shut and pushed home the bolt. It was of brass and, like the door, solid. I had bought myself some time – but not much.

The handle was already turning as I tore the thin flimsy sheets of writing paper into small pieces and dropped them into the pan. He knew I was here, so there was no point in pretending. I flushed the toilet and, with a sense of release, watched the last fragments of Claire's letter disappear. I had achieved my major objective.

There was a subdued knock at the door and a voice said: 'Who is that in the bathroom? Please to come out, at once.'

I didn't answer. I had opened the other envelope and was skimming through what Bronwell had written. It was not what I expected, not the denunciation of myself that he had promised. Instead it was a kind of apologia for himself. It outlined and tried to justify his actions, from his early conviction that communism was the only relevant political philosophy, through his recruitment at Oxford as a sleeper and his eventual activation, to his gradual disenchantment and his determination not to become a scapegoat. He vehemently denied any connection with the theft of the gas grenades that had been used on Massacre Day, and he gave the name of the man he suspected of having stolen them. I stared at it in disbelief and horror.

'You must come out of there. You must do what I tell you. I am the manager of the Albury Hotel.' He rattled the door to emphasize the lie. 'You have no cause to be afraid.'

I wasn't afraid. I was too stunned by what I had just read to give any thought to my own safety. Bob Finton. Dr Robert Finton, the eminent scientist and administrator, who was just taking over as Research Director at the manufacturers when the theft took place two years ago. Now rumoured to be in the running for a 'K' for services to government research in industry. It wasn't possible.

I started to tear it up. It was on thicker paper than Claire's letter so the pieces would have to be smaller. But I had to destroy it though it was no direct threat to me. I could keep nothing which showed that I knew the true identity of 'Mr Clarke', and in any case it condemned Claire as a sleeper. I watched the little scraps of paper swirl around the pan and disappear.

I turned my attention to my own situation. It wasn't too good. By this time the man on the other side of the door had abandoned his pretence to be the Albury's manager and was hissing like a snake.

'You, you listen. You come out *at once*, with your hands above your head, or I shoot the lock off. You understand what I say?'

'Yes. I understand. One minute.'

There was nowhere in the bathroom to hide the gas grenades. However, a window suggested a possibility. As silently as I could, I opened it. The sill, coated with London dirt, sloped outwards but it was broad enough. I hoisted the box outside and shut the window. Luckily the glass was frosted and only an indeterminate shadow showed through. I could but hope it wouldn't be noticed.

'Last chance. I shoot.'

'No. Don't do that. I'm going to unlock the door.'

'One step back when you've unlocked it and your hands up. I shall open the door myself. I don't trust you.'

'All right.'

I didn't trust him either, but there wasn't much I could do about it. I fingered the pen the gadget man had provided. It was one thing to contemplate using it against a complacent Bronwell who believed I was prepared to do as he wanted, and quite another to think of attacking this character, already suspicious and angry at being thwarted. I had seen the professional way he had searched the sitting-room and I was sure he had only hesitated to break into the bathroom because of the noise. He wasn't to be treated lightly.

I released the bolt, took two steps backwards and lifted my hands in the air. I was too elated at what I had achieved to be badly frightened, but my adrenalin was running fast.

The handle swivelled. The door swung slowly inwards. All I could see was a fist holding a small, blunt gun, a flick of black hair, the edge of a profile outlined in white. He had tied a handkerchief over the lower part of his face. It didn't make him absurd.

'Empty your pockets, quickly but carefully, with your left hand. Drop the things in front of you. Then turn round, spread your legs, lean over the bath, and support yourself with your hands against the far wall.'

I did as he ordered. When I was in the classic posture of helplessness he came into the bathroom and patted me down. Satisfied that I had no weapon, he inspected my belongings. I heard him grunt with amusement.

'What are you doing here, Mr Camplin?'

'I came to visit Mr Clarke.'

'Mr Clarke?' He mocked me. 'You mean Alan Bronwell, don't you?' His tone changed. 'You were searching his rooms, Mr Camplin. You found something. What?'

I didn't answer and he stuck the gun in the back of my neck. I winced but I still said nothing and he began to screw it into my flesh. I clenched my teeth in order not to cry out.

'Tell me, Mr Camplin. Don't be a hero.'

I had no intention of being a hero, but I had an idea that if I gave in too quickly he wouldn't believe me. Besides, I was now hoping for the Special Branch to appear; they were supposed to be watching out for me. What the hell were they doing? 'For God's sake, don't!' I said. 'I'll tell you.'

'Good.' He released me. 'You may stand up straight, but clasp your hands on the top of your head.'

'Thanks.' I stood upright and took a deep breath. My neck was fierce with pain. 'I was looking for letters that Claire, my wife, wrote to Bronwell – compromising letters. They – they'd been lovers.'

'You found and destroyed them?'

'Yes. I flushed them down the toilet.'

'I heard you. Did you find anything else?'

'No.' I was glad I was facing the tiled wall and couldn't be tempted to glance at the tell-tale shadow. 'What were you looking for?'

He didn't answer. He must have been considering whether to believe my story about the letters or not and, in either case, what to do with me. He made up his mind quickly. He knew his time was running short.

'Turn right and kneel down, Mr Camplin.'

'Why?'

'Because I am a compassionate man and I don't wish you to brain yourself on the bath.'

I wasn't aware of him hitting me, but only of falling into a long, black void . . . My next conscious thoughts were of the discomfort of my limbs, the throbbing of my head, the smell of talcum powder in the carpet. Then I remembered, and almost laughed aloud. Alan Bronwell had always had luxurious tastes; he would have expected a carpeted bathroom in his hotel suite.

'Christ! It's Mr Camplin.'

I opened my eyes. Above my head a face floated, a face with a large nose, vaguely familiar. I focused with difficulty. It was the Special Branch man I had last met at Claire's funeral. He bent over me anxiously.

'Why the devil were you so long?' I said. 'I could have been killed.'

He grinned in relief. 'I'm sorry, Mr Camplin, sir.' He helped me to sit up with my back against the bath, tut-tutting when he saw what the gun had done to my neck, and squatted beside me. 'How are you now? All right?'

'I've known occasions when I've felt better.'

He nodded sympathetically. 'I'm sure. You've been coshed, and you've a nasty wound on your neck. You must see a doctor, sir.'

Gingerly I touched the place on my neck. It was soft and left blood on my fingertips. The pain was excruciating. And my head was throbbing madly.

'Later. I've got to get to the MOD – Mr Harworth's waiting for me – but I'll need your help.'

'Of course, sir – if you must.'

I pointed at the window where the silhouette of the box I had hidden on the windowsill still darkened the frosted glass. 'Bring that in, will you? But be careful! Whatever you do don't drop it into the street. It's full of gas grenades.'

He gave me a look, part surprise, part amused respect, and did as he was told. I watched with triumph. Everything had turned out better than I could have hoped. Bronwell was dead, and his accusations with him. Though the manner of his death had shocked me I wasn't such a hypocrite as to pretend I was sorry about it. And now that Claire's letter and Bronwell's apologia were somewhere down in the London sewers I was wonderfully content. Of course, the question of Bob Finton still remained, but that didn't affect me personally, or my family. Considering what might have happened, a sore neck and a minor concussion were a small price to pay.

My euphoria lasted well into my meeting with Mat, to whom I told as much of the truth as I could. At last I was able to admit to knowing who 'Mr Clarke' really was; my assailant had told me. The only disturbing thing was Mat's acceptance as proven that Bronwell had stolen the grenades – something I knew to be false if Bronwell himself was to be believed. I had no objection to blaming him, but I couldn't let the enquiry come to a dead end, especially if Finton was in any way involved. I argued with Mat.

'You don't even know if the grenades came from the same source.'

'That'll be easy enough to find out.' He opened the box and frowned. 'Philip, how many grenades did you say were missing?'

'One. Why?'

'Because there are only four in the box.'

'Four?' I felt suddenly deflated. I hadn't been as clever as I thought. 'Damn the man!'

'Quite. Your assailant appears to have been most efficient.' Mat paused to light a cheroot. 'It's a pity we don't know what's happened to the missing grenade, isn't it?'

I agreed, though I wasn't really interested. However still I kept my head – and I had to keep it very still to avoid rubbing my bloody neck against the collar of my shirt – little hammers continued to play on the inside of my skull as if it were a steel drum. And it was becoming more and more difficult to concentrate on what Mat was saying.

'. . . assume that his masters thought Bronwell was going to re-defect to us. Otherwise why should they have killed him? They must have arranged this "Mr Clarke" charade in order to blackmail you, Philip, but Bronwell decided to turn it to his own advantage – except he didn't get the chance, did he? Philip!'

But the hammers had reached a crescendo. My eyes were slitting shut, my body sliding down the chair. The air was full of cheroot smoke and I couldn't breathe. The floor was hard, surprising.

A voice said: 'Grenades could've been planted so that Bronwell blamed. Bronwell expendable. Real villain protected. Bob. Dr Finton.'

The voice sounded like mine, but it came from a long way off. Must have been someone else speaking. Not me. God, but my head hurt!

The next morning I swam very slowly to the surface of consciousness. I wasn't in my own bed but I knew where I was; the bedroom door was ajar and I could hear Patrick and Denise chatting over breakfast. Why I was sleeping in their flat instead of my own was another matter. I could think of no reason why I should be staying with them.

I yawned and immediately became aware of the dressing on my neck. Now I remembered. Everything was clear up to the time I collapsed in Mat's office. After that my memories were intermittent and hazy – and I was filled with apprehension. What had I said to Mat in my half-conscious state?

I called out and both Patrick and Denise came running. Their concern, followed by their relief when they saw I was all right, touched me. I grinned at them weakly.

'A lightly boiled egg, tea and toast for the invalid,' Patrick said. 'Doctor's orders.'

'I'm not an invalid. I – I had an accident.'

'So Mat Harworth informed us, but you're to stay where you are for forty-eight hours. Denise will take care of you.' He patted his wife fondly on the bottom. 'Go and get his breakfast, love.'

When she had gone he sat himself on the end of the bed and regarded me with unusual seriousness. 'Philip, I have something to say, and you may not like it. You see, Mat was more forthcoming than I – er – implied while Denise was with us. And we're worried about you – Harworth and me – though I suspect for rather different reasons.'

'There's no need.' My retort was sharper than I had intended.

'No need? Dear God, brother! During the last few weeks you've been shot at, your car's been blown up, Claire . . .' He shook his head as if in pain. 'Yesterday you were concussed and some foul thing was done to your neck and – and you tell me not to worry?'

'Sorry. I meant – '

He cut me short. It seemed he wasn't interested in what I meant, but only in giving me the astonishing news that both he and Mat Harworth thought I should consider resigning from my job at the Ministry and from the Civil Service.

'. . . Mat agrees it could be the sensible thing for you to do, Philip. He'll hate to lose you, of course, but – '

Amazed and angry, I let my temper flare. 'Like hell he will! He's my senior in the hierarchy, but he doesn't employ me. He didn't hire me. He can't fire me. And I'm damned if I'm going to resign. Why should I? I've been a Civil Servant for twenty years, ever since I came down from Oxford, and the life suits me. I've made a success of it. I don't find it dull. I like it!'

'Dull?' Patrick smiled grimly. 'No! Dull is not the word I'd use either, Philip, not after the antics you've been taking part in recently. But you can't go on like this and as your Washington job seems to be off – '

'What? How do you know that?'

'Mat told me, when we were talking.'

It was a bitter blow, even though I had been half expecting it, and to learn of the decision in this casual fashion made it twice as hard to bear. As far as I knew the appointment was still classified information, which was why I hadn't mentioned it to Patrick. But Mat Harworth had seen fit to discuss it with him. Then between them they had cooked up the idea that I should change my way of life. I wished them both to hell.

'Philip, from what Mat said I'm sure you don't have much of an alternative. Either you're to be dusted away into some dreary job in a dreary place where you'll die of boredom before it's time for you to retire, or you resign now, voluntarily, and start a new career, which could be terrific for you. You know you can count on all of us to help. William and Andrew – '

'I don't want anyone's help. I don't want a new career. I'm perfectly happy with the one I've got. And if you'll stop trying to interfere, I'll get on with it, and with my present not unimportant job.'

'Don't be a damned fool! That's no longer a viable alternative.' Patrick was angry himself now. He got to his feet and towered above me. 'Don't you understand, Philip? What with all the publicity you've had recently and the unpredictable way you seem to behave, you've become a danger to yourself and a liability to Mat, though he was too generous to put it like that.'

I stared at him blankly. 'Get out!' I said at last, through clenched teeth. 'Get out, Patrick. And in future mind your own bloody business.'

He didn't argue. To give him his due he didn't even suggest that since I was occupying a bedroom in his flat I was the one who should get out. But, in the doorway, almost colliding with an astonished Denise bringing my breakfast tray, he turned and said bitterly:

'Philip, if you go on as you are at present, you'll get yourself killed, and it will be your own fault.'

He was gone before I could struggle out of bed and Denise frustrated any further efforts on my part by planting the tray firmly on my lap. The front door slammed. Denise looked at me in disgust.

'Philip, I don't know why you've been quarrelling with Patrick, but it's too bad of you. You might be more considerate.

He's been up half the night with you, and he's got a heavy load of work today.'

'Up half the night with me? Why?'

'We both were. You kept on crying out in your sleep.' Her expression softened, changed to one of pity. 'You weren't well, Philip dear.'

'What did I cry out about?'

'Come on, Philip, eat your egg before it gets cold.' She poured coffee for me. 'It was just a jumble.'

'Denise, stop treating me like a child and tell me. I want to know.'

'It was a jumble,' she insisted. 'You were grieving for Claire, but you seemed to include all the people who had been killed or hurt on Massacre Day. Then there was something about a pebble in a stream making wider and wider ripples, and a fire, and how you could put out the fire if you knew who had thrown the pebble.' She grinned suddenly. 'You were determined to find out, Philip. You became quite violent. Patrick had to hold you down at one point.'

'I'm sorry, Denise, terribly sorry.' I managed a feeble grin in response.

'Forget it.'

I nodded. But it wasn't so easy. After what Denise had told me I could understand Patrick's concern for me, and I regretted my earlier outburst. I owed him an apology. Mat's behaviour, however, remained inexplicable and inexcusable. I wanted to know the reasons. And there was only one person with the answers.

SIX

In spite of Denise's protests I got up as soon as I had finished breakfast. The floor was inclined to tilt and inanimate objects weren't as stable as they should have been, but I could manage, though it needed concentration. I went upstairs to my own flat.

It was impossible to hurry and I didn't dare have a bath, but I washed, shaved with my electric razor and put on clean clothes. The shirt was a problem. The pad on my neck prevented me from wearing anything tight, and I had to settle for a silk handkerchief to hide the dressing. The result was not what I would have chosen. I looked distinctly raffish.

And the effort to achieve this had cost me dear. There was a thin film of sweat on my skin and I was shaking. I had to sit down. I looked longingly at the whisky decanter but it was only half past ten, and I couldn't give Mat such an obvious excuse for disregarding what I intended to say to him. I waited until the dizziness passed.

When I felt better I went downstairs and leaned against the railings outside the house until a taxi came along. The traffic was heavy and slow-moving, my driver bored and talkative. I was a captive audience. I listened.

For my sins his main theme was Ireland, for which he claimed to have the perfect solution. Everyone, except the true Irish, should be deported and the whole island sealed off while the natives fought it out amongst themselves. If there was a blood-bath, too bad. At least they couldn't blame anyone else for it.

'What do you think, guv?'

'It's an idea,' I said, and refrained from adding that it wasn't original.

'And a good one, though I say it myself. Why should our boys get hurt trying to stand between them? Four killed last night and others wounded, in that pitched battle at Baly – Baly –

whatever the place is called, where the family of that little boy Kevin lives. There'll be more trouble too after the American woman's offer.'

'What offer was that?'

He had certainly got my attention now. I had neither listened to the news nor seen a morning paper. I knew nothing about these latest troubles. But I remembered Hal Runce's warning, and Hal had a habit of being right.

'She's one of these rich birds, and she wants to take the whole of Kevin's village – all five hundred of them – to the States,' my taxi-driver explained over his shoulder. 'She's willing to match dollar for dollar whatever can be raised, here or over there, and she's put down a lump sum to start the campaign. She says they've got to be saved from what she calls British persecution. Me, and a lot like me, call it British soft-heartedness towards a bunch of murderers.'

The traffic opened suddenly and he had to concentrate on his driving, but he had left me with some unpleasant thoughts. The campaign might be genuine, but I doubted it. More likely it was a communist ploy; it would be the source of further conflict and misery and violence to the Irish, and in the States a propaganda vehicle to urge support for American intervention. I wondered what Hal would have to say about it.

'Here you are, guv.'

I was so lost in contemplation that I hadn't noticed we were bowling down Northumberland Avenue, and we had drawn up in front of the Ministry before it occurred to me that this wasn't an ordinary day. Possibly I wouldn't even see the latest telegrams on Ireland. I hadn't come to work. I had come to confront Mat Harworth.

I went straight to Mat's office. I would have been glad of a rest first, perhaps a cup of coffee, but I didn't want him to have advance notice of my arrival in case he decided not to be 'in' today. As it was the main surprise was reserved for his secretary.

'Why, Mr Camplin! I – I thought you were on sick leave.'

'Is he in?'

'Yes, but – '

I was in no mood for excuses. In spite of my game leg I can move quickly and I was past her desk and at the door of the inner office before she could stop me. But she was a competent secretary. As I turned the handle and entered the room, I heard her announce me on the intercom.

If Mat had needed the warning it wasn't apparent. He expressed some surprise, which was reasonable, but mostly he showed a genuine anxiety on my behalf.

'Philip, my dear chap, what are you doing here? Oughtn't you to be in bed? Come and sit down.'

He pulled up his most comfortable chair, usually reserved for important visitors, and I sank into it gratefully. I could feel the resolve begin to drain out of me. I had known Mat for a long time, and he had been a good friend. If I couldn't trust him . . .

'I gather that, after all, I'm not to be posted to Washington,' I said conversationally.

'Your brother, Patrick, told you?'

'Amongst other things, yes.'

'Damn!'

I hadn't chosen a good moment. Mat was standing at the cupboard he used as a bar, his back to me. He was pouring us whiskies. I wasn't sure I liked this VIP treatment – it made a stranger of me – but I should be glad of the drink.

'Is it true?'

'Yes. I'm afraid it is, Philip.' He put my whisky down beside me and went to sit at the desk. 'I'm sorry you heard about it this way. I meant to tell you myself yesterday evening but, as you know, there was no opportunity.'

'You told me the posting was definite. Why was the decision reversed?'

Mat regarded me gravely. 'Political reasons. The Minister considers that there's been so much publicity recently connecting you with Northern Ireland that you might not be able to do the Washington job properly.'

It was fair enough. I couldn't really object. Nevertheless, I sensed that Mat wasn't being completely frank with me. He had chosen his words too carefully. I sipped my whisky and felt its warmth gentle my insides. My anger had evaporated. I needed some Dutch courage to go on.

'So, what would you say my prospects are now, Mat? Would you advise me to resign?'

He wasn't as startled by the question as I had hoped he would be, but it was half a minute before he spoke. Even then he didn't answer me directly.

'Washington was a plum, which you deserved, Philip. I believe you were the best possible choice, but circumstances were against you. You know as well as I do that there aren't many such plums, and they're not easy to get. As to your chances in the future . . . ?'

He shrugged. It wasn't clear whether he was commenting on plums or on my personal future. He picked up the case from his desk, took out a cheroot and replaced it. That he should consider me to this extent was a bad sign. Something was seriously wrong.

'I think your brother's right, you know, Philip. Claire's death and everything you've been through in the last few weeks have had more effect on you than you or anyone else has realized.' Mat smiled to take the sting from what he was saying. 'Honestly, can you imagine yourself a year ago ducking up to "Mr Clarke's" suite and searching it?'

I hesitated; it was impossible to explain my behaviour. 'No. Perhaps not. But I did find the grenades, Mat.'

'You did indeed. To my mind that confirms Bronwell's guilt, though, as you pointed out last night, they could have been planted there.'

'I suggested that?'

'Yes. Just before you blacked out. You said it was possible Bronwell was being made a scapegoat, and we should get hold of Bob Finton. I suppose to check on his staff again. You were fairly incoherent.'

'I'm sorry. I don't remember.'

I passed a hand over my face. It wasn't altogether play-acting. I was feeling decidedly unwell, but on one point at least I was reassured; I hadn't implied anything incriminating about

Finton – and probably not about Claire. As for the other things Mat had said, I would have to think about them – later. There was something going on that I didn't understand.

Mat got to his feet. 'Philip, I don't want to push you out, but I really am extremely busy. In addition to the complications that Bronwell's masquerade as "Mr Clarke" has caused, there's been a fresh flare-up in Northern Ireland. I expect you've heard. What's more, the forecast isn't good. We're in for trouble, especially if this great American benefactor can't be controlled.'

'Of course.'

I had stood up too quickly and the room was spinning. I wondered if I had been stupid to drink whisky. Concussion and alcohol didn't mix well.

'. . . find you a taxi,' Mat was saying. 'You must rest, Philip, and take care of yourself. Next week, if you're fit, I'd like you to go and have a talk with Mrs Rose Bronwell. There's no hurry. But once she's over the first shock of her husband's death, she might be glad to see you – and you might learn something useful.'

I suppressed the grin that threatened to split my mouth. Mat's assumption that next week I would be back at my old job was enormously encouraging. True, I had lost the posting to Washington and Mat was behaving in his usual devious fashion, but I wasn't to be shunted into some backwater. The question of resignation didn't seem to arise seriously. Patrick must have been mistaken. Happily I told myself that I had got steamed up about nothing.

By Friday afternoon, except for a certain lethargy, I was back to normal. Patrick – with whom I'd made my peace – and Denise were going to some 'do' at Nicole's school, and I faced an empty weekend. Having considered the possibilities, I phoned John Telsey, who sounded surprisingly glad to hear from me. Bette Aylwyn was visiting him, but she was staying at The Mitre, and his guest-room was mine.

'You're sure I won't be in the way, John?'

'Positive. Bette has Lance with her. She's hoping to get him into the College. Considering it's notorious rather than famous at the moment, I can't think why. Incidentally, we're more under siege than ever here – but I suppose you knew that.'

I hadn't known. I put down the receiver thoughtfully. I assumed from John's remark that Rose Bronwell had returned home and was staying with the Provost and Lady T., at least temporarily. And, in addition to Mat's request, I had reasons of my own for wanting to see Rose. Bronwell's accusation of Bob Finton was nagging at me like a toothache.

The problem of what to do about it occupied my mind for most of the drive down to Oxford. I knew Dr Finton casually. We attended some of the same meetings and, though we didn't seek each other out, we usually had a brief chat at the official parties afterwards. He was an agreeable man. I admired his ability. The last thing I wanted to do was throw unjust suspicion on him. Nevertheless, I couldn't ignore Bronwell's accusation. As far as I could judge from the cursory reading I had given his apologia before I destroyed it, it had been a truthful statement. Why then should he have lied about Bob Finton? Just possibly, it had occurred to me, Rose might know the answer, but this was a long shot, and if it failed . . .

I parked Denise's Renault in the Broad and went along to the College. I had to wait at the lodge while the porter phoned John to confirm I was expected. The Special Branch man, having logged my arrival, eyed me with interest. I wondered what he would do if I suddenly sprinted for the Provost's house.

'All right, Mr Camplin,' the porter said.

'Thanks, Hopkins.' I returned his smile, excluding the SB man, and set off across the quad.

John was waiting for me at the bottom of his staircase. 'Hallo, Philip. Good to see you.' He seized my overnight bag. 'You wait there. I'll run this up. Unless you want – ?'

'No. I'm all right.'

He was back in a minute and, supposing that we were going to lunch with Bette and her son, I turned towards the porter's lodge. John redirected me. We went past the chapel and into the small quad, where he unlocked a door in a high wall. He had walked fast, ignoring my question, but I knew where I was.

It was no surprise to find myself in the Provost's private garden. As an undergraduate I had been allowed into it on at least one occasion, and had probably penetrated it a couple of times since. But it was a surprise to see the Provost kicking a football around the lawn with two identical little boys.

He desisted as soon as he caught sight of us. He was probably glad of the interruption, for he was red-faced and panting. Otherwise he looked much as usual, a large lumbering man, not a fine scholar but a good administrator who had done well by the College during the last twenty-five years. He would be angry that this scandal had hit him – and the College – when he was on the edge of retirement.

'Ah, John, you've brought him. Good for you. Morning, Camplin.'

'Good morning, sir.'

The Provost didn't offer to shake hands though it was a habit of his, and it was left to John to introduce the twins who were crowding around him.

'This is Telsey, my godson, in the blue shirt, and Clarke, who's older by five minutes, in the red shirt – that is, unless they've swapped.' John beamed on them. 'Boys, this is Mr Camplin, an old friend of mine.'

Unlike their grandfather, they solemnly offered me their hands. Alan Bronwell's sons were attractive small creatures, fair-haired, blue-eyed, sturdy. I was glad they were too young to know what their father had done. Years before they were adults it would be forgotten – unless, when the findings of the Special Enquiry into Massacre Day were made public, he was blamed for procuring the gas grenades. In that event the name of Bronwell would be recalled with opprobrium for a very long time. Which was another reason why I couldn't ignore the charge Bronwell had made against Bob Finton.

'Rose is in the morning-room,' the Provost said. 'Will you show Camplin the way, John?'

He looked at me as if he were about to add something, but he changed his mind and nodded brusquely instead. Dismissed, I followed John across the lawn, through the conservatory and along a passage. John pointed to a door.

'You'll find Rose in there, Philip. Don't pay any attention to the Provost. The old man would like to shut her up in an ivory tower for the rest of her life.' He gave a helpless, irritable shrug. 'Anyway, she wants to see you, and she tells me you know about Alan and Claire, so – '

I knocked on the door and went in. Rose came forward to meet me. She was wearing a pink skirt, tight-belted, and a candy-striped shirt. She had made no attempt at mourning, but grief had refashioned her. She was no longer the plump pretty girl who had accosted me at Claire's funeral. She had lost weight, her features were more finely honed and she had an air of determination. I would hardly have recognized her.

'Hallo, Philip.'

It was typical of the change in her that today she could use my first name without embarrassment. We shook hands and she gestured me to a chair. I murmured something about being sorry we always seemed to meet in unhappy circumstances.

She smiled sadly. 'Sherry, Philip? Light or dark?'

'Dark, please.'

It was a ludicrous situation. I felt like an undergraduate paying a formal call on the wife of his tutor. Neither of us could think what to say. For a minute or two we spoke in platitudes, about Oxford and how it had changed since I was up, about John Telsey, about the twins. To my chagrin Rose was more at ease than I, and it was she who, after a lengthening pause, said:

'Philip, you were there when Alan was killed and – and you had lunch with him a few days before. I'd like to know about it, everything you can tell me. You see, I've got to start again – because of the twins – but first I want to tidy up all the ends. Do you understand?'

I did understand, at least in part, for there were ends of my own not yet tidied up from the aftermath of Claire's death. I had to keep on reminding Rose, and myself, that I had met Alan Bronwell as 'Mr Clarke'. And there were some things, such as what 'Mr Clarke' had wanted of me, that I couldn't explain to her. It wasn't easy, but I told her as much as I could.

Rose was disproportionately grateful. 'Thank you, Philip, very much.' She managed to smile.

'My dear. I'm only sorry – '

'Mr Harworth said you'd be understanding, and you have been, wonderfully.'

'Mat Harworth! He said that to you. When?'

'On – on Wednesday. They took me up to London to identify Alan's body.' Her voice shook and for the first time she seemed on the edge of tears. She took a moment to get control of herself. 'Mr Harworth said he was terribly busy, but you'd be coming to see me and you'd tell me whatever was allowed. He said you probably knew more about what had been going on than he did.'

'Did he?' Suddenly I was uneasy. 'I doubt he meant it.'

'No, perhaps not. He knew a lot about Alan – more in some ways than me – and considering what Alan had done he was very sympathetic.'

'You're talking about Wednesday?'

My voice was sharp, and Rose looked at me in surprise. I rearranged my features to appear merely interested. My unease had become apprehension, though I couldn't have said specifically why. It was a gut reaction.

'Wednesday, yes. But mostly last Sunday. I was at home then, hoping and praying Alan would come back. I didn't believe this stupid story that he'd drowned himself. He always hated water. And Mr Harworth arrived.'

I nodded. I would have found it difficult to speak. On Saturday morning I had given Mat my version of what had taken place between me and 'Mr Clarke' at the Albury Hotel. He had shown no sign of doubting it. But the following day, a Sunday, he had gone to visit Rose, the wife of a known agent. This was an incredible action for Mat to take. He was much too senior for such an expedition. But I could imagine him chatting up Rose. He would be courteous in an out-dated manner, considerate, kind, and by the time he said goodbye he would have learnt everything he wanted.

I said: 'I suppose he asked you about Alan's relationship with Claire?'

'Yes. He explained his belief – I know I mustn't mention this to anyone but you, Philip – that just possibly Alan's disappearance was connected with what's been happening in Northern Ireland. If so, it might be tied up in a roundabout way with the attacks on you and Claire.'

'It sounds far-fetched to me,' I said, though it was near enough to the truth to make me sweat.

'Mr Harworth admitted that himself. Still, Alan was dreadfully upset when Claire died. In fact, we had a row about it.' Rose flushed. 'I was always jealous of Claire. It's no use pretending I wasn't. Oh, I know Alan had a lot of girl-friends, but Claire was somehow special. After you were shot at in Dublin and your car was booby-trapped he used to read the newspapers from cover to cover in case there was some reference to Claire. He didn't say so, but I knew. And he was seeing her again.'

'What?'

'You didn't know, Philip? A neighbour of ours saw them lunching together in Soho.' Unexpectedly Rose began to cry. 'It's silly to mind now, isn't it, when they're both dead? It's not important any more.'

Not important! I couldn't tell her that if she hadn't hanged me, she had buried me. Ironically it was I who had first put the idea that Claire was a sleeper into Mat's head; but Rose was the one who had convinced him, though he couldn't prove that 'Mr Clarke's' blackmail threat had substance. Claire had been a sleeper, a communist agent. That condemned me out of hand. Washington apart, I would never get another positive clearance. Whether I resigned or accepted some backwater job, my career was over. Mat had made that plain by his seeming indiscretions to Patrick. Whatever his personal feelings – and he would guess why I had tried to trick him – he could never wholly trust me again. And, since words would have compromised him, he had sent me to visit Rose so that I would understand. It was typical of his deviousness.

I would resign, as he expected me to do. He had even made it easy for me. He had suggested a long sick leave. Resignation on grounds of ill-health would follow naturally. There would be no scandal and only I would pay, not the rest of the family. Which was as it should be. I had no right to complain.

SEVEN

Saturday passed somehow. I ate a little and drank a lot and endured dinner with John and Bette and Lance. Bette was being maternal and Lance, though an amiable lad, obviously and not surprisingly found the three of us a strain. I took a double dose of sleeping pills when I went to bed. I woke, sodden and miserable, about four o'clock. The rest of the night was interminable.

John had planned a day on the river for the four of us, but at breakfast I decided I couldn't face the effort. Besides, the river held too many memories of my youth and of Claire.

I saw John off, and settled to the Sunday papers. Ignoring the stories about Alan Bronwell, I concentrated on the Northern Ireland news. It was bad. There had been more shootings and Kevin's father had only narrowly missed being killed. He said that he and his family didn't want to leave their home and go to America, but the fund being raised for that purpose was growing hugely. A petition urging the President to give it his support had been signed by thousands. There had been a demonstration outside the White House demanding that British brutality should end and that the Brits should be compelled, by force if need be, to leave the Province. Having read a long article supporting this view, I threw the newspapers down in disgust and went for a walk.

On a Sunday it was still possible to enjoy strolling the streets of Oxford. Traffic and pedestrians were at a minimum. Church bells were ringing. A pale sun was shining. I found myself relaxing and my spirits rose a little. Once I had decided what – if anything – to do about Bob Finton, I could leave the Ministry with a clear conscience. Others could struggle with my problems. I wasn't irreplaceable. And, as Patrick said, I could try to make a new career for myself – though God knew in what.

However, the questions raised by Bronwell's accusation of Finton had to be answered first. Rose had been no help. She said that Bronwell had preferred Finton to the former Research Director and had been sorry to leave the firm, so spite could probably be ruled out. I didn't know what to do next . . .

'Hallo, Mr Camplin. How are you?'

I stared at the young man who had come swinging purposefully out of St John's College. He looked familiar but I couldn't place him. Then suddenly my memory clicked. He was the doctor who had treated Claire at the Radcliffe after she had eaten the poisoned liqueurs.

'Hallo, Dr – er – Collins, isn't it?'

'Yes. That's right.' He hesitated. 'Mr Camplin, I was sorry to hear about your wife. It was a dreadful thing to have happened. One of the nurses told me. I never read newspapers, never have the time, which is why when we last met I didn't know about the troubles you were having.'

'It made no difference. You did everything necessary.' I didn't want to rehash the events of that night. 'Are you on your way to the hospital?'

'No. I'm off duty. I was just going around to my local.' He eyed me speculatively. I guessed what he was thinking. I wasn't merely the husband of a patient whom he'd met on one panicky occasion. I was Patrick Camplin's brother and I remembered him saying that he and Patrick sometimes had a drink together.

'If you'll lead me there, I'll buy you a beer,' I said, 'unless you prefer whisky.'

He grinned at me. 'Thanks, Mr Camplin. I'll settle for a pint.'

We crossed the road, went down a slit of a lane by Pusey House, and into a cobbled yard where The Cock and Feathers stood. New since my day, it was obviously very popular, but Collins managed to acquire a couple of window seats. We chatted amicably. Over our second drink I made some reference to his remark that he never read newspapers.

'Not as a rule, but I have recently. This business of Alan Bronwell fascinates me.'

'Did you know him?' I don't know why I was surprised. They were much of an age, and could well have been at the university together.

'I met him a few times, mostly at Dick Havant's. Did you know Dick? He was an ex-schoolmaster who lived in North Oxford. He had lots of bread, and was always giving parties. I must say, I have wondered – '

'What?'

' – if perhaps his house was used as a sort of meeting place for – for agents. I mean, it would have been a good cover. All sorts of people went there.'

'Including me, and my three brothers before me,' I said sardonically. 'Dick was a friend of ours.'

'Yes.' He was embarrassed. 'I'm not saying Dick knew. He was old, and by the time I'm talking of he was dying of cancer.'

'What are you saying exactly?'

'I – ' Dr Collins buried his face in his beer mug. 'I expect I'm being silly,' he said finally. 'But it did strike me as odd, and since Alan Bronwell . . .'

Dr Collins was a mixture of common sense, shrewdness and extraordinary naïveté. It took him a while and another pint of beer to tell a simple story.

Rather a favourite of Dick Havant's, he had been invited to drop in when he liked. On one occasion, having taken Dick at his word, he found himself interrupting half-a-dozen people who seemed to be holding some kind of meeting. However, they had been welcoming enough. When he left, Bronwell and a don had offered him a lift. Subsequently he received a succession of invitations from the don. But this was a difficult time for Collins. He was working desperately hard for his finals and he was having problems with his girl-friend. He had refused almost all the invitations.

'I think I told you before, Mr Camplin, if it hadn't been for your brother I'd never have got through my exams. I was a nervous wreck at that point, in no mood for socializing. Next term, when I started as an intern at the Radcliffe, I might have been glad for some invites, but when I chanced to run into this chap, he pretended not to know who I was. And that's all.' He laughed at himself. 'I'd almost forgotten about it. It wasn't until Alan Bronwell turned out to be a spy that I wondered if there was anything behind it.'

There almost certainly was something behind it, for the don Collins mentioned was the man who Bronwell said had been responsible for his recruitment, and who had subsequently been killed in a car crash. By the way he had told the story I surmised that Collins wasn't being completely truthful. No one likes to be made much of, then dropped like a hot chestnut, but I guessed there had been more to the incident and its consequences than he had suggested. He was far from being a fool and it was possible that some attempt had been made to recruit him. I remembered Bronwell's words: 'Few are called and even fewer are chosen.'

'What about the other people at this meeting?' I asked. 'Did you ever see any of them again?'

Dr Collins shook his head. 'Not to speak to. There were four of them actually. Dick Havant wasn't there, you know. They said he was working in his lab and couldn't be disturbed. Two of the men I never set eyes on again. The woman I saw once, soon after. She must have been a member of the university, because she was leaving your brother's consulting-rooms – that is, assuming she was a patient. She could have been a doctor, I suppose. The fourth – ' He paused to grin ruefully. 'This makes a nonsense of my story, I know. The fourth was Dr Finton.'

It was like a blow to the solar plexus. Dr Collins was wrong. His story hadn't been a nonsense. On the contrary, it had become immeasurably important.

He misread my expression, and hurried to offer what he thought might be an explanation. 'Obviously Dr Finton isn't a communist. I – I wouldn't suggest it for a moment. That time at Dick Havant's he made my arrival an excuse, as if he'd been wanting to leave. And a few days later, I saw him cut Alan Bronwell dead in Turl Street. I wondered if perhaps they'd been trying to persuade him to support some cause, so that it would look good, and he'd realized they were trying to use him.'

Dr Collins seemed to have been doing a good deal of wondering, and his memory of what had taken place about seven years ago was amazingly clear, even if his logic was not of the best. Subjected to a professional interrogation, he would probably produce a lot more hard facts. At the moment, however, there was only one fact that concerned me.

'You're certain it was Dr Finton, Dr Robert Finton, the present Research Director at – '

'Positive.'

I frowned. 'I thought he was a Cambridge man. What was he doing here?'

'He had a visiting Fellowship. He was working near Aylesbury, on some project for the Government – I'm not sure what – and he used to come up to Oxford every week to lecture. Jolly good lectures they were too. I couldn't possibly have been mistaken.'

My last doubt resolved, I glanced at my watch. Dr Collins had told me all I wanted to know. I could now pass on the information and bow out gracefully, thankful that I wasn't in Bob Finton's shoes. The rest would be up to Mat.

I went back to the College, packed my overnight bag, wrote John a note explaining that as I felt unwell I had decided to return to London and collected the Renault. Driving with circumspection – after four whiskies and no lunch, I didn't want to face a breathalyser – I set off over Magdalen Bridge.

It was probably because I was taking extra care that I noticed the driver of the Ford. He was wearing a bright yellow shirt. There had been a man in a bright yellow shirt in The Cock and Feathers. He had gone into a telephone booth as I left the pub.

I tried going slowly, but he refused to pass. I put on speed and he accelerated. He followed me to the outskirts of London, and there I lost him. Presumably someone else took over but, in the congested traffic, I failed to spot him. I was worried. I didn't believe these were Special Branch men; the shirt had been too careless a give-away.

When I got home, I parked Denise's car at the kerb and let

myself quickly into the house. Then I hurried into the waiting-room on the ground floor. From here I had an excellent view up and down the street. For five minutes I watched a black Mini that had drawn up some thirty yards behind the Renault. No one got out. No one got in. Nothing happened. If my tail was waiting for me to reappear, he was going to have a long wait. Thoughtfully, I went along to the lift.

As I started up the last flight of stairs I heard the telephone ringing. It stopped the moment I put my key in the lock. Frustrated, I shut the front door and took my bag through to the bedroom. The phone rang again.

'Hallo! Is that Mr Philip Camplin?'

'Yes, it is.' I didn't recognize the voice; the accent was pure Boston.

'Good.' The sigh of relief was audible. 'I've been trying to contact you since yesterday.'

'I've been out of town. Who's that speaking?'

'You won't know me, Mr Camplin, but I'm a friend of Hal's. He asked me to give you a message, as it were. It's kind of important to him.'

'Yes?'

'In person.'

I hesitated. I was tired, I was hungry and, as well as a letter to Mat that would have to be carefully worded, I needed to write a memo on my conversation with Dr Collins. Besides, I had no idea who this individual was. Anyone could say he was a chum of Hal's. I thought of the black Mini parked in the street below.

'I'm sorry,' I said, 'but in that case it'll have to wait till tomorrow. I've had a tiring drive and I'm still recovering from an accident I had last week.'

'Accident? What kind of accident?' He had fastened on to the word.

'I slipped in the bathroom and concussed myself slightly.'

'Ah!' It was an enigmatic monosyllable. 'But I could visit you, at your apartment. In half an hour, say.'

'Tomorrow!' I insisted.

'Now, see here, Mr Camplin, I won't be available tomorrow and, as I said, this is important to Hal.' There was an edge to his voice.

'You think I should be prepared to welcome anyone who claims to be a friend of Hal's.'

'Mr Camplin, Hal said that if there was any difficulty about getting to you I was to mention that time at Oxford you and he . . .'

'Okay.' I laughed, relieved that he had established his bona fides. 'I'm waiting. Come along as soon as you can.'

Though I was no longer hungry, I made myself eat some bread and cheese and drink a mug of instant coffee. The CIA man arrived before I had finished, a smallish, compact character, light on his feet, his face lined with fatigue. As I let him into the house I saw that the Mini was still there.

In the flat he sat down without waiting to be asked, took out a packet of menthol cigarettes and lit one. I didn't object. He looked as if he were on the point of collapse. I found him an ashtray, poured him a strong scotch and let him add the water. He swallowed half the drink. He hadn't spoken except for 'Thanks', to indicate his wishes, and I was having difficulty controlling my impatience.

At last he said: 'We're keeping it very quiet, on purpose, but Hal wants you to know what happened to him.'

'For God's sake, what do you mean?' I said. 'Is Hal all right?'

He said: 'Last Wednesday we were in Belfast. We came out of the hotel and were getting into our car. I went round to the far side so as to drive. Hal already had his door open. A woman called his name and of course he turned. She threw acid in his face.'

'Christ!'

'He tried to dodge, but he was much too slow, and there wasn't a thing he could do. I got a good view of the bitch, and I'm going to find her. And when I do, believe me, Mr Camplin, she'll regret the day she was born.'

I believed him, but I felt no pity for the woman. 'What about

Hal? How is he?'

'Maybe if he'd gone to a hospital right away – I don't know.' The anger had left him and I could hear the pain in his voice. 'He wouldn't let me. Somehow he scrambled into the car, and I drove like hell to – to the house of a friend, where we fetched him a doctor.'

'But why? Why wouldn't he go to a hospital?'

'The woman was laying for him personally. There was no doubt about that. She called him by name. He figured the communists had set the thing up, intending that later some anonymous Brit should claim credit for doing the interfering American. Think what that would have done for relations between the States and the UK, Mr Camplin.' He made a despairing gesture. 'As it is, there's nothing to claim credit for. He beat them. Maybe he was expecting something like this to happen. But if it were up to me, which it isn't, Hal Runce would be awarded the Congressional Medal of Honor.'

I nodded. 'You haven't told me how he is.'

'As of now I can't. He's in the Naval Hospital in Bethesda, Maryland. We hired a private plane to fly him to England. He's supposed to have had an accident here; no mention of Ireland. The US Air Force shipped him to Washington. But when I last saw him – Jesus Christ!' He drew a long shuddering breath. 'He'll live, I guess. They'll patch him up somehow, but his sight has gone – and his face . . .'

After he left I sat for a while staring at the stubs of his cigarettes in the ashtray. I didn't think about Hal. I thought about Dr Robert Finton. By stealing the gas grenades that had been used on Massacre Day – and for me his guilt was no longer a matter of conjecture – he was the cause of an immense amount of human misery. Hal was only the last of his victims.

But there was no proof against Finton. Moreover, though I could provide enough evidence to make Mat dig, proof might not be obtainable, however hard the digging. Yet Finton had to be shown to be guilty if blame for Massacre Day was to be put where it belonged – not on the British Army, but on the communists. As Hal had said, nothing would ease the Irish situation as much as producing the actual traitor.

Earlier in the day, I had been prepared to leave everything to Mat. It had seemed to me that I could scarcely do anything else. I was, after all, on my way out of the Ministry. Now I had changed my mind, or rather the message from Hal had changed it for me. There was something I could do and I proposed to do it.

I had a fair knowledge of firearms but I didn't possess a gun. Patrick did. He had managed to get a licence for a pistol eighteen months ago after someone had broken into the house through the basement. Nothing much had been stolen, and we had had no trouble since, but I knew he had kept the gun. What I didn't know was where, and neither Patrick nor Denise was at home.

There was no problem about getting in. I had a key to their flat, as they had one to mine. I didn't like the idea of rooting around without first asking, but I had no choice.

I started with Patrick's den, which was a minute room containing a chair, a table piled with books, and a filing cabinet. This was where Patrick did the research for the learned articles he sometimes contributed to psychiatric journals. I thought it the best bet.

The gun wasn't in the desk, but I found it in the filing cabinet, at the back of the bottom drawer, behind some papers. With it were two cardboard cartons and, thinking I should need cartridges, I took one of them, broke the tape which sealed it and pulled off the lid.

Inside was a gas grenade. As far as I could tell it was similar to those I had found taped under Alan Bronwell's bed at the Albury Hotel. There seemed a good chance that it was the grenade my assailant had removed from the box I had hidden outside the bathroom window. I stared at it in dismay.

My dismay turned slowly to horror. My first reaction – that the grenade had been intended somehow to incriminate me, but had been planted in Patrick's flat by mistake – was absurd. There had been little attempt to hide it, and the two cardboard boxes – the second did hold cartridges – were identical.

As in a black dream, I thrust a handful of cartridges into my pocket, seized the gun and the grenade, and left my brother's flat. I felt physically sick. Upstairs the lingering smoke of the CIA man's cigarettes turned my stomach completely. I went into the bathroom and vomited.

Some time afterwards I returned to the sitting-room, but I couldn't stand the smell. I needed air. I threw open all the windows and took myself out on to the roof garden. It was a beautiful summer afternoon.

I slumped in a chair. I couldn't think clearly. Half my mind was searching for a possible, or even an impossible explanation. The other half was remembering.

Dr Collins had been Patrick's patient. Dr Collins had seen the woman who had been at the meeting in Dick Havant's house leaving Patrick's consulting-rooms. Alan Bronwell had been referred to a psychiatrist for the rash on the back of his hands; he had told me this himself, as if it were a joke. Since he had been a student, he too would probably have been one of Patrick's patients. Who better than a psychiatrist to judge potential agents, and what better place to interview them than a psychiatric couch?

Claire? Had Patrick arranged the threats and attacks and finally her death? It would have been all too simple for him. He knew all about us, our plans, our movements. Such intimate knowledge was what had made Mat suspect John Telsey. Naturally no one had thought of Patrick, though he was much closer to me. And recently he had taken to asking questions. Denise said it was because he was concerned for me. Denise – and the children, Jack and Nicole. The rest of the family – dear God!

Patrick couldn't have stolen any of the gas grenades. It wasn't possible. He had no opportunity. That must have been Finton. So there was a connection between Patrick and Finton – Oxford and Cambridge. What connection? It was unlikely Patrick had recruited Finton, or even knew him. For that matter, had Patrick recruited anyone? Was my brother really a communist agent, or had I fabricated the whole story on the basis of finding a grenade in his filing cabinet? Why shouldn't he possess a grenade? He was a consultant to the Army and –

I caught my breath. Consultant psychiatrist to Oxford University. Consultant psychiatrist to the British Army. What, if any, was the significance? Had Patrick's interest in the lieutenant who had committed suicide because of his part in Massacre Day been more than professional? Hopelessly, I buried my face in my hands.

It was a minute or two before the sounds in the flat impinged on my consciousness. Startled, I lifted my head and listened. Someone was walking quietly from room to room as if making sure that no one was at home. The footsteps were those of a man, and the only man with a key to my front door was Patrick, but Patrick was supposed to be in the country with Denise, visiting their daughter. As I waited for him to come up the three steps that led to the roof garden I thought of the grenade and the gun I had left on the table in the sitting-room.

'Hallo, brother.'

Patrick pulled up a chair and sat down facing me, his back to the glass doors that led into the flat. He was between me and my only means of entry into the house.

'I warned you, Philip,' he said gently. 'Why didn't you listen? I told you that if you went on snooping you'd get yourself killed. But you paid no attention, did you?' He shook his head reproachfully. 'I didn't mind you visiting John Telsey but I bet you had a long cosy chat with our Rose while you were in Oxford. And then this morning there you were, pouring beer into Dr Collins. I'd love to know what information you got out of him to make you dash back here so precipitately. Not that it matters any more, I regret to say.'

Idly he picked a small stone from a tub of flowering shrubs, and flicked it over the edge of the roof. In the seconds before the stone shattered on the paving of the courtyard below I was aware of him watching me. He knew I was afraid.

'I intended the grenade for you, Philip. You would have died in your sleep. It would have been a nice, peaceful death, and no bother to anyone afterwards. The verdict would have been heart failure of some kind.' He picked another stone from the tub and started tossing it in the air. 'Unfortunately that's not possible any more. You've been too clever, brother. You've caught me out. So you'll have to go a different way.'

His meaning was clear. He didn't need to throw the second pebble off the roof. He dropped it back into the tub and we looked at each other. I forced the saliva into my mouth.

'Why, Patrick?' I said. 'Why?'

EIGHT

'You mean, why do I have to kill you?'

'No. That's self-evident. I mean, why – everything?'

'Philip, you're not by any chance playing for time, are you?' Patrick smiled regretfully. 'It's no use, you know. No one's going to interrupt us. Denise isn't with me. She's spending the night at the school and coming back by train tomorrow. I arranged it like this so as not to disappoint Nicole, and to spare Denise the – er – the immediate shock of your death.'

'I see.'

I wet my lips and shifted in my chair, moving it a few inches. I wanted a better view of what was on my left. I would never be able to get past Patrick. He was bigger and stronger than I. But if I could distract him somehow, I might manage to scramble over the roofs and either crash through a skylight where he wouldn't dare follow me or draw someone's attention. Explanations would have to be invented later. For the moment all that mattered was to stay alive and, with my game leg, the odds weren't exactly in my favour.

'I'd still like some questions answered,' I said, 'for my own satisfaction. Surely that's not too much to ask, is it, Patrick?'

'What do you want to know?'

'Claire – why did you ever involve me with her?'

'Ah, Claire! That was altogether a mistake. I agreed to recruit her, and Bob Finton suggested marrying her off to you. Unfortunately, I was in no position to object. Bob and I were having a private power struggle at the time, and he thought he'd come up with a winning gambit. I had to disabuse him.'

'Bob Finton?'

I wanted him to go on talking. I didn't care what he said. I had spotted a possible means of escape. At the end of the little terrace on which we sat, a cement urn, full of geraniums, offered a stepping stone to the roof of the adjoining house. Given a head start, perhaps I could scramble up the slope, dodge between the chimneys, and . . .

'Yes, Dr Robert Finton, my brother in the Party for many a year. We first met in Moscow, while we were undergraduates, and we've worked together ever since. Does that surprise you?'

'I'm beyond surprise, Patrick.'

'You knew about Finton?'

'Yes.' I was calculating distances; I would need that head start. 'Alan Bronwell left a sort of apologia with the box of grenades.'

'Which you destroyed, I'm told. Why?'

'It explained that Claire was a sleeper. I wanted to keep that secret.'

'Poor Philip!'

His pity was genuine, and it infuriated me. To hide my anger I thrust my hands into my pockets, clenching my fists. And the fingers of my right hand closed around the cartridges I had put there and forgotten. If I threw them straight at him, he would dodge instinctively. Even if they failed to hit him, he would be thrown off balance, which might give me a lead of two or three seconds. But I would have to time the attack very nicely.

'Did you tell Harworth, or anyone, about Bob Finton, Philip?'

'No. I wanted to make sure he was what – what Bronwell said he was.' I had spoken without thinking, and at once regretted it.

'Good.' Patrick was pleased. 'Finton's extremely important. If anything happened to me – if I fell under a bus or had a heart attack – he'd take over as Co-ordinator.'

'And what exactly do you co-ordinate, Patrick?' I tried to keep the acid from my voice.

'Anything and everything that may lead to the second conversion of Ireland. What St Patrick did for Christianity in that country, I hope to do for communism – and in the not too distant future.'

I hesitated, my throwing hand half out of my pocket. Now was the moment for me to act, when Patrick was lost in self-satisfaction. Once he started to amplify what he had said, he would watch me closely to savour my reactions. But I couldn't pass up the chance of learning his plans. If by a miracle I did escape from this hideous situation, I had to be in a position to act.

Reluctantly I slid my hand back into my pocket and relaxed my grip on the cartridges. 'Are you planning some sort of coup?' I said to encourage him.

'Of course, to complete what Massacre Day nearly achieved. This time the US President will have to interfere. We're already increasing the pressure on him, so that when there's a second British atrocity nothing will damp down the outcry across the States. And if the Americans, why not the Russians? By request, naturally.' He laughed. 'Whether the Brits go or stay, there'll be chaos throughout Ireland, and from chaos will come communism, as has happened in so many countries. Now – '

Unexpectedly Patrick pushed himself out of his chair and stood. Taken by surprise I got slowly to my feet. My chance of surprising him had gone. It wasn't difficult for me to express horror and fear.

'Surely you're not planning another Massacre Day?' I said.

'I don't know what they'll call it.' He shrugged. 'There'll be rumours that the Brits are drugging the political prisoners in Northern Ireland to make them docile. The odd few will be taken ill. Then the whole lot will die – an overdose, an accident.'

He spoke without emotion. And I stared at him, in complete disbelief. This was Patrick, my brother whom I had known all my life, whom I had loved and admired. He was mad. It was the only conceivable explanation.

'God help you,' I said.

He didn't seem to hear me. 'Philip, I – I wish you'd just step over the edge. But, if you can't, I'll have to push you. It'll be a quick death, I promise you.'

Oddly enough I found it easier to accept that he was going to kill me than that he could be indifferent to the immense suffering he intended to cause. I was actually moving towards him when the instinct of self-preservation reasserted itself. I clutched the cartridges tight. This was it. If I failed I would know nothing about it. If I succeeded . . .

I hurled the cartridges in his face with all the strength I had. I don't think any of them touched him but he jumped backwards, throwing up his arm to protect himself. It gave me valuable seconds in which to reach the end of the terrace, step on the urn of geraniums and from there heave myself on to the neighbouring roof.

The slope was steeper than I had expected, and I hit it hard. Momentarily I was winded. I lay against the tiles, gasping. My leg hurt like hell. I forced myself to scramble upwards. I wasn't an athletic type and what would have been simple for some men was almost impossible for me. My built-up shoe with its metal heel and toe-tips didn't help me climb. But I was within a foot of the chimney when suddenly I found myself slipping.

Patrick had recovered quickly and was already catching up on me. The climb, I thought bitterly, would be child's play to him. He even had breath to speak.

'Come back, you little fool,' he said.

This was precisely what I was doing, but not of my own will. I had to stop my slide. Desperately I flung out an arm and wedged my hand in a gutter. At the same moment I felt Patrick's fingers close round my left ankle. I fought to free myself, but it was useless. Patrick's grip was firm. My hold on the gutter began to weaken. He was pulling me inexorably towards him.

As I struggled, my body swung outwards, and I caught a glimpse of the neighbouring courtyard, paved like ours, and a long way below. I shut my eyes tight, but I couldn't blind my imagination. Sick with fear, I made a last frenzied effort.

Patrick had immobilized my left leg, my good leg, but the right was still mobile. I drew up my right knee and, violently straightening the leg, thrust it down and back in what I hoped was the general direction of his head. Patrick screamed. I had caught him squarely in the face and, though there can't have been a great deal of force behind the blow, by an ironic chance it had been delivered with the foot on which I wore the built-up, metal-tipped shoe.

I heard him slithering down the tiles behind me. I tried to turn. I would have saved him if I could, but it was too late. His screams diminished as, in spite of clutching fingers, he disappeared over the edge. His body struck the ground with a dull, heavy thump, like a bursting sack of flour.

I pressed myself against the slope of the roof and shook as if with ague. It was a minute before I could regain control. Even so I was trembling as I let myself very carefully down the roof, past the smashed geraniums and on to the safety of the terrace.

Kneeling by the parapet, I was able to see most of the courtyard of the adjoining house. Patrick lay spreadeagled directly below me. There was no doubt that he was dead. I looked around. Except for a ginger cat walking along a wall, nothing stirred. The probability that on a summer Sunday no one had seen what had happened was good. Patrick might lie there, unobserved, till tomorrow morning. By then I might have killed another man.

I stood up. I was calm now – the trembling had ceased – and able to think clearly. I searched for the cartridges. Not only might I need them, but if they weren't collected they would add a bizarre note to the scene. I found what I hoped was all of them and returned them to my pocket. I picked up a chair that Patrick had become entangled with. I could do nothing about the broken geraniums, but otherwise the little roof garden looked normal.

In the flat I brushed my jacket and trousers, and changed my shoes. I would never wear that particular pair again. I loaded the pistol and studied the gas grenade so that I knew how it operated. I then put the pistol, the grenade and the remaining cartridges in various pockets. As an afterthought I added a small bottle of surgical spirit from the medicine cabinet. I was ready to go.

But I didn't leave at once. Instead I made myself sit down quietly and slowly drink a whisky. I thought of the new disaster threatening in Ireland, of the prisoners and their families, of Hal Runce. After twenty minutes I went downstairs to the patients' waiting-room. Standing in the window I looked up and down the street. The black Mini, presumably on Patrick's instructions, had gone. Everything was peaceful and orderly. There was no sign of police cars or ambulances or untoward activity. The authorities hadn't been alerted, which could only mean that no one had seen Patrick fall. Thankfully I left the house.

Dr Robert Finton lived in a modern one-storey house, set well back from the road in about two acres of land. It was within five miles of the laboratories where he worked, convenient for London but very private. Visitors could come and go unobserved, which was lucky for me. No one saw me turn into the lane that served as a driveway.

I had had some difficulty finding the place. I couldn't ask for directions and my maps were not too helpful. As a result I had got lost twice and it was after nine when I rang the doorbell. I waited anxiously.

Finton was unmarried, and I had no idea of his domestic arrangements. I hoped he didn't have a housekeeper. To judge from the grounds, which were beautifully manicured, he employed contractors to look after the garden. This could mean that he preferred not to have resident help. But he might have guests for the evening or a girl-friend staying with him.

My considerations were halted by Finton opening the door himself. Of medium height, he was balding, bespectacled, with a thin intelligent face. There was a smear of egg beside his mouth and I guessed I had interrupted his supper. A sweater and an old pair of slacks suggested it was a solitary meal.

'Why – Philip Camplin. This is a surprise.'

'I'm sorry to disturb you, but – '

'Not a bit. Come in.'

He held the door wide and I went into the hall. Someone was playing Bach – *Jesu, joy of man's desiring*. It had to be a recording, possibly Myra Hess. Otherwise, the house was quiet. There was a strong smell of burnt toast.

I sniffed, and Finton apologized. 'Sorry about the stink. My factotum's on holiday and I'm having to do for myself. I'm afraid I'm not much of a cook.'

He led the way into a long room with french windows opening on to the garden at the back of the house. It was a pleasant room with shelf upon shelf of books and a grand piano. In other circumstances I might have enjoyed being there. Finton turned off the hi-fi and gestured to a chair.

'May I get you a drink?'

'Whisky and soda, please.'

'Ice?'

'No.'

There were bottles and glasses on a butler's tray and, while he busied himself with these, I slipped on the thin driving gloves I had brought from the car and strolled across to his desk. As if it were the most natural thing to do, I began to open the drawers. Finton swung round.

'What on earth are you doing?'

The amazed indignation, nicely tempered with restraint since I was a guest, was convincing. The frown, the hesitant smile, the glass of whisky in each hand, all added up to a beautiful act. The only give-away was that he hadn't spilt a single drop.

'Put the glass in your left hand on that table,' I pointed, 'and sit down there.'

Not taking his eyes from me or the pistol I had produced from my pocket, Finton obeyed. I was prepared to bet he wouldn't react till he knew what I was after, but nevertheless I intended to take every precaution. Hurriedly I riffled through the rest of his desk. There was nothing in it he could use as a weapon. I threw the onyx calendar, the matching penholder and a glass paper weight into the waste-paper basket. The top was now clear of offensive weapons.

'Philip, what do you want?' He was still playing innocence.

'A written confession.'

'Of what? My dear chap, what is it that you think I've done?'

I ignored his interruption. 'A confession, first that you've been an agent since you were at Cambridge. Secondly, that it was you and not Alan Bronwell who stole the gas grenades used on Massacre Day. Thirdly, that it was you who organized the actual catastrophe on behalf of your communist masters.'

'You must be crazy. I can't imagine where you got hold of such absurd ideas.'

'I have them on the best of authority, that of my brother Patrick.'

It must have been a shock to him. Yet he did no more than raise an eyebrow. His self-control showed how right I was to deal with this myself. The authorities would have stood no chance on the basis of the slim evidence that was all I could provide.

'Now I know you're sick, Camplin.' Calmly Finton took a sip of his drink. 'Unless this is some outrageous joke.'

'No joke. There's something more I need – a statement on the next disaster you and Patrick intended for Ireland.' I paused, and added slowly: 'I'm talking, Dr Finton, about the plans you have to poison the prisoners in the North, and blame the British for this casual barbarism.'

Finton brought his head up slowly and looked at me. His mouth was a slit, his nostrils thin, his expression blank. I wished I knew what he was thinking.

Suddenly he shrugged, relaxed. 'All right,' he said. 'You seem to have won a battle – quite an important battle. What has happened to Patrick?'

I wasn't to be tricked into talking while he planned to outwit me. I didn't have Patrick's self-confidence. I backed towards the french windows and, keeping Finton well covered, shut the two that were open.

'Why did you do that?' he asked conversationally. 'If you're afraid of a neighbour strolling across the lawn, I don't have that sort of neighbour.'

I didn't explain. I said: 'Clasp your hands behind your neck. Go over to the desk. There's paper in the top drawer. Take it out. Start to write.'

'And if I refuse, you'll kill me.'

'Eventually, yes. You'll suffer first.'

'Don't be silly, Camplin. You don't want to spend the rest of your life in prison or in some mental home, do you?'

'I've already killed Patrick, who was my brother; I shall have far less compunction about killing you, Finton. As the saying used to go, one can only hang once.'

'I see.' He didn't comment on Patrick's death. 'Well, in that case you'd better get on with it. Shoot me, if you must. I'm damned if I'll write any confessions for you.'

This was the moment I had dreaded, the moment when he called my hand. It wasn't that I had any scruples about shooting him. God knows, I had enough personal reasons for hating him, and with him and Patrick both dead it was unlikely that the mass poisoning of prisoners would go ahead. But, at the same time, unless he signed a statement, all hope of proving that Massacre Day had been a communist conspiracy would be gone, and that was something I was not prepared to accept.

'You'll change your mind,' I said levelly.

'I very much doubt that, Camplin.'

'Do you, Finton?'

I put the pistol down on the corner of a table within easy reach if he made a sudden move. Then, with extreme care, I took the bottle of surgical spirit from my jacket pocket. I unscrewed the cap.

I said: 'You know what happened to Hal Runce, don't you?'

He didn't answer, but he was swallowing hard. He had a large Adam's apple, and I could see it working up and down. His eyes were wide, staring at the bottle. I was ashamed at the surge of pleasure I felt as I recognized his fear.

'Shall I start with a few splashes on the bottom of your face, around the mouth and nose?' My voice was hard. Mat was right; I had changed since Claire's death. Six months ago I couldn't have threatened a man like this. 'Of course, I can't promise to be accurate. You may get a spot or two in your eyes.'

'No! Don't! Not acid.'

'Write those statements.'

He looked at me. Then his eyes fell to the bottle in my hand. Involuntarily he shuddered. The thought of acid seemed to fill him with a peculiar horror. There were beads of sweat on his upper lip.

'All right.'

He stood up, and I told myself to be extra careful. Now, when I believed I had won, he could be most dangerous. I moved to keep a safe distance between us as he went to his desk.

'Hands behind your neck,' I said harshly.

He nodded and did as I asked. When he was seated, I screwed the cap back on the bottle, and picked up the pistol. Oddly enough I felt less secure with a real weapon than with the spurious acid. The reverse was true of Finton, who regained some of his confidence.

'Well, what do you want me to write?'

Deliberately he glanced at his watch and, though I was sure this was a ploy, I found it unnerving. It was going to be a laborious business getting him to put on paper exactly what I wanted. I was tired, emotionally exhausted, and the muscles of my game leg kept on going into spasm. I wouldn't be able to stand for much longer.

Making a long arm I hooked a chair towards me and sat. Finton's face was immediately mask-like, but the mask disintegrated as I again uncapped the bottle of spirit.

'What are you doing?'

'Taking precautions. You write. As you finish each page, bring it and put it on the piano here, so that I can read it without moving. Don't try anything clever or you'll get the acid straight in the face. Do you understand?'

'I understand.'

'Don't waste time either. I've a long drive home after this.'

'And what happens to me when you've got your statements? I suppose you'll kill me?'

'Not unless you make it necessary, but that's only because it might be difficult to stage a convincing suicide. No, once you've done what I want, you can make a run for it. And the quicker you are now, the more time you'll have.'

'Why so generous?'

'Patrick was my brother. If you're out of the country my family should escape the scandal.'

Finton smiled contemptuously. It was a plausible argument,

but he knew I was lying.

'Okay.' He sounded resigned. 'Let's get down to it.'

In spite of Finton's reluctant co-operation, it was after midnight before he produced an acceptable text. In it he admitted he was an agent and, as such, had been responsible for Massacre Day. He also explained the plan for wholesale poisoning of prisoners in Northern Ireland. But I had to bully details out of him and nothing would persuade him to divulge names.

Reasonably satisfied with what I had achieved – if there were any discrepancies in what he had written I hoped they would be attributed to his mental condition – I made him put the confession in an envelope, address it to the Chief of the Special Branch and add sufficient stamps. The tension between us was now very high.

'Before I give you this envelope what guarantee do I have you won't shoot me?' he said.

'None. But you don't have a choice, not while I have the acid. Hurry up.'

He came forward, placed the envelope on the corner of the piano and walked back to the desk. On the way he picked up the glass of whisky, which I hadn't touched.

'Cheers,' he said, and drank.

I had been too slow to stop him, but his casualness didn't deceive me. He hadn't gone behind his desk. He was planning to hurl the heavy glass tumbler in my face and then rush me. Either he had grown suspicious of my bottle of acid or he believed this was his last chance. He knew I couldn't let him live. The minute I left the house he would be on the phone to his thugs to get me stopped at all costs. Even if they failed, he would swear to Mat that I had gone out of my mind and forced him at gun point to write a nonsensical statement. And he might get away with it. I dare not take the risk.

Thrusting the envelope inside my jacket, I quickly screwed up the bottle of spirit – too quickly and carelessly. I saw the anger darken Finton's face. He knew he'd been tricked. He lifted the glass.

But he didn't expect a lame man to move with such speed. I

was at the door. The bottle was in one trouser pocket. The pistol went into the other. I saw his mouth open, his belief begin to unfold, the hope start in him. Against all odds I was going to walk out and leave him unharmed, or so it must have seemed to him. He was lowering the glass when I threw the gas grenade.

The grenade struck the desk. There was a soft plop as it exploded, a hiss of escaping gas. Finton clutched his throat and fell, choking. He must have died within seconds. I slammed the door and ran.

I felt neither triumph nor compunction. Both would come later. At the moment I was overwhelmed by a terrible weariness that deadened every emotion. I only wanted to sleep.

Once I had mailed Finton's confession I felt an enormous relief. I had done all I could and achieved all I could hope for. At the very least, a second major catastrophe in Ireland had been averted. It was time to think of myself.

I turned up on Mat's doorstep at two in the morning in a state of exhaustion. My story was that, overcome by depression, I had tried to do away with myself during the afternoon. Patrick, in an effort to restrain me, had fallen to his death. Since then, I had been driving through the countryside in a state of near amnesia. What should I do?

Mat was incomparably sympathetic. He coped with everything and persuaded the authorities to close ranks against untoward publicity, not that there was much interest in me or Patrick, with Finton hogging the headlines. To this day I don't know to what extent Mat put together Finton's death, Patrick's fall and my 'breakdown', and added them up to some approximation of the truth. He said nothing, but subsequent events suggested that he might have had some inkling.

As for me, the family rallied round as always. I had three months' sick leave. Then, judging that I didn't have much of a future in the Ministry of Defence, I offered my resignation. I thought of going to Washington, to live with Hal Runce, to forget Claire and the past, to help Hal face his new blind life. We would have made a good pair, the walking wounded of an incomplete campaign. But the Ministry – perhaps because of Mat's intervention – had other ideas. Ironically, they seemed to like the new image I had acquired; my experiences, even the suspicions that had attached themselves to me – all became assets in the minds of those who plan unrecognized wars. Nominally I did resign, but in fact I left England, to play another shadowy role in yet another battle, equally obscure, equally imperative.